GAMES
PEOPLE PLAY

GAMES
PEOPLE PLAY

Shelby Reed

HEAT | NEW YORK

THE BERKLEY PUBLISHING GROUP
Published by the Penguin Group
Penguin Group (USA) Inc.
375 Hudson Street, New York, New York 10014, USA

USA I Canada I UK I Ireland I Australia I New Zealand I India I South Africa I China

Penguin Books Ltd., Registered Offices: 80 Strand, London WC2R 0RL, England
For more information about the Penguin Group, visit penguin.com.

This book is an original publication of The Berkley Publishing Group.

HEAT and the HEAT design are trademarks of Penguin Group (USA) Inc.

Library of Congress Cataloging-in-Publication Data

Reed, Shelby.
Games people play / Shelby Reed.—Heat trade paperback edition.
pages cm
ISBN 978-0-425-26506-2
1. Erotic fiction. I. Title.
PS3618.E4358G36 2013
813'.6—dc23
2012046049

PUBLISHING HISTORY
Heat trade paperback edition / June 2013

PRINTED IN THE UNITED STATES OF AMERICA

10 9 8 7 6 5 4 3 2 1

Cover design by Jason Gill.
Cover photograph of couple: Sean Neal / Shutterstock.
Text design by Laura K. Corless.

For my dear critique group, Inkplots, the support of the La-la-la's, Cate Rowan, Vicky Ardito, and Leslie Ann Dennis. And special thanks to my agent, Laura Bradford, who believed in me from the start.

CHAPTER ONE

She moved through the crowded gallery, slim, tall, cool, oblivious to the stares of the art reception attendees. *A swan in a swamp*, Colm Hennessy thought, and for a moment he forgot his purpose.

That single-minded goal returned with a vengeance when the swan approached a man in a wheelchair surrounded by clucking socialites. Only when she reached him and placed a glass of white wine in his hand did her detached expression shift. Vulnerability. A vague frown. He said something to her and reluctantly took the wine, as though she'd brought him the wrong beverage.

"So that's the woman of the hour," Colm muttered to himself as his date, Azure Elan, arrived at his side with two flutes of champagne. "I'd pictured someone different." Someone less controlled. The artist who'd created the lurid paintings around them should be the proverbial wild-haired pseudo-Bohemian, not this remote creature who stood a pointed distance from the Svengali in the wheelchair. She'd allowed herself to be closed out from the group surrounding the man, her arms crossed over her breasts as though to guard her heart.

In certain Washington circles, blond-haired, blue-eyed Sydney

Warren was a guilty pleasure, and it had little to do with her celebrity looks. For the last three years, fair-weather connoisseurs had scrambled to get their claws on her explicit landscapes. Now that he'd seen her, Colm couldn't quite picture her in a paint-stained smock, splashing erotic visions on canvas. And yet, according to the district locals, she had more than created the paintings. She'd rendered erotic art a high-priced commodity.

He glanced at a nearby canvas so massive it nearly swallowed a single display wall. Who'd have thought erect penises, lined up like rows of cornstalks, could be considered a landscape?

Azure slid her arm through Colm's and broke his trance, her signature jasmine perfume filling his senses. "You're scowling. Don't you think your new friend is stunning?"

Of course she was stunning, but Sydney Warren was no friend and never would be, no matter how deep he got inside her before this job was over.

"Consider yourself lucky to have landed this assignment." Azure's well-practiced, sultry tone gained an edge when he didn't answer right away. "I picked you specifically, Colm. To reward your excellent attendance, the high compliments of your clients, your devotion to—"

"Fucking?" he finished, and after raising his glass to her in salute, washed the foul word down with a mouthful of Dom Pérignon.

Her features tightened. "Don't drop your mask quite yet, darling. The show hasn't even begun."

"I'll be good." As a waiter passed by them, Colm swapped his empty champagne glass for a full one. "I'm always good."

"Indeed." She let her pale gaze slide over his sports coat and down his gabardine pants as though measuring the quality of the merchandise, and he forced himself to stand under the inspection and feel nothing. Azure was at her gorgeous worst tonight, dressed in a black catsuit and stiletto boots that answered to no fashion rules, only to the primal senses of men and women alike, her long black hair pouring down her back. She was his savior and his own personal demon.

She was his pimp.

When her appraisal reached his eyes again, her expression hardened just enough to relay the warning she didn't speak. "Sydney Warren is a gift. A beautiful one."

He tilted his champagne glass to his lips again and took another look at the artist through its crystal distortion. Max Beaudoin spoke to her again from his wheelchair, a cajoling expression on his sallow face. Colm read the placement of her hand on the man's shoulder, the brush of her sleek blond bob against her cheek as she bent to listen to him, the way her attention left him only long enough to acknowledge passing fans. She was the star of the evening. This was her show, and yet she deferred to her invalid lover as though they were the only two people in the gallery.

The two unhappiest people in the gallery.

Thanks to a quick briefing back at Avalon, the pleasure club where he worked under Azure's careful eye, he knew the basic history of Sydney and Beaudoin's relationship. They'd met four years ago when Beaudoin was a thrill-seeking art dealer and Sydney a twenty-something ingénue just tapping into the local scene. As an artist she'd initially ridden her older lover's coattails. Then two years ago, when a rock climbing accident landed him in a wheelchair and he shuttered himself in black reclusion, Sydney had clawed the rest of the way to her own unquestionable success—with mixed-media penis landscapes and lithographs of naked, moisture-beaded breasts.

Hey, whatever works. Sensationalism was a drug to these people, and Sydney Warren knew it. Colm wasn't sure she was talented, but there was no question she was smart as hell.

He stepped aside to let two chunky women pass and watched the synchronized swish of their heart-shaped asses as they beelined for Beaudoin. The man might be a shadow of his former self, but he still held impressive sway over the female gender. Colm wondered how many times Max had betrayed his "beautiful gift" in the past, and if the man's guilt had anything to do with why he'd hired a prostitute to see to Sydney's pleasure.

He drained his glass, set it on a nearby butler's tray, and glanced at Azure. "Ready?"

"Not until you put on your pleased-to-meet-you face, darling. If the alcohol won't improve your mood . . ."

He shook his head. "I don't need anything to improve my mood. I'm just aware of the futility of all this. I hate to rain on Beaudoin's parade, but that woman will never agree to this little arrangement. I know her kind. She'd rather spend a lifetime as his nursemaid than admit to her own needs."

"I beg to differ." Azure's fingernails lightly scraped his wrist beneath the sleeve of his suit jacket as she drew him toward the subjects of their surveillance. "Sydney will do whatever makes Max happy, and *you* will make Max happy. And that will make *me* happy . . . and then I will make you very, *very* happy."

Wrong. Sex with Azure wouldn't make him happy. The money would. He was the top of the twenty flavors at Avalon right now, but it was just a matter of time until she turned her attention to another of her boys and Colm was relegated back to the harem. He wouldn't mind one bit. The thought of her displaying any affection toward him deeper than the merely sexual bothered him.

And Max Beaudoin was no harmless sweetheart either, despite the wheelchair and wasted legs. Dealing with someone in a wheelchair was a part of Colm's life, but the man was something different entirely from what Colm understood. Beaudoin might be paralyzed from the waist down, but he could move his arms. His fingers. His lips and tongue. He didn't need a cock-for-hire to pleasure his girl-friend.

A sudden suspicion grabbed his gut and stopped him cold. He pulled Azure aside under the guise of viewing an abstract ménage à trois. "Does Beaudoin get off on watching her with another man?" When she merely looked at him, he added, "It's one thing to screw three diplomats' wives in one night at Avalon, but I didn't sign on for anything like what you're implying when I agreed to do this out-side job."

"You're being paid more than any companion in Avalon's history to do this outside job." The generic amiability fled her face, momen-tarily exposing the demon behind it. "Say the word and we'll be done here. And you'll never see this kind of money again, you un-grateful wretch."

Wretch.

Fifteen hundred dollars a day for two weeks, and all he had to do was seduce Sydney Warren. He stared at the ménage à trois painting, at the luminescent flesh of two women crawling over a faceless man. He'd almost forgotten what it meant to be attracted to a woman, forgotten the hunger for soft skin, soft touches, soft cries. Sex was mechanical now, but he stuck with it for the money, for the brief exorcism of ghosts it provided, for a night's relief from the memory of screeching brakes, twisting metal, Jill and Amelia screaming and screaming . . .

And then the silence, the eternal, excruciating silence that stalked his dreams . . . when he actually slept.

Wretch.

He could do this one thing. This one woman. He could fuck her and walk away. Whoring suited the black tar pit his road had become.

"Darling?" Azure wrapped a hand around his neck and nuzzled his ear.

He jerked from his trance.

"You'll pleasure her wherever and however she wants it," Azure said.

He glanced from the painting to Sydney Warren.

"You'll pleasure her without asking questions."

He closed his eyes and then opened them. Sydney was still there.

"Even in front of her boyfriend," Azure prompted.

Colm didn't reply, but Azure's gentle smile said she'd obviously heard the acquiescence he couldn't bring himself to speak. "Besides, you assume too quickly that she knows who and what you are, or has any inkling of what Max has arranged for her."

Colm frowned. "She doesn't know?"

"Time to introduce yourself, darling."

As if on cue, Beaudoin glanced in their direction, looked away, and then let his narrow gaze drift back to them. The smile on his face turned brittle, and he gave a subtle nod.

Azure slid her arm through Colm's again. "On second thought, maybe I'll make the introductions myself."

"I don't need a bodyguard," he said.

"Of course not." They skirted around men in suits and women in pearls and silk. "But humor me. You know how I like to be a fly on the wall."

He avoided looking at Beaudoin as they approached, choosing instead to focus on Sydney. Her face was half turned as she talked to a gaunt matron with hair the color of eggplant. Her graceful hand gestured toward yet another ménage à trois painting behind them as she spoke.

I call this painting Two Guys Fucking One Lucky Gal, Colm

imagined her telling the middle-aged socialite, who would reply, *It would be perfect over my Louis XV settee!*

The urge to laugh constricted his chest and he coughed against a curled fist. It was easier to concentrate on seducing a client when sequestered in his quarters at Avalon without Azure breathing down his neck. Out here in the real world, his job seemed like a game. Absurd and pretentious.

And this time, somehow, treacherous.

As he and Azure reached the circle of people surrounding the couple, the low murmur of Sydney's voice floated to his ears.

". . . At times I use a camera since the models can only hold the pose for so long."

Gliding ahead, Azure took advantage of the lull in the women's conversation. She paused behind Sydney, and to Colm's amazement, brushed her fingertips down the artist's spine left naked by the seductive drape of her black dress . . . an utter invasion of personal space that only the pleasure club owner could get away with.

Sydney stiffened and turned.

"The work is exquisite, Miss Warren," Azure said smoothly. "The artist herself even more so."

Sydney's blue eyes appeared almost silver up close; striking, but not icy like Azure's. They searched Azure's benign expression, and then she offered a curious smile. "I'm sorry. Have we met?"

Before Azure could respond, Beaudoin lurched forward and planted his wheelchair between them. "I see you received my personal invitation, Ms. Elan. Sydney"—he reached up and caught Sydney's fingers—"this is an acquaintance from my past, Azure Elan."

"What an unusual name," Sydney said faintly. "It's a pleasure."

"In more ways than I can say, Sydney." Azure let her gaze drop to the gentle curve of the blonde's breasts. "May I call you Sydney?"

"Of course."

Azure's smile widened in a manner that amused Colm as she glanced around the erotic art display, then returned to appraise Sydney's face. She could seduce a eunuch monk with those diamond eyes, and the artist was no exception. Sydney's willowy form swayed ever so slightly toward her, a reed drawn into a mini-cyclone.

"I hear you're making an honest man of our Max, dear Sydney," Azure went on in a conspiratorial tone.

Colm's eyebrows shot up. *Our Max?* Azure hadn't known Beaudoin until seven days ago, when the silver-haired art dealer wheeled through the doors of Avalon, intent on his odd and perverse quest.

"This is *my* honest man," Azure was saying as she glided her fingers along Colm's jacket sleeve. "Colm, meet Max Beaudoin and his companion, Sydney Warren. The artist."

With methodical ease, he extended his hand first to Sydney, but Beaudoin thrust his own hand between them and grasped Colm's with bone-crushing pressure.

Jesus Christ. Colm gritted his teeth and endured the discomfort with a dry smile, holding the man's flinty gray gaze until Beaudoin released his grip. Then Colm returned his attention to Sydney.

The instant their eyes locked, her lovely features went blank and she averted her gaze, even as she dutifully grasped his hand. Her fingers were dry and cool, a little rough from too much turpentine and paint, he suspected, and they lingered barely long enough to render the gesture polite before withdrawing.

For a moment, Colm was at a loss. She wouldn't even look at him. Women didn't usually dismiss him so quickly. Or ever.

"Your work is amazing, Miss Warren," he said, ducking his head to recapture her gaze.

"Thank you." Her eyes shot to the left; his followed. She glanced to the right, skirted past his stare and up to the ceiling.

Azure was right. He wasn't in the mood for this. "My name is Colm." He tried again, lowering his voice, not too much, just a note for intimacy. "I'd like to know more, Sydney."

Her attention fixed past his shoulder as though what lay beyond him was infinitely more interesting than their exchange. "More about . . . ?"

"More about what drives you to produce this kind of art."

"Most critics think the answer is obvious." She finally smiled, though it didn't reach those silver-blue eyes. She had long, incongruently dark lashes, left naked of cosmetics, but her full mouth glistened with pale pink gloss. So soft to be so remote. If she excused herself from the conversation, Colm wouldn't be the least bit surprised. This woman had taken one glance and decided she wanted nothing to do with him. How the hell was he supposed to screw her to kingdom come if she didn't like him on sight?

He clasped his hands behind his back and fisted them to maintain control. "But these paintings are about more than sex," he continued, aware now of being surreptitiously observed by Azure and Beaudoin, and that the sudden surge of adrenaline rushing through his veins had more to do with the challenge Sydney presented than the nakedness of being onstage.

"There's humor here," he added, glancing back at the field of penises he'd noted earlier. "Maybe anger, too." He shrugged. "I want to know more." He wanted to know what she didn't like about him. He wanted to know why she was the only female to look past him in forever, this reluctant child to whom he was being presented like a toy with a big red bow. And most of all he wanted to know if her skin was as soft as it appeared, shining like dusky gold in the display lights. Gritting his teeth, he waited in the excruciating silence that had fallen over the small group, his attention unwavering on her face. She *would* look at him, damn it. She would look at him, or he'd be out of a job. Azure let escorts go for much less than lack of enthusiasm on a client's part.

At last Sydney met his eyes and blinked as if awakened for the first time, her lips parted. "I'll have to think about your question . . ." She hesitated as if searching for his name.

"Colm Hennessy," he repeated.

"Most people don't bother to see beyond the surface of my work. To be honest, Mr. Hennessy, I'm not sure there is anything beyond the paint on the canvas. But I assume you have your theories."

"I do." A smile lifted one corner of his mouth as he read the vague flush seeping into her cheeks. Just like that, the tension drained from his muscles. She was self-conscious for a reason, and in that instant he understood why she treated him so remotely.

It had nothing to do with dislike.

Beaudoin's chair rolled forward another few inches, a vague and nonsensical threat to block Sydney from the gigolo he'd paid to seduce her. "Sydney, why don't you give Colm the grand tour?"

"Yes," Azure added. "Max, darling, you and I have some catching up to do after ten long years."

His thin lips curved. "Has it really been that long? It seems like yesterday."

He'd paid yesterday. In cash. Colm had stood at the top of Avalon's grand staircase and watched the transaction take place in the lobby below. Not only had Max bought a sexual partner for a woman who could hardly look a male in the eye, but that woman had no clue what was in the gift box.

This was going to be a real walk in the park.

CHAPTER TWO

Sydney preferred a little imperfection in a man, the character inherent in a subtle lack of balance. The artist in her appreciated a well-proportioned body, but only from a distance, appraising him as a potential object for the canvas.

The male standing beside her, studying the flowing composition of female genitalia she'd entitled *The Garden*, challenged that belief. He embodied everything she disliked—and yet he stunned her like the first Michelangelo she'd ever seen. Tall, broad-shouldered, with chestnut brown hair and light green eyes, he was classical.

It wasn't his good looks that tilted her decorum, or the way every passing woman seemed to have the same visceral reaction as Sydney.

The instant her gaze had met his a few minutes ago, she'd felt . . . exposed. She didn't know how he did it, but the brief, excruciating inventory he'd taken of her face—without ever once skimming down her body in the clichéd visual assault some men offered—told her she couldn't fool him. He'd somehow grabbed hold of her cool disguise and yanked hard enough to send it pooling around her ankles, and yet they'd hardly uttered a word to each other.

Then, before she could recover, Max had thrown her to the wolves. He'd sent her off to play with this incredibly attractive stranger while he stayed behind to visit with his "old friend," the one with the long raven hair that poured down her back like Chinese silk. The one currently standing too close to his wheelchair with a hand caressing his shoulder as they laughed over some joke Sydney would never share.

She swallowed and turned back to the canvas without seeing it. The low hum of gallery-hushed voices around her, the faint scent of expensive perfume and spilled champagne filled her senses. So did her returning awareness of the man beside her.

The piercing focus he'd aimed at her earlier was now fixed on the painting, a perfect opportunity to steal a glance at his profile. He looked about thirty. His brown, clean-cut hair was shot through with golden highlights only the sun could bestow. His nose was straight and unextraordinary, his mouth sensuous with that wonderful bow at the top of his upper lip, a detail she prized in faces. The faint beginnings of a beard shadowed his strong jaw in a way no razor could quite banish. He was confident without being cocky, and just beautiful enough to make that confusing. Usually his kind wore their appeal like a Technicolor dream coat. This one, though . . . she couldn't quite figure out.

She let her gaze drop down the smooth expanse of his charcoal sports jacket and wondered about the physique beneath it. Hard lines, she guessed. Hard flesh, no give. His gabardine pants looked expensive and broke perfectly atop Italian leather loafers.

When he moved suddenly, she startled. If he knew she'd been staring, he didn't show it. He smiled at her and reached out to grab two champagne flutes off the tray of a waiter standing nearby. "Thirsty?" he finally spoke, holding out a glass.

"Thank you." She took the champagne and sipped it, nearly choking when the bubbles tickled her dry throat.

They lapsed into silence again. The female genitals painted on the canvas stared back at them. Sydney hadn't experienced shyness over her choice of subject before, but suddenly she couldn't get away from this painting fast enough.

"Let me know if you have any questions," she said dutifully as they sauntered toward the next painting. *Oh please don't have any questions.*

He didn't. They stopped beneath a display light that glared directly on a four-foot-high clitoris painted in varying shades of fuchsia and lavender. She'd forgotten about this one; it was a study in the most unforgiving secrets of female flesh. He looked at it, those green eyes tracking back and forth, top to bottom, like a dot matrix printer. What was he thinking?

She peered past him at the next canvas. A field of penises. "I like this next one better," she said, trying to move him along.

He didn't respond, didn't even glance in the direction she indicated. He stood rooted, his gaze fixed on the clitoris painting, while Sydney rubbed an aching spot between her eyebrows and tried not to look at him.

Damn it, but he was gorgeous. Beneath the fine lines, though, she saw only an unpredictable animal through the eyes of a woman who didn't feel comfortable with men in general. Her mother, who'd never married Sydney's father and rolled through a wild slew of boyfriends, had spoken of the male sex as though they were creatures in some exotic zoo. *Wolves*, she'd called them. *Thieves. Liars.* Love and hate.

Even Max, the only one Sydney had loved in her twenty-nine years, had proven himself equally deserving of both.

Once again, her gaze was drawn over her shoulder to her lover and his female friend. Max had always done the enamoring when it came to the fairer sex, but now he seemed lost in the force field of charisma Azure Elan radiated. And despite the hard-won healing that had taken place between him and Sydney since his accident—despite all the indications that he was a better, more honest man—Sydney recognized what was obviously a flirtation.

A sick feeling curled in her stomach, reawakened vestiges of the old days.

Wolves. Thieves. Liars.

Suddenly the silence between her and the undesired guest beside her seemed to roar in her ears. She turned back to him. "Have you two been dating long?" Her question rang out, disjointed and lacking key information.

He stirred from his meditation on the painting. "Who . . . you mean Azure and me?"

Azure. It sounded like a stage name, but it suited the woman's exotic beauty. That hair of hers—its darkness reflected the light, blacker than black, as though it had been dipped in Egyptian ink and combed through. She wore it like a priceless accessory.

"We've known each other a couple of years." Colm sounded distracted as he swirled his glass by its slender stem, the champagne sliding dangerously close to the lip. "She's a friend."

Sydney looked at him, threw back the remainder of her drink like a shot of whiskey, and coughed. "Really?"

"Really."

"She's stunning."

He shot a look over at Azure, shrugged, and then returned his attention to the painting. "I'm not sure how I feel about this."

For a moment she didn't follow. She was too busy entertaining a searing image of him and the stunning Azure wrapped in a tangle of linens, limbs, and lust. When she realized he meant the painting in front of them, she straightened her spine. "You don't like it?"

His mouth quirked. "You really want to know?"

"I always want to know what people think about my work."

"I like your work very much."

"Thank you." Something about the compliment told her a "but" was en route.

"But this one—it's not quite accurate. A woman's flesh is softer. The edges here are too bold. Too harsh."

She took a harder look at the composition, trying to see it through his eyes. For heaven's sake, she knew what a vulva looked like. What could possibly be inaccurate about her depiction? This particular canvas was the least abstract in the exhibit.

As if on cue, he added, "Is it supposed to be abstract?"

She winced. "Actually, Mr. Hennessy, no."

He finally abandoned the canvas and turned to her. Face-to-face they stood, Sydney hugging herself against the threat of a too-honest, too-beautiful man, and he with his hands tucked in his pants pockets, the edges of his gray sport coat caught behind his forearms. He didn't smile. He gazed straight into her and down into the empty place she thought was capped off for good.

"The grocery bagger called me 'Mr. Hennessy' today," he said. "And the doorman."

"I was always taught to address strangers politely."

"Am I still a stranger?"

"Of course," she shot back too quickly.

"I'd like to change that. We can handle this first-name issue you have when I see you again."

He was flirting. She wasn't. "You think you'll see me again, do you?"

"I don't *think*," he said. "I know."

If he'd smirked, shown the slightest hint of conceit, she would have walked away. But the sincerity in those striking green eyes brought out her six-shooters. "It's likely you won't. I may soon fall out of favor with Georgetown art aficionados."

"Why do you say that?"

Her chin lifted. "I'm supposed to be an erotic artist, but apparently I have my parts all wrong." Her earlobes went hot behind the pearl studs she wore. She knew better than to say what was coming, but she couldn't stop herself. "Tell me, are you a gynecologist?"

This time he did smile. Then he laughed. Only a little, but enough to elicit an embarrassed giggle from her own chest—and with it, a wave of ease.

"This is the silliest conversation I've ever had at one of these things," she said, tucking her hair behind her ear. "You're a piece of work."

"I've been called worse. And I'm not a gynecologist." They stood in silence that instantly turned awkward before he spoke again. "Did you use a model for this painting?"

She bit her lip and averted her eyes. "Well, yes. Me."

His dark brows shot up.

The experience had been brutally personal, but she would keep that to herself.

He cast another glance at the painting before his gaze returned to search hers. "At the risk of insulting you a second time, I stand by my original statement. A woman's flesh is softer than what you've painted here. And I'm willing to bet, Sydney, that despite what you see when you look in that mirror, *you* are softer, too."

Sydney blinked. She couldn't possibly be standing here talking about her own genitals with a total stranger. And what disarmed her most was the feeling that he referred to more than just her female anatomy.

This wasn't funny anymore.

He made it worse. "You're beautiful when you laugh. I don't think it comes easily to you, and that's a shame."

How could he know that laughter had become as alien to her as a foreign language? He'd committed a mortal error being so discerning, and an even worse one to throw a compliment into the mix.

"It's time to say goodnight," she murmured, staring into those pale green eyes and seeing twin reflections of a ghost. "Thank you for the stimulating conversation, Mr. Hennessy."

He inclined his head. "Thank you for the tour, Sydney."

And she left him standing before her naked self-portrait with its too-harsh, too-bold lines, each one a possibility that after all these years she still couldn't see the truth in the mirror.

CHAPTER THREE

Sydney rested her forehead in her hand and tried not to look at the buttered toast that Hans, the valet, had set in front of her. A storm thundered behind her eyes. When was the last time she'd suffered a hangover?

Champagne always made her sick, but last night it had been blessedly close at hand. She'd returned to Max's side, smiling politely, guzzling bubbly and shivering inside, while Azure and Max wound up their cozy conversation. When Azure finally bid goodbye and glided over to rejoin Colm, Sydney watched with narrow interest as the man laid a solicitous hand at the small of his date's back to escort her out. *Just friends*, he'd claimed, but Azure's serpentine confidence said Colm was all hers. It didn't matter. Somehow Sydney knew he would look back at her—something sick and petty in her wanted him to—and in the end he hadn't disappointed her. He'd cast a humorless glance over his shoulder at Sydney as he ushered Azure toward the exit, and then they were gone. Magical, inhuman creatures, vanished from her sight, and she could breathe again.

Sydney touched a fingertip to the crust on the toast. It came away glistening with melted butter. Nausea crept around her stomach and her mouth watered. The early sun had shifted enough in the last five minutes to dump its insidious spotlight through the French doors and over her head.

Across a table big enough to seat ten, Max finally lowered the wall of newspaper and snapped it closed into a neat square. He set it beside his plate, pressed it into a rectangle, and lined it up with his untouched grapefruit spoon.

"Are you sick?" he asked lightly, his pale hand smoothing the paper over and over in the odd ritual he performed every day.

She forced herself to take a sip of coffee, the slight tremor of her fingers causing dark liquid to slosh into the saucer. "A little hungover, maybe."

He raised his brows. "Do you want Hans to bring you aspirin?"

"I think I've swallowed half the bottle already." She grimaced. "It'll pass. I didn't realize how much champagne I put away last night."

He seemed hypnotized by the movement of his own hand as it continued to stroke the folded newspaper. "What would possess you to drink something that always makes you ill?"

Sydney thought of the handsome man from the reception and a fresh spear of pain pierced her skull. "Nerves, I guess. The show was pretty explicit, even for me." Such a lie. They both knew she aimed to be as brutal as possible in her depictions of eroticism.

A hint of surprise crossed Max's aquiline features, and then his expression eased into concern. "Maybe you need to throw yourself full force into the canvases for the next show. Begin immediately. You seem to need the escape."

On the heels of what had happened last night after they got home, anger grabbed her by the throat. "What do you mean?"

His gray gaze shifted to the sunlit windows. "I don't know. This drinking champagne thing, for example. And last night after we came home . . ."

"Yes, Max, that fiasco might just go down in infamy." She gave a choked laugh and fought a fresh wave of nausea. God, she'd made a fool of herself. On the drive out to the suburbs, sequestered in the back of Max's limousine, she'd felt strangely awakened, alive, hungry. How long had it been since she'd had sex of any sort? Six months? Seven?

Max hardly seemed interested anymore, and guilt edged her frustration. She understood he was fragile despite his smooth demeanor, but last night she didn't want to feel compassion or pity for him. She wanted a lover. Their relationship was tattered and threadbare, but they were still together. She wanted—needed—to be touched, and Max could do that. Despite the distance between them lately, she could make him want her again.

Once home, she'd accepted his perfunctory goodnight kiss, then headed to her bedroom and thrown on one of the sheer nighties he'd bought her in the old days. Then she tiptoed down the corridor to his room, pulse pounding as though she were disobeying some kind of unspoken law. When she tapped on his door and peeked in, he'd already hoisted himself into bed by the metal bar mounted above the four-poster, the coverlet and sheets neatly folded on his lap.

Like the newspaper, she thought now. Every part of every day the same. Every morning, the same poached egg and toast on his plate, the same grapefruit he never ate but insisted Hans serve him. Why did he waste the fruit? *Because he could.* Why did he waste her? *Because he could.*

"Max," she said from behind her hand. "When did I become the grapefruit?"

The clang of his juice glass bumping the side of his plate made her jerk. "What?"

"The grapefruit." She let her fingers slide away from her face. "You never touch it. It sits in its bowl in front of you. You look at it. Maybe you think about tasting it, but you never do."

Last night he'd actually flushed at the sight of her standing so brave and transparent in his doorway. All he'd done was stare at her in her pathetic see-through nightie without uttering a word. Could a dearth of desire be as consuming as lust? It had felt that way in the passage of those excruciating seconds. After a moment, she'd backed out of the bedroom and closed the door soundlessly behind her, too mortified to cry.

"Why didn't you say anything to me last night?" she asked from her sun-drenched spot at the other end of the table, a thousand miles away.

The frown creasing his brow deepened. "You caught me off guard."

"I was trying to fix what's wrong between us lately."

"Do you know what that might be?" he asked with a faint, regretful smile.

She sighed. "Besides lack of sex?"

"I wasn't ready last night when you showed up. I was tired."

"Okay. But can't you simply sleep beside me? I hate our separate bedrooms."

"I keep you awake at night, especially if I have to get up for something."

"I wouldn't mind," she said.

"But I do. Look, Sydney . . . all couples go through rough spots. You know I—"

The jarring gong of the doorbell pealed through the house, followed by the *shushing* sound of Hans's footsteps as he crossed through several rooms to answer it.

The interruption hardly permeated Sydney's focus. By God, she was feeling something . . . something good and bad and arctic, like she'd been doused with ice water. Something besides guilt for the first time in two years.

"Max? I don't need more than just a touch."

"I can have sex if I choose," he said flatly, as though she'd accused him of being impotent. After the accident, they'd gone to great lengths together to regain his abilities, trying Viagra and even a miraculous medical vibrator that allowed him to climax. For a while, it had given them back their lovemaking. So why had he become so distant? What had she done to deserve it?

"I know you can have sex." She picked up her coffee cup again just to give her hands something to do. "Why don't you? With me?"

"We'll talk about this later."

"I think now is a good time."

He didn't reply, just stared at her in stony silence as though willing her to drop the subject. And in the glare of the sun, a flash of ebony hair like Chinese silk darted across her memory.

Her back came off the chair and she braced her forearms on the edge of the table. "Are you sleeping with that woman from the reception last night?"

He let out a bark of laughter. "Don't be ridiculous."

Sydney had been *ridiculous* before, of course. The many nights before his fall from the cliff, when he would come home late and she'd question him. *Ridiculous*, he would say. *You're being silly and insecure.* A week before the accident, Max's accountant came to Sydney on the sly, unable to hold the truth any longer. He'd confirmed Max's relationship with the office receptionist, the one who looked so innocent and peppy with her fawn eyes and fawn ponytail that swung to and fro. Love, sex—Sydney didn't care what had compelled Max to cheat. She packed, moved into a pathetic rental, and locked herself in, trying to plot out a life without the man she'd loved and thought she knew.

And then, while supposedly drowning his remorse on the West Coast, he had plunged off the sheer face of a mountain in a futile attempt to save a climbing buddy, who died in the fall anyway. Max had dropped one hundred fifty feet and shattered three vertebrae. Maybe it was pity that drew Sydney back to him; maybe it was the fact that she hadn't had time to get over their breakup before he was injured, but against her better judgment, she went when he reached for her. At first his remorse for his past infidelity, his newly loving manner, fed her trust like gentle summer rain. But now, the fragile peace they'd forged trembled like the coffee cup in her fingers.

"You don't have to have sex with me at the drop of a hat," she told him in a low voice as approaching footsteps grew closer. "But you *do* have to talk to me. And you do have to be honest."

His expression softened and he stretched out a hand toward her, even though he couldn't reach her from where he sat. "I will. I'll— *we'll* talk about this," he promised, just in time for the valet to reappear in the breakfast room doorway.

"Mr. Hennessy is here," Hans said lightly. "The houseboy is putting his bags in the guesthouse."

Sydney glanced between the two men. *Mr. Hennessy?*

"He's early," Max said, wiping his unsmiling mouth with his napkin. "But show him in."

And before another thought could cross Sydney's mind . . . before she could draw another breath . . . Mr. Hennessy materialized in the doorway.

Colm stood at the threshold and watched the color in Sydney's face drain away and return as two red spots on her cheeks. *Nice*, he thought. Beaudoin hadn't warned her. To her credit, though, she pushed back her chair and rose, graceful, slim, immaculate. No makeup. She stood golden in the autumn sun that streamed in the windows behind her.

"Hennessy." With a boisterous enthusiasm most likely for Sydney's benefit, Beaudoin wheeled back from the table and rolled toward Colm. "Welcome! Sydney, do you remember our new friend?" He directed the question without even looking at Sydney, but Colm glanced her way.

She definitely wasn't happy. "What a pleasant surprise, Mr. Hennessy," she said. "Max didn't tell me we were expecting you."

The left wheel of Max's wheelchair brushed the leg of Colm's jeans. When Colm looked down at him, the man's hand was extended, waiting to crush the hell out of anyone idiotic enough to take it. Colm let a grudging smile touch his lips as he accepted the handshake and Max once again gripped like a steel trap. He was a strong bastard, there was no question. His arms were lean and muscled from pushing himself around.

"Sydney," he said, without turning his cool gaze away from Colm's face, "meet your birthday present."

Colm cleared his throat and looked at her.

She'd seated herself again, fingers white-knuckled on the arms of her chair. "What?"

"Colm is an experienced art model, darling." Max's voice echoed in the massive room, sounding unnaturally friendly and somewhat higher than Colm remembered. "I thought it might be nice to have you work from the real deal rather than go into the city and snap photos of college kids. Your work comes to life when you use live models."

Sydney's pleasant mask never faltered, but her blue eyes narrowed. "When did you arrange this?"

"A couple of weeks ago."

Her eyebrows drew down. "But last night you two acted like you didn't know each other."

"We didn't want to ruin the surprise," Colm said, coming to the rescue. "We felt it was a good time to see if you'd be receptive."

"And was I, Mr. Hennessy?" She was speaking to Colm, but she glared at Max. "Receptive?"

"I thought you and Colm would get along fine or he wouldn't be here," Max said.

"And now it's my turn to decide the same, I suppose." Irritation shortened her words.

"Absolutely, darling." Beaudoin's good humor returned, high wattage and out of place. "Come in, Colm, and have some breakfast."

Colm pulled out the chair at Sydney's right elbow and sat. "Just a cup of coffee would be great."

With timing as impeccable as his high-shined wing tips, the valet appeared with a tray holding a mug and a silver coffeepot, and set the mug before Colm.

Colm eyed the bar in the corner. The half-filled decanters winked at him in the morning sun.

"Last night you didn't tell me you were a model, Mr. Hennessy." Sydney held her cup steady while the valet poured. Her tone held a slight note of accusation, but when Colm glanced at her, she smiled sweetly and sipped her coffee.

"Max was being kind when he called me experienced," he said. "I pose occasionally at the colleges in the area. There's not much to being a model."

"I beg to differ. You have to have strength, stillness, and patience to hold the poses, especially for me. Do you think you'll be able to manage standing buck-naked in a drafty studio, unable to move for an hour at a time?"

The ornate antique chair squeaked as he sat back to meet her direct gaze. "You can't scare me off that easily."

"How do you feel about working with other models intimately? Have you ever done anything like this? Remember, it's erotic art."

"Colm and I have discussed all this, Sydney," Max said from the other end of the massive table. "This is your birthday present. No interrogation is necessary." He added a smile, but Sydney didn't return it. She looked from one face to the other, then wadded her napkin and set it beside her coffee cup.

"Well, it appears you've thought of everything."

"And yet you don't seem pleased," Max added, his mild expression fading. "Would you like me to ask Colm to leave?"

Colm swallowed a mouthful of coffee and waited as hot color flooded Sydney's face anew. Beside her plate, her hand clenched the napkin. "What if I said yes?"

"Sydney—"

"I'm just stunned, especially since you know how I feel about working with only one model in the studio."

"We can bring in more from the city," Max said. "Would that suit you?"

She appeared to think about it and then stared out the window, the light limning her profile.

Max glanced at Colm and gave his grapefruit bowl an impatient nudge. "Sydney? Is this yes or no?"

Jesus, Colm thought. Sydney was tired of the toys Daddy brought her. Maybe if Daddy would ask her what she liked once in a while . . .

"I see this as a challenge, Max," she finally spoke. "I'll take your suggestion and get started on the next show immediately. Let me go upstairs and change into my work clothes." She stood again, elegant and cool in her white sleeveless blouse and unwrinkled khaki shorts, offered Colm a polite smile, and headed for the door leading to the foyer. When she reached it, she paused. "I didn't ask if you were ready to begin so quickly, Mr. Hennessy."

"I'm ready," Colm said, feeling Max's gaze on him.

"Wonderful," Max said. "I'll show you to the studio while Sydney gets ready."

I'm not going to ask how you plan to do this," the man in the wheelchair said, his tone cold and clipped. "Just do it and do it quickly."

Colm folded his hands behind his back and walked alongside Beaudoin as they crossed a rocky section of yard leading toward a stone cottage. The terrain was uneven and when Max hit a rock he couldn't maneuver over, he cursed and pushed in vain at his wheels.

Automatically, Colm reached to help the chair forward, but Max's head snapped around and he shot Colm a venomous glare. "Don't touch the chair. Ever."

Hands held aloft, Colm stepped back and picked up his pace, a cold knot forming in his gut. This was a hell of a game. Why would Beaudoin want to trap Sydney in infidelity, anyway? Had she already had affairs? She didn't seem like the kind. She didn't seem like any kind except closed off, pissed off, and probably lonely. Colm knew what it was to love someone in a wheelchair, to ache over the vibrant being that person once had been, and the agony of guilt that followed. It was possible things had cooled between Sydney and Beaudoin, but if Colm read her right, it had little if anything to do with the wheelchair. Max was a real bastard.

He reached the cottage door and waited for Beaudoin to catch up with him. Max was panting as he rolled around Colm to unlock the studio door. A twinge of sympathy seized Colm for an instant, but he banished it. This man wasn't pitiful. He was underhanded

and manipulative, cut from the same cloth as so many of the people
Colm had met in the sex trade. Colm was no better. He recognized
his own self in Beaudoin, and it sickened him.

The pungent smell of turpentine filled the air as they entered the
building. A ramp led down into a single, sprawling room floored in
golden oak planks, its walls white-washed and hung with myriad
canvases.

None were erotic. They were portraits: old men and women with
craggy features, smooth-faced children and cherubic babies. Lithe-
some figures of women. *Rubenesque*, Colm thought, studying one
painting of a chubby woman whose mouse brown hair had slipped
from its bun and snaked down her milky back.

His fingers fisted and unclenched. He wanted to touch; the tex-
tures and features were so tactile. There was a luminosity to each
work here that her erotic art didn't yield. Colm pictured Sydney's
brush lovingly stroking the ivory-smooth flesh of the Rubenesque
painting, the passion in her face as she worked, the fierce concentration that would be there, such a disparity to the coolness she wore
like a costume—and fought the urge to adjust himself in his jeans.
The image was more erotic than anything he'd seen in the gallery
last night.

He stepped off the side of the ramp and wandered to the center
of the studio, where he examined the easel covered with a paint-
spattered sheet, the rickety-looking side table beside a seventies barstool where she sat to work; the outdated boom box which boasted
a CD and cassette player. That, too, was splashed with paint. Beyond her station, toward the middle of the room, sat a naked wooden
stage. The model's platform. He wondered how many hours he
would spend equally naked atop it before he reached for Sydney and
she came to him. Maybe they would have sex right there on the bare
wood. It would dig into their skin, but he wouldn't feel the splinters.

He would bury himself as deep in her as he could and feel nothing but the pleasure. No guilt. He would play the game Beaudoin's way, and Sydney would lose.

". . . And I don't need to tell you drugs are strictly forbidden," Beaudoin was saying from the top of the ramp. Colm had nearly forgotten the man was there.

"I don't do drugs," Colm said. "An Avalon rule."

"This isn't Avalon. Azure isn't your pimp here. I am. Keep in mind who's paying you and we'll get along just fine, Hennessy."

Colm was squelching the urge to tell him to screw himself when the man added in a more subdued tone, "I'm aware you're curious about this situation."

"It's none of my business."

"No." Max's mouth twisted into a smile. "I'm going to tell you anyway. If Sydney passes this test, I plan to ask her to marry me."

Holy shit.

"Sydney is everything to me. I molded her into what she is today—beautiful, talented, polished. I took her for granted once, but now I see the value of what I nearly threw away. I'm certain of what I want, and I want her. But not unless she's as trustworthy and loyal as she appears."

Colm wandered back to the easel and fingered the edge of the sheet. "Has she done anything to make you think you can't trust her?"

"I don't like the way she looks at other men. Deep into their faces, like she could swallow them. I've never seen such intensity. She did it with you last night. Surely you noticed it."

All of a sudden it became clear. Weren't cheaters always the first to suspect infidelity in others? "She hardly looked at me," he said, and meant it. "She seemed skittish and uncomfortable last night."

"Well, you could have fooled me. Like most women, she's no doubt vulnerable to . . ." He looked Colm up and down. "Something

like you. I don't want her to be like most women. She has to prove
that she isn't."

"Wouldn't a prenup be easier?" Colm murmured, running a finger
beneath the sheet to peek at what was beneath. Looking at the man
was twisting his stomach.

Max ignored the question. He wheeled backward to open the
door. "Do what you're supposedly so goddamned good at and if she
folds, come straight to me."

Colm nodded. "I do have one question. You've paid me to do this
whether I succeed or not. How does that work for you?"

"I'll pay you double if you succeed."

"You mean intercourse, not just foreplay."

"If you want to walk out of here with your hands full of cash. Do
it right and I'll pay you and you'll go. No long good-byes. No emotional bullshit. She might be hurt, but I can hurt her much worse
than you ever could, Hennessy. Do your job and get the hell out.
You have two weeks."

This really wasn't about money—or trust. It was about keeping
Sydney up high and pretty on her shelf. For an instant Colm was
tempted to go easy on Sydney. Even if he didn't, even if she didn't
pass the test, she'd probably be better off without Max. Then he
thought of the money. Double what he'd been told, and all to take
a woman to bed like he did at Avalon nearly every night. All to wrap
himself around a rare beauty like Sydney and then be done.

He thought of Amelia. Of the bills, and his dream to quit Avalon.

Two weeks. He would do the job and then get the hell out.

CHAPTER FOUR

Sydney paced the long expanse of the studio while Colm changed in the small bathroom. She'd given him a robe for the sake of modesty, and for her own sanity. She didn't need him naked to begin the portrait, but by God, if this is what Max wanted, this is what Max would get.

Challenge, indeed. Why had he done this to her? He knew how she felt being alone in a studio with a man. She always, always worked with two or more models, and he *knew* that. He knew her past, knew what she'd gone through with her mother's boyfriend and the fathomless, insidious damage, so why had he disrespected her this way? Her stomach somersaulted for the fiftieth time since Colm Hennessy walked into the dining room. Maybe Max didn't know her after all. She thought herself utterly transparent, but maybe they had lost each other. She'd always looked to him for guidance to steer her in the right direction, much as she considered herself his partner and protector when he was vulnerable. She'd trusted him blindly too often.

And perhaps he'd trusted her just as mindlessly. She wasn't

the same young fool from four years ago, or the sympathetic, still-enamored woman who came back to him after he fell. Not anymore. She didn't want an agent or a father figure. She wanted love; she wanted to be allowed to love, but Max was playing games she didn't understand, loving her in fits and starts, and she hated it.

Sometimes she hated him.

When Colm emerged from the bathroom, she jerked awake, averted her eyes, and returned to her easel, where she fiddled with her brushes in the pregnant silence. He sat on the edge of the modeling platform and waited. After a painful length of time, in which she felt she'd adequately built a barrier between them, she looked up. "Let's get started."

He stepped up on the stage, but when he started to disrobe, she shook her head. "Just as you are for now. I expect you need time to adjust to the situation."

"Not really." Who knew such light green eyes could give off heat?

"Well, I do. In fact . . ." She strode to a small, retro-looking cabinet and rifled through it. "There's a bottle of something in here . . . here it is." She withdrew a bottle of red wine. "I know it's early, Mr. Hennessy, but do you like Shiraz?"

"I do."

She pulled out two plastic tumblers and poured a splash in each, then returned to him and handed him his cup. "Cheers," she said, lifting her tumbler in an age-old gesture.

He held up his cup. "Here's to me getting naked and you being comfortable with that."

Sydney gave a huff of laughter. "Have you forgotten eroticism is my subject of choice? My choice, Mr. Hennessy. I like erotic art."

Colm glanced around at the chaste portraits and lifted an eyebrow at her.

She took another gulp of wine and drained the cup. A little hair of the dog, but its bitter fruitiness only tilted her stomach. "Here's to us making the most of an awkward situation."

"And you calling me something other than 'Mr. Hennessy.'"

"I can't say that will ever happen. Are you finished with your wine?"

He handed her his cup, which she discarded in a nearby trash can. Then she returned to her easel, picked up a piece of charcoal, and clipped a practice sheet of newsprint to the board while he returned to the center of the platform.

"Where do you want me?" His voice echoed in the vaulted-ceilinged room. She liked the sound of it: low but not baritone. A little husky.

"Right where you are." Shifting her attention from his green eyes to his body did little to alleviate her discomfort. "Just stand still and let me get in some warm-up sketches."

He stood dutifully still, hands at his sides, shoulders stretching the robe so that it gaped at the chest, which rose and fell with each breath. He kept his lashes mostly downcast except for stealing one glance at her, which went through her like a tiny electric jolt.

Her charcoal faltered on the page, then resumed. After a moment, the wine curled warmth through her limbs. The lines were coming more fluidly now as she finished a study of his uncomplicated stance. His bare legs were strong, muscled. As she'd suspected the night before, he was well-proportioned. A perfect model for her work—both erotic and otherwise.

She set down the charcoal, tore out a new piece of newsprint, and looked at him, her heart hammering, mouth gone dry. When his eyes met hers, she said flatly, "You can disrobe now, Mr. Hennessy."

He shifted his weight and shrugged out of the robe, tossed it aside, and resumed his stance.

Oh, Jeez.

She tried not to look at anything but his shoulders. They were a good place to start. Then his chest, a study in celestial musculature. Over his heart was a tattoo, a cursive word she couldn't discern except that it started with *A*. Her gaze dropped lower. He had a six-pack, naturally. Wonderfully defined flanks.

Even his penis was just right.

"Do you have a pair of boxer shorts?" she asked, redirecting her attention to her disaster of a drawing.

"Back at the cabin."

"Bring them next time. I don't always know what I'm going to do at first. I change my mind frequently and abruptly. Just now, I think I've decided to work on certain parts of your body instead of the whole thing."

That didn't come out quite the way she'd planned. His surprised hesitation filled the room before she hurried, "I mean, turn your back to me." That might keep the blood in her head instead of running amok to other places.

Bad idea. His backside belonged to Michelangelo's David, sculpted and pale like alabaster where the sun hadn't touched him. He obviously worked out, although she had a feeling that kind of physique was also a case of excellent genes. And the way he stood, at ease, head slightly lowered, made her think he was giving her the chance to look at all of him, to savor what they both knew was stunning.

Heat slid through her veins, a heat she hadn't felt since before Max's accident. And God, it was a welcome sensation. She shifted on her barstool and rubbed her free hand on her denim-covered thigh. She could hardly sit still, suddenly.

"Wrap the robe around your waist," she ordered a little too sharply. "I want the material, the . . . the extra element of . . . you know what I mean."

He grabbed it off the floor and did as he was told, then secured the belt low on his hips so as not to interrupt the drape of material. He was experienced. Maybe even a magazine model, the idealized variety she couldn't stand.

"Have you modeled before?" she asked lightly, studying the play of light on the tanned skin of his back. "Fashion magazines, that sort of thing."

"When I was in college I gave it a shot. I hated it."

"Even the money? The gorgeous women?"

At the cynicism in her tone, he glanced over his shoulder at her, and she winced. She was being a bitch and didn't know why. Max was the one she was angry with, not Colm. It wasn't his fault he was so damned hot.

For a long time he didn't speak, letting her bathe in her own shame. She half expected him to pick up his things and excuse himself. She would deserve it.

Then to her surprise, he said, "Can I ask you some questions now?"

"Okay." She'd sketched his back and buttocks, even though she'd started out trying to do a portrait study of his head and shoulders. She'd drawn them all wrong, too. Starting at the top again, she pressed hard to banish the previous lines.

"Tell me where you're from," he said.

"Nebraska." She feathered the charcoal along the sides of the image's spine to capture his musculature. "You?"

"Virginia."

"From around here?"

"Southwest Virginia."

"You have no accent."

"It was hammered out of me." Before she could press for more information, he said, "You do incredible portraits. Are you formally trained?"

"Homegrown, I'm afraid. My aunt taught me. She was a successful artist in the sixties—Lila Warren. Have you heard of her?"

"No, but then I don't hang out in artists' circles."

"What about the art modeling?"

"It's been awhile, and it was mostly for students." He moved, a
natural shift brought on by relaxation. Fluid, graceful. Her charcoal
faltered, and she forced herself to objectify the slight shine of perspiration on his skin. Just sweat. A human body's natural response
to heat. Despite the drafty studio, the lights aimed at the platform
radiated warmth. Her own brow was damp, too. Maybe the heat
was why her lines ran all over the place. This was already a mess and
they'd only just started.

Drawing number two in the garbage.

"Why do you do this?" he asked suddenly.

She hesitated in the midst of pinning up a fresh sheet of paper.
"What do you mean?"

"Why do you choose erotic art over portraiture, when you obviously have an affinity for people's faces?"

"Sex sells." She stroked the charcoal down the length of his
image's spine. "You can't argue with that."

He said nothing.

"There's no shame in it if you can rise above it and do what you
have to do," she added.

His head turned slightly, a smile curving his mouth. "Really?
Not even a little?"

Sydney swallowed. The practice drawing was turning into a disaster. After another futile attempt, she sighed, set the charcoal in
the tray, and turned off the work light. "That's all for today."

Colm glanced at the clock. "We were only at it a few minutes."

"I'm just trying to get a feel for your body." A new blush warmed
her face. "You know what I mean."

He flashed her a grin. "What are your plans for the rest of today?"

"I need to talk to Max," she said quickly. "Then I'm going into the city."

"To photograph models?" At her nod, he added, "You really are uncomfortable being alone with me."

"You're a stranger, Mr. Hennessy."

"I won't be for long if you'll give me a chance. Let's be friends."

She sighed and glanced at the last drawing. It looked like something a ten-year-old could produce. "Look, I know you're trying, and I'll do my best to . . . to meet you halfway. Today I don't need to photograph models. I just need more people for the idea I have for this project. I'm going into the city to pick the right models to work with you."

"What's your idea?"

"A ménage à trois."

"Right." He stepped off the platform, stripped the robe from his hips as though being naked was the most natural thing in the world for him. Sydney closed her eyes and wished for that same lack of inhibition, but it would never happen. When she opened her eyes, he'd disappeared into the dressing room.

"Two women and me?" he asked from behind the curtain. At her silence, she heard him laugh. "It was worth a shot."

"Are you too shy to pose with another man, Mr. Hennessy?"

"Not too shy. I just like women."

"I can easily find someone else to do this if you—"

He stepped back into the room with jeans on, barefoot and shirt unbuttoned. "No. I can handle whatever floats your boat. Boss," he added, although the humor in his words didn't reach his green eyes.

"Don't call me Boss."

"Don't call me Mr. Hennessy."

"I'll let you see yourself out." She started for the door.

"Sydney."

She paused on the ramp, her heart pounding. The way he spoke her name made her feel like they shared a secret.

"I might know someone you can use," he said. "A male model, anyway. He's a friend of mine. Maybe I could save you some of the search."

She rested her hand on the latch and was silent for a long time. Then without looking at him, she said, "Is he as fit and good-looking as—is he fit and good-looking?"

"From a guy's point of view, yeah, I'd have to say so. He usually has women all over him."

"Lovely. Then talk to him and let me know what he says. I'd like an answer as soon as possible."

". . . Colm."

"Colm," she conceded. But she left the studio without looking back at him again.

CHAPTER FIVE

She found Max in the house's gym with a new massage therapist, a young sandy-blonde who looked pale and nervous as she cradled his head in her hands and gently moved it side to side. Sydney knew he often had muscle spasms, and she prayed his temper wouldn't run this therapist off as it had the last three.

"You finished early." He jerked his head aside and brushed the woman away to look at Sydney from his prone position on the table.

"I wanted to talk to you before I go into the city. I need more models for this particular project," she added quickly, before he could ask about Colm. "They'll have to come out here for a few sessions, unless you wouldn't mind me working in the city."

"I'd rather you work here, naturally. And what about Hennessy?"

"He'll be part of it, of course. But while we're on that subject, I have something to say."

Max raised a hand to stop her and glared at the massage therapist, who, to keep from being in the way of the conversation, had gone to work gently limbering his legs. "For Christ's sake, Tina, are you trying to shove my knee down my throat?"

She murmured an apology and resumed bending his leg more gently, but her hands shook around his bony knee.

Sydney couldn't stand it anymore. "I need to speak to you in private." It was the truth, but she also felt sorry for the therapist and wanted to give her a break. "Give me five minutes," she told the woman.

When the grateful-looking therapist had washed her hands and departed, Sydney came around the table and perched beside Max. "Why did you hire Colm?"

He looked at her, his gray eyes searching her face, and then sighed. "I'm aware of your restlessness lately. I wanted to encourage you to start again as soon as possible. Between shows, you seem lost. This time, I thought—"

"But why didn't you tell me this before? And warn me? I would have listened to your idea, even if the thought of having a single model out here in my studio makes me uncomfortable. And why a male one?"

"Hennessy seems like a superior specimen." His gaze shifted away, his mouth thinning. "Surely you can see that. I'm a man, and even I can recognize that he's art on legs. I thought having a male model might help you work through some of your idiosyncrasies."

Hurt bolted through her, stinging her eyes. "My idiosyncrasies? They're fears!"

"And when will you get help for them, for Christ's sake? When will you let go of the past?" Max reached out and grasped her wrist when she went to jerk away. "Sydney. You talk about our lack of a sex life, but I never know who you're thinking of in bed with me— that bastard who took such advantage of you years ago, or me."

She dropped her head and squeezed back the tears. She never thought of that man from so long ago, but she couldn't convince Max of it. She'd tried counseling a couple of years ago to rid herself of the bad memories, but it had only seemed to feed them. Then the accident happened, and since then, she hadn't had time to think about the past, her youth, anything much but Max, his needs and her own for him. She couldn't explain it. She didn't know if she loved him anymore—maybe hadn't since the night he cheated on her—but he was her stability.

Until lately. Until Colm Hennessy.

"I don't want you to run off to the city," he said, caressing the wrist he had grabbed. "Every time you go, you're gone all day. You're so far away. Maybe I've hired this man for selfish reasons, but only because I miss you. I need you out here, Sydney. *I need* you."

Sydney hesitated, her chest pulling tight. She didn't often see beyond his cheerful, steely bravado, but the plea in his gray eyes now grabbed her anger and ran off with it. He seemed smaller, lying on the massage table with two useless limbs and that prison of a wheelchair hovering ever near.

She sighed. "I'll try to recruit a couple of women models to buffer things. I know you meant well by hiring Colm, and I'm trying to understand."

He offered her a smile that didn't quite warm the piercing way he studied her. What was he thinking when he looked at her like that? She fought the urge to fold her arms over her heart, to protect herself, and yet this was Max. The same man she'd known and loved for four years. When had it all become so strange?

He broke from his trance and squeezed her hand. "I've got to finish this damned massage therapy, but tonight I'll take you out and we'll talk more. We'll have dinner in Middleburg at that inn you love. Would you like that?"

Mixing food with discussions of their relationship issues didn't exactly appeal to Sydney, but she wouldn't dash his well-meaning intentions. "I would. And what about Colm?"

Instantly Max's expression hardened. "He isn't a guest here, he's an employee. He can find his own meals when he isn't invited to join us."

Sydney pressed her lips together and nodded.

"Now will you tell Theresa to get back in here? I want this hellish session over with."

"I think her name is Tina." She bent to kiss his lips and to her amazement felt the touch of his tongue, just for an instant. "I'll see you tonight."

"Yes," he said. "If it's good for you."

She didn't know what was good for her anymore, only that something had to change, *was* changing, and she couldn't stop it.

With the afternoon off, Colm buried his frustration in a long run around the estate. The gold and russet trees canopied the soft path, the call of unseen wildlife soothing his irritation. He hated every moment of the situation with Sydney and Beaudoin. He hadn't deciphered Sydney yet, but his knowledge of the finer sex had become honed in the last three years, and he recognized an easy mark when he saw one. She reminded him of the myriad clients who'd passed through his doorway since the whole Avalon thing had started. Lost women too long neglected, beautiful, untouchable except with a total stranger between the sheets. Then they came apart under his hands, a double-edged sword that spoke to his male ego but also left him feeling empty and desperate.

Long gone were the days of worshiping and designing civil architecture. He'd been so self-important then. Another Louis Henri Sullivan or Frank Lloyd Wright. He'd thought the world spun solely for him.

Amelia's face floated through his mind, and he picked up speed.

This was all for her. Maybe one day when they were old, he would tell her what he'd done to keep her in good care and she would understand. He couldn't help Jill now, but his sister . . . she was the life that remained. Real life.

Tears stung his eyes as the unseasonably cold wind assaulted him, and he sprinted faster, leaping over logs and debris, mindless and driven, until his lungs threatened to rise into his throat and choke him.

He circled the entire estate without realizing the distance he'd covered until the house and its outlying buildings came into view. Then he half-stumbled to a stop and braced his hands on his knees, panting and nearly sick. When he glanced at the mansion, the draperies in the living room wafted aside and he found himself the object of Beaudoin's unyielding regard. He didn't bother to raise a hand in greeting. He looked away, caught his breath, and then walked the rest of the way to the guest cabin.

The shower beat down on his head, washing away vestiges of his run and lingering waves of pain. He dressed, and with his hair still damp, climbed into his black Ford Explorer and headed back toward the city, past mansions that rivaled Beaudoin's whitewashed brick behemoth, past worlds he couldn't possibly understand except when the ladies of the house crawled into his bed at Avalon. Then he lived and breathed their opulence, and it echoed with empty restlessness.

Near his home in Silver Spring, he stopped at the usual flower stand and purchased a bouquet from an old man, who said, "Mums today? What happened to the usual roses?"

Colm smiled and took the bouquet. "I like to keep her guessing."

The house was chilly. Amelia's nurses were changing shifts and

though they both greeted him, the one departing—the new one—
spoke a little more warmly than the other. Colm recognized the
smile all too well. He returned it, holding her gaze just long enough
to ensure maybe an extra kindness or two for Amelia. There were
times that head-to-toe appraisal bolstered him. He'd come to rely
on slow looks for all sorts of twisted reasons.

He didn't realize how tired he was until he stepped into his sister's bedroom and set the flowers on the bedside table. Her closed
eyelids didn't flutter. She was so still, her dark lashes like smudges of
ashes against her cheeks. For one horrifying instant he imagined her
dead, even though he knew better. She always slept deeply after particularly taxing physical therapy sessions. But the same jolting fear
woke him up a lot of nights, soaked in sweat and heart pounding.

Sleeping. She's just sleeping.

The world shrank, drawing in its ragged edges until it was just
the two of them, siblings against the world. Their world, the strange
and wonderful one they'd forged as twins. But now . . . he was a
whore. She was a quadriplegic, and nearly unrecognizable. He was
responsible for all of it, and here he stood, offering a damned bouquet of flowers, a sad symbol of the bright promise they'd both displayed once upon a time.

Sinking to the chair, he glanced around and sighed. Three years
ago this room had been his home office. Cluttered computer desk
and drafting table in the corner near the window, no blinds or curtains, sunlight flooding the space. Plans on that drafting table.
Dreams. Now the room felt arctic, its cold seeping through his gray
Henley shirt, and the place smelled like Pine-Sol.

He grabbed an extra blanket from the foot of the bed and spread
it over Amelia, then focused on her face and reached out to finger the
dark silky strands on the pillow. She had always been petite, but now
she was as small as a child, and so damned pale. Grief welled in his

chest and he laid his forehead on the bed near where her hand lay. "Just sleep," he whispered. "Rest." As long as she slept, she escaped her reality, and he could find a moment's respite from the guilt.

It's always about you, isn't it?

The knot in his throat grew. Usually he could keep it together when he was home, but today he felt so beaten. Maybe it came from being inundated with Beaudoin's malice and the knowledge of Sydney's inevitable victimization at Colm's own hands. Maybe it was the fact that on a rain-soft night three years ago, he and Jill had been arguing about nothing in the car—with Amelia in the backseat, unbelted, the stubborn fool—and he was more interested in his own irritation than the wet bridge, and when their Lexus hydroplaned into oncoming traffic, he hadn't been able to stop it. Maybe it was because he still missed his wife sometimes, not the fighting, but the way they had been in the beginning . . . and maybe it was because in three years' time he had nearly screwed her out of his memory.

"You never feel anyone else's pain, do you?" Jill had accused him. *"You're like an automaton. What will it take to wake you up?"*

The last words he'd heard before the collision. They stayed with him. *What will it take to wake you up?* He was the one sleeping now, not his sister.

Without warning his shoulders started shaking, and he pressed his face against the sheets by Amelia's hand. Every time he thought he was cried out, the emotions surprised him. He was so empty, but the tears—they lurked, each one a scalding reminder of his and Amelia's destruction.

When the nurse came in to check on his sister, he kept his head down. The nurse acted like she didn't notice, and he was grateful. He liked this warm, heavyset woman who watched over his twin. Hell, she took care of him, too, when he needed it.

After a while he regained his decorum, snatched a tissue from the nearby box and wiped his face. "How long has she been asleep?"

"An hour," Jane whispered. "She'll sleep into the evening. She had a rough day."

He swallowed and looked at Amelia's hand rather than at the nurse. His sister's skin reminded him of rice paper. The veins marked a diminutive map beneath it. "I can't stay long enough to see her awake," he whispered back. "I'm working out of town for the next couple of weeks, but I'm still as close as the phone. All you have to do is call and I'll get here, Jane. Any issues, any problem, and—"

"You'll know immediately," she said gently.

"Tell her I was here when she wakes up."

Jane smiled and cast a glance at the bright bouquet he'd set beside the bed. "Oh, she'll know."

Though the grief sat like a stone in his chest and guilt assailed him, he finally left Amelia and headed over to Avalon, where he parked a safe distance down Connecticut Avenue from the large, innocuous-looking trio of town houses.

Inside the pleasure club's main building, he picked up his mail from Azure's secretary and rifled through it. Two notes from women thanking him for the best sex of their lives, one of which read like *Penthouse* Forum. So different from the mail he got at home. He swallowed as he thought about the daily bills for Amelia's care, a familiar anxiety tightening his chest. He was almost caught up, thank God, but Azure had him enslaved, and she knew it. She reveled in it. In typical clairvoyant fashion, she appeared at the end of the corridor, wraithlike in a gauzy white pantsuit, her black hair woven back in a soft braid. Colm knew what the outfit meant. She was in a benevolent mood.

"Colm, darling. Tell me this is not bad news."

"On the contrary." He forced a smile. "I think Sydney and I are off to a good start. She needs more models, though. I figure at least one of the guys might be agreeable to earning a little money on the side."

Azure reached him and smoothed the front of his button-down shirt with a gentle hand. "I'm sure that's doable. It's a quiet week here." She started into her office, then paused and looked back at him, her catlike eyes unreadable. "You're asking Garrett in particular?"

Jesus, she was a mind reader. "Is he here?"

"He's got appointments tonight."

"Sydney won't need him tonight."

"Then you'll find him upstairs. Don't keep him long if he's resting. I want him ready for a most important guest."

An important guest on a quiet Sunday night. Colm's mouth quirked. He could picture the client. *Church first, family brunch, take the kids shopping, tuck them into their canopied beds, then off to the fuck palace.* Sometimes he hated the cynical bastard Avalon had turned him into. Sometimes he walked into this place and felt its embrace, felt the orgasm building even before he'd touched his first client of the evening. He belonged here. He would stay until Amelia recovered some mobility, or Azure let him off his tether.

He strolled through the Baroque-decorated lobby, weaving around circular settees and gold-leafed tables to the great curved staircase, where he took two steps at a time to the second floor. Someone was burning incense, patchouli and cedar. He breathed it in and thought about college. Another life. Ashes of memories.

Garrett answered his apartment door in a towel, his light brown hair wet and messy. "What are you doing here?"

"I got dismissed a little early today."

"Trouble already?" He let Colm into the room and went to his dresser to pull out a pair of jeans. He was probably hooking up with Dana Cherlow, an attractive Broadway actress in town for a Kennedy Center gala. She liked her men in ripped jeans and T-shirts. Bad boy shit. She liked it rough and relentless.

"No trouble yet." Colm leaned against the doorjamb. "Sydney needs another male model for some kind of erotic ménage à trois canvas, and you're the only one I'd put up with. And even that's minimally."

"You know you want me." Garrett dropped his towel and smacked himself on the naked ass.

"Jesus, Garrett. Don't do that."

"Sorry." In the fashion Dana Cherlow favored, he pulled on a pair of snug jeans without underwear, fastened and zipped them. "Talk to me on the balcony before my appointment gets here. I need a smoke."

They moved down the long hall, passing rooms where not a sound echoed, even though Colm knew there might be an early bird or two experiencing the eye-rolling orgasms Avalon promised. Congresswoman Margaret Vale was usually one of them at this hour. She liked a sweet, short fuck and made methodical rounds, sampling Avalon companions, one whore a week. Colm had entertained her two weeks ago, and it hadn't been half bad. She was sexy in a cougarish way, even if he hadn't gotten off when he was with her. It took a lot to get him to that point anymore. Two or three clients back-to-back, or a general weariness, and then he would climax. The clients loved it and took smug credit for it, although few requested it from him. And after three years, coming was just a physical response to which he was completely disconnected.

The autumn sun shone its direct rays on the two men as they stepped onto the back balcony. The wrought iron–surrounded terrace was one of Colm's favorite places in the town house. He often brought his voyeuristic clients out here, although no passerby could really see what took place. Azure owned the two lots behind Avalon and had demolished the row houses that sat on them, then surrounded the land and its gardens with high, manicured hedges. The elite pleasure club had made her incredibly wealthy, enough to shoo off underpaid law enforcement when suspicion reared its inevitable head.

Facing away from the chilled breeze, Garrett lit a Turkish cigarette, took a long drag, and offered it to Colm in a cloud of sweet-scented smoke. Normally Colm didn't like cigarettes, but he was wired, driven. He took it and sucked in a lungful of smoke. Closing his eyes, he held it for a moment then exhaled with a shiver. The smoke scraped his throat and spun the world around him.

"So what's this group sex thing?" Garrett asked, leaning an elbow against the balustrade. "You, me, and one chick posing?"

"Right." Colm looked away. He was a whore, but certain ideas were still new to him, especially when it came to his friends. He'd never touched another man, never wanted it, not even in his darkest fantasies. Azure had asked him point-blank his limitations when she'd interviewed him for the job, and he didn't have many, but he preferred women. He craved them. Nothing could take the place of soft skin and being lost in deep, wet heat.

"Hmm." Garrett rubbed his bare stomach beneath his T-shirt. "I don't know."

"Garrett. It's just posing. The entire female population of this city has seen your dick. Don't go shy on me now."

"I don't mean that." He passed the cigarette back, the breeze rifling his light brown hair. "I mean, will you respect me in the morning?"

Colm took a drag and tried not to laugh, but it came out in a smoky burst anyway. "This won't affect our friendship from my standpoint as long as you remember I don't swing both ways."

"Jesus God, you're the most hetero guy I know."

Colm's humor faded to a smile. Garrett was heterosexual himself, but if a client wanted to engage two men at once, he obliged with a shrug and a grin. Sex was sex. It all felt good. It all paid well, too.

This was a hell of a life.

"It doesn't matter what I am," Colm told him. "And I don't judge your crazy ass."

Garrett took back the cigarette and rolled it between his fingers. The air between them grew thick with smoke and something strangely like sadness. "I wouldn't do anything to make you uncomfortable."

"I know." For a moment they were silent. The day had been so full of anguish, Colm couldn't stand even a little sentimentality. He changed the subject. "Max Beaudoin is an evil bastard."

Garrett's eyebrows went up. "So why is the woman with him?"

"I haven't figured it out yet, but she's broken. I'm only going to make it worse in the end, and I try not to give a shit, but—"

"But you're James Hanford, a good guy masquerading as a whore Azure dreamed up. James Hanford," Garrett added, "with a sister you would give your life for. And you have. You've given your life. What's one more job, one more lonely woman? Do the job, Jimmy, and put it behind you. You can do this. I'll help however I can."

Colm looked away, toward the high hedges that blocked out the real world beyond Avalon. Who the hell was James Hanford these days? After three years of this shit, he'd nearly forgotten his own name.

Garrett puffed smoke into the air and grinned. "Jesus H. I can't quite picture us sharing the same chick. You're such a control freak, you'll be telling me every little move to make, from where to stick my tongue to where to put my damned hands."

"Just swear to keep them off my cock," Colm said, grateful for his friend's sense of humor.

"Unless your illustrious artist tells me otherwise."

"I'm telling you otherwise."

Garrett laughed and carefully stubbed out the cigarette on the concrete floor, then blew on it and stuck it in his jeans pocket. No littering at Avalon. No cigarettes unless the client requested it. Dana Cherlow would watch Garrett smoke half a pack tonight.

"So when are you free for this thing?" Colm asked, straightening from the balustrade. Dusk was falling and he felt a strange, urgent tug back to Beaudoin's estate.

"Normally Wednesdays are three-fuck nights, but this week's quiet." Garrett adjusted himself in his jeans and squinted at Colm. "Will that work for this woman—what's her name?"

"Sydney. Sydney Warren."

"Don't say that too tenderly or I might think the worst."

"There is no worst. And I'm looking forward to her ménage idea like a kick in the balls." Colm shoved a hand through his hair. "It's late. I gotta go."

"Leaving me all alone in the funhouse, huh?"

"You're the only one I know who still thinks it's fun." Even if Garrett did look kind of alone, standing there in the out-of-character clothing some rich bitch had chosen for him. "I'll call you with the time as soon as I talk to Sydney. And thanks, man. Your being there will make things a lot more bearable."

With a shrug, Garrett lit another cigarette and let the smoke snake through his lips. "See you Wednesday, Jimmy."

CHAPTER SIX

Sydney found her female model by posting help-wanted flyers on bulletin boards at Capitol University, and within two hours she had five responses. Dark-haired and body-pierced in ears, brow, and tongue, Cherise Ford was a junior art student who had heard of Sydney in local art circles. Cherise loved the idea of working in Sydney's private studio, not to mention the generous pay. Sydney liked her immediately, her youthful enthusiasm, her coltish movements, as though she had only just finishing growing and didn't know what to do with her long limbs. And the sparkle of those piercings all over the place—they would read as erotic instead of gauche on the canvas. For the first time, excitement tickled Sydney's muse awake. This project might well turn out to be the right combination of portraiture and sensuality she'd always sought.

After a day of small triumphs, her evening with Max was a different story. Normally Sydney loved the eighteenth-century stone inn in Middleburg where they went for dinner, a charming place where they used to spend evenings talking art, music, the life they would make together. But this conversation was abysmal, filled with awkward silences.

And somehow the image of Colm Hennessy sat between them, as vibrant and hot as the flickering flame of the candle by Max's elbow.

"I've thought about what you said," Sydney told Max when she couldn't stand the silence, or thoughts of Colm, anymore. "About . . . counseling. You're right. I've made arrangements to see someone in the city next week."

"I'm glad to hear it." He smiled at her and drained his bourbon on the rocks, the ice cubes knocking in the glass. In the background filled with the clink of dishes and the low murmur of diners, Mozart spun his magic through the low-ceilinged room. Sydney closed her eyes, searching for the serenity she normally experienced in this tiny inn, but nothing came to her. Nearby, a waiter's tray clattered to the floor and the noise jerked her back to the world.

Max's gaze had wandered, first to the clumsy waiter, then to the flickering candlelight around them, never landing on one particular thing for more than an instant. "I've got a couple of trips coming up in the next few weeks," he said abruptly, arranging his utensils alongside his plate.

"Oh?" She swallowed a bite of filet mignon and set down her fork. "Really? Where?" What she really wanted to say was, *Take me with you. Free me from this mess.* Except Max was the biggest tangle of all, and a trip together wouldn't change that. Sitting across from him on this strained date, she understood it now. Without some kind of help—counseling, a shared, truthful dialogue—soon they would have nothing left, and Max didn't seem to recognize the danger whatsoever.

"San Francisco," he was saying, "Chicago." He paused and

smiled. "You look so wistful. You weren't thinking about coming with me, were you? You've only just started working with Colm."

"And I'm anxious to keep working," she said flatly. "This is a challenge, remember?"

But God, she was confused. It didn't bother Max one bit to leave her alone with a strange man—a devastatingly attractive one. Max hadn't always been so free with her. Until recently, he'd been mildly possessive, even though she'd figured it had more to do with their agent/artist relationship than their romance. Why was this time so different? What lay in California or Chicago that would tug harder at him than his usual need to guard what he felt was his?

"Max—?"

Before she could finish her question, he withdrew a blue velvet box from inside his suit pocket, laid it on the table, and flipped it open. Pearls. A single strand. Luscious and priceless. "These might encourage you to finish what you've started. You can wear them to your next opening."

Shock flooded Sydney's face with warmth. He occasionally gave her gifts for no reason, but this was different. She touched a fingertip to one of the pearls. "They're lovely . . ."

"Would you like to try them on?"

No. *No.* It was the last thing she wanted, pearls, gifts, shells of proclamations rather than the spoken sentiments and communication she so craved.

But the moment held an odd intimacy, so she gave a short nod. He wheeled around to her side of the table and drew the strand around her neck, fastened it, then dropped a kiss on her shoulder bared by her spaghetti-strap dress.

"You are the lovely one," he murmured. Sydney pulled back to meet his eyes. In the candlelight they shone the color of gunmetal.

In the candlelight she might believe he desired her still, that the old love between them still existed. She couldn't ask herself if she felt the same. Not with Max's pearls hanging on her neck.

"Thank you, Max. I'm so surprised."

He wheeled closer and bumped the table, jostling the glasses so that Merlot splashed crimson onto the linen cloth. "Can't you see it, Sydney? Can't you see how much I love you?" His voice was low and nearly grim, the words clenched with a strange determination she'd never seen before. "Everything I do is for you, for us. You are my world. You must know that."

Her pulse pounded beneath the strand of pearls as she stared into his eyes. "But you don't have to buy me gifts to show me. Just talk to me. Come with me to counseling. We could start there."

He wheeled back. "It brings me pleasure to dress you, to give you pretty things. How does that merit counseling? Oblige me tonight with . . . this."

So she did; there was nothing left to say.

They rode home in the limousine without speaking and went their separate ways with the usual brief kiss goodnight. Sydney methodically undressed, sat down at her vanity to brush her hair . . . and burst into tears. But a part of her she'd never accessed had awakened and didn't join in the grieving. Her world was crumbling to expose something new and not altogether unwanted, although she couldn't yet read its abstract composition.

She slept until just before dawn, then went to the studio, where she stared at the beginning drawing she'd done of Colm. It was obvious she hadn't been concentrating yesterday. The static lines also told her she'd been frustrated. She ought to dismiss him, let him go back to his life in the city and leave her to her own issues. He was too much of a distraction. She should let him go and forget pleasing Max for even one more day.

No, damn it. The paintings she was about to create would continue to support her financially and even more, she'd be doing the kind of work she really wanted to do—completely unassociated with Max for the first time. She had to see it through. And if she could say one thing about Max, it was that he was right about her work coming alive when she used live models. No more photographs. It was time to get over her fears.

Maybe she should thank Max after all.

When the day's early sun streamed golden through the studio windows, a brief knock sounded at the door and Colm stuck his head in. "Good morning."

Sydney slid off her barstool as though she'd been caught doing something illicit. "You're up incredibly early."

"I saw your lights on."

She offered him a wry smile. "Your enthusiasm is without measure."

"I like this job."

Warmth crept up her neck. Before she could respond with something dismissive, he said, "I need coffee. The machine in my room doesn't work."

"I'll have Hans replace it." She studied his damp hair and thought about him standing under the showerhead just minutes before. Her gaze ran over his untucked blue shirt and jeans. There was a hole in the left knee of his Levi's and they were terribly faded. Terribly sexy, too.

He nodded at the small coffeemaker on the table where she kept jars and extra supplies. "I know you serve Shiraz around ten a.m., but how about Starbucks at seven?"

Good Lord, why hadn't she offered him her coffee yet? She was standing there like a besotted fool. "Will Folgers do?"

"Sure." He stepped inside and shut the door behind him, then meandered down the ramp to where she stood at her easel. "Is that drawing what you did on our first session?"

"I kept only this one warm-up sketch. The rest are in the garbage."

"You should never throw away a single work you do, Sydney. I'll take them rather than see you do that." His hair was a darker brown when wet, the chestnut highlights muted. He smelled like Irish Spring and shampoo. If she ever smelled the same scents again, she would remember this moment when a man would fish her crappy drawings out of a trash can rather than see them go to waste.

"What are we doing today?" he asked.

"I haven't decided yet." As she went to the table that held the ancient coffeemaker and poured some in a chipped mug, she spoke more brightly. "Did you talk to your friend about modeling?"

"I did. His name is Garrett. He's available Wednesday night and Thursday in the morning." He took the mug from her and sat on the edge of the platform. "He understands the nature of the project and he's very . . . malleable."

"Good." She returned to the easel and set a blank prepared canvas on it. Today she would work on a portrait of Colm since they couldn't start on the ménage until Wednesday. She wanted to gaze at his splendid male beauty and use her finest, most honed artist's skill to render the perfect portrait—an ever elusive goal, but the drive was stronger than ever. She glanced at the play of shadow cast from her work lamp on the left side of his face. Her pulse thudded. A long time had passed since her heart had begun painting before she did.

"How do you need me today?" he asked, setting aside his coffee mug.

She jerked awake. "Oh . . . just as you are."

"More warm-up drawings?"

She made a face. "Not today, since they obviously warmed up a whole lot of nothing yesterday."

The way he smiled told her that had somehow come out wrong, but she waved his humor away.

"You know what I mean. I want to do another study of your face and shoulders today. Maybe work on it for the next two days until our models can get here and we begin on the ménage."

"So I don't need to change."

"No," she said. "Well, maybe remove your shirt."

The slide of material on skin teased her ears and she focused hard on her toolbox as she picked out a piece of charcoal.

The wooden platform creaked.

Sydney peeked.

Colm had done as he was told, hanging one leg off the side of the stage, the other knee crooked, his bared upper body gleaming in the light. Sydney wanted more of that. His skin was so tactile, his musculature so sleek. But something about his face today . . . not as smooth and perfect. A weariness about the eyes and mouth she hadn't noted before. Secret unhappiness in a beautiful man. It seemed like a fascinating premise to capture on canvas.

She wanted more of the shadow touching his chin and nose and left eye, so she adjusted her lamp, rose from her barstool, and approached him. "I'm going to pose you, okay?"

"Sure."

Her fingers threatened to tremble as she gingerly touched his chin and tilted his head ever so slightly away from the light. He'd obviously shaved, but what little shadow remained prickled her fingertips. When she left a smudge on his jaw, she used her other hand to gently wipe it away. "Sorry—charcoal."

The whole time he watched her with those all-seeing green eyes, and suddenly she couldn't help herself. She let her gaze slide down his tanned throat to his chest.

And there it was, up close. The tattoo over his heart. *Amelia.* Nothing more than that. A shrine on flesh.

"Who's Amelia?" she asked, staring at it.

He glanced down, realized he'd broken the pose she'd created and resumed it. "Someone who means a lot to me."

Sydney backed away. "Is she still your . . . ?" *Jeez.* "I mean, is she still in your life?"

"Yes."

Her fingers rolled the charcoal back and forth, back and forth as she moved away and seated herself again. She'd never seen him more solemn, and something told her not to push the subject, although a strange sensation had fisted in her solar plexus, a sort of burn in her that stole her breath.

She didn't put on any music; they didn't talk, nor did he ask any questions this time. They worked in sweet, heavy silence, and her charcoal sketch gradually took on the features of the man sitting in such obedient stillness six feet away. The only thing Sydney couldn't quite capture was the expression in his eyes, but she told herself that would come with the actual painting.

"Would you like to stretch?" she asked after she'd finished the preliminary sketch.

Colm got to his feet, paced a few steps, and raised his arms over his head. The muscles of his back flexed and he yawned, giving a shuddering, full-body stretch. Sydney tried not to watch, but she couldn't stop herself. Even now, knowing she was still with Max and Colm was a man in love with a woman named Amelia, the female in her couldn't stop ogling. *A work of art on legs*, Max had called him. Yes, indeed.

When they resumed working, she felt restless and distraught.

Squeezing beads of paint on her palette, she tried to distract herself. "Tell me about your friend Garrett."

Colm half smiled. "He's a good guy. Walks the wild side. That's why I thought of him for your project."

"He's uninhibited?"

"In every possible way."

Sydney smiled. "Are you?"

His gaze shot to hers and she grimaced. She needed to stop talking or she would humiliate herself. Women probably fell all over him, and it wasn't her style. She wanted to be different. She *was* different. "You don't seem like the type to have wild friends."

"You don't know me yet," he said softly.

She quickly returned her attention to the canvas. "To quote your earlier declaration, I'd like to change that fact. So I have a few more questions."

"Shoot."

"What gives you that expression in your eyes?"

He hesitated. "What do you mean?"

"There's a somberness about you I didn't see before. I know I'm prying, but it might help me with my painting. Do you mind?"

"Your boyfriend paid me to do whatever you want. Pry away."

Something about the edge to his words told her to shut up, but she couldn't. Her curiosity controlled her like a puppet master. "Tell me more about your background."

His fingertips went to the tattoo. "I grew up with one sister, a twin. My mother died of cancer when I was eighteen, my dad of a heart attack when I was twenty-five."

She stopped in the midst of mixing flesh tones. "I'm so sorry."

"Thank you."

She felt his eyes on her, stripping away her defenses when she was the one asking the probing questions.

"How old are you?" she continued, without looking at him.

"Thirty-one," he said. "You?"

"Twenty-nine. My thirtieth birthday's on Friday."

"Ah. Sad about kissing your youth good-bye?"

She couldn't help but smile. "I'm asking the questions, Mr. Hennessy."

"Don't start that name thing again."

She pressed her lips together and lapsed into silence again, studying the way the light fell across the bridge of his nose and defined the beautiful bow of his upper lip, the shadowed dip below his full bottom one. She sensed his attention on her all the while, and when she looked into his eyes, his gaze caught and held hers. And like a fool, she said, "I assume you're not married."

The right corner of his mouth tugged up. "What makes you say that?"

"Well . . ." No explanation would come. Her throat tightened, then she blurted, "Well, you're free to come here for two weeks, for one thing."

"Maybe I have an understanding wife at home."

"You don't wear a ring."

"I don't like jewelry."

She knew he didn't have a wife at home. For all his clean-cut appeal, there was something of an untethered animal about him, as though he'd broken away from his keeper but didn't know where he wandered.

A stray.

"Have you ever been married?" she asked as she applied a shadow to his image's jaw.

"Once," he said, and that was all.

The curiosity burned her in the dearth of conversation that followed until she thought she'd burst out of her skin. "Colm." She laid down her brush and looked at him. "I'm curious about you. I know it's none of my business, despite how much Max is paying you—"

"It's fine." He shrugged. "We're getting to know each other, which will relax you and make it easier for you to do your work. Right?"

"Right." But the awkwardness had crept back, drawing her attention from the canvas to his face again and again, not for the sake of her work, but for the masochistic sweetness of looking at him without being able to read him.

Intimacy swirled around them, a hot tension drawing them tight together, and the questions burst forth again. "Was Amelia your wife?"

"No. Jill was my wife." He moved suddenly, straightened from his pose. "I'm a widower."

Surprise stole Sydney's breath. "Oh, Colm. I truly am sorry." He'd lost so many loved ones. Now she understood the weary look about him today. Maybe he'd lain awake last night, missing Jill. Or missing some beauty named Amelia he had loved enough to engrave her into his skin.

He'd said Sydney could pry as she wished, but the vibe in the room had changed. She finally gathered her wits. "This is coming along nicely. The painting, I mean."

"Plan to finish it before you begin the ménage project?"

"I'd like to. Do you have that many hours in you?"

He smiled. "Sure. Can I take a break and see what you have so far?"

"Of course."

He hopped off the platform and came around to look at the canvas. He stood there a long time, studying it with the same intensity he had when he'd looked at her work two nights ago at the gallery.

Two nights ago. Had it only been that long? The minutes passing between them had been so full of . . . she didn't know. Something electric and rich. Something that was changing her. She didn't feel guilty. Her interactions with Colm, her thoughts and growing fantasies belonged to a sacred, secret part of her.

"It looks just like me," he said at last, and Sydney released the breath she'd held.

"It wasn't difficult. You have beautiful eyes."

Colm glanced at her.

"Unique," she hurried.

"You do, too. So blue. They catch the light."

Sydney tried to look away, but she couldn't. He'd snagged her. She felt drawn in, caught, paralyzed, even her heart. Then it resumed its beat, hammering now, and she licked her lips. "Have you had a long enough break?"

"Sure." Wearing a faint smile, he returned to the stage and sat again on the edge.

She picked up her brush and went back to work. It was too quiet now; she should have put on music. The clean scent of his bare skin still lingered around her and teased her senses. And this painting—it was one of her finest, she could already see it.

"Sydney," he said into the quiet.

"Yes?"

"My turn to pry."

She hesitated. "I reserve the right to pass on anything inappropriate."

She thought he might laugh, but his expression was serious. "Do you get lonely?"

You already know the answer. "What makes you ask?"

"I'm not sure. You seem like an only child."

She released a breath. He was talking about her lack of siblings, not her relationship with Max.

"Do you?" he repeated, shifting just the slightest bit, his head tilted in a beguiling way she wished she'd captured before she started painting.

"Sometimes. And I *was* an only child. There was just my mom and me." Maybe in another time, another place, she would tell him the whole story. But not yet. Not after just two days.

"You miss her?"

Darkness swept through her, left her cold. "Not really."

"Something else, then?"

She didn't reply. The question was dangerous.

"What are you missing, Sydney?"

She opened her mouth to reply, to ask him politely not to pursue the topic, but then the studio door swung open and Max rolled in, the gilded morning sunlight silhouetting his form.

"How's it going in here?" He wheeled down the ramp, the door closing behind him with a particular slam that made Sydney feel chided for her wayward conversation with Colm. This creeping intimacy between them had to be palpable to someone as astute as Max.

"It's going fine," she said, her tone light and cheerful. "Come see."

He wheeled himself to her easel and gave the painting a cursory glance. "Where's the eroticism?"

Colm rose from the platform. "She does amazing portraiture."

Max's lip curled just a little, but Sydney quickly said, "This is just to tide us over until the models come on Wednesday."

Disapproval darkened Max's expression. "Colm's got an unexpected vacation until then? How fortunate for him."

"No, we're absolutely working," Sydney said. "This portrait—"

"I'm doing my job," Colm spoke at the same time.

Sydney wanted to groan for both of them. *Thou dost protest too much.*

Max merely smiled. "I actually came by to ask Colm if he'd like to join us for dinner tonight. Colm? How about it?"

"Sounds great." Colm's features were unreadable, but he was nothing if not gracious, even in the face of thinly veiled contempt.

"We'll grill outside," Max added. "I make a mean New York strip."

Sydney stared at him. They never grilled outside. Steaks appeared magically on their plates, full of hickory flavor and compliments of Hans's fine service.

"I didn't know you could grill, Max," she spoke when no one offered a word.

"Maybe there's still a thing or two about me you don't know, my love." He pivoted the wheelchair toward the ramp. "Cocktails at six, dinner at seven. Carry on." But when the door closed behind him, Sydney laid down her palette and sighed. The magic was shattered. The painting didn't look as tactile and promising as it had moments before.

She thrust her brushes in the jar of water. "You can go, Colm."

"Okay," he said, rising from the platform. "But this cutting out early is starting to worry me."

"It shouldn't. I work in fits and starts, remember?"

"I hope that's it. I hope we're not done here."

She watched him put on his shirt, the double-sided comment echoing in her brain. Only when he left did she realize she had tensed every muscle, ready to flee.

CHAPTER SEVEN

Dinner was quiet except for the soft clang of utensils against china. Colm glanced at Sydney more than once, but she kept her gaze mostly downcast as though concentrating on her food, even though she only pushed it around on her plate with her fork. Her short blond hair fell forward, a protected, curtained place from a world where she was so obviously unsafe.

Most of all, unsafe with *him*. Guilt speared his gut. He knew desire when he saw it, and she wanted him. He wanted her, too, so much it took running thoughts of algebra equations and football to keep the erections at bay when he was alone with her in the studio. Only a little while longer and he'd have her. Physical attraction was only one small step with a woman like her; she had layer upon layer of emotional barriers, but they toppled quickly with a little careful attention.

She was making it much easier than he'd guessed she would.

Max broke the silence. "This is a celebratory dinner, by the way."

"Really?" Sydney tucked her hair behind her ears and looked at him, surprise altering the distracted expression she'd worn all evening. "What are we celebrating?"

"A new artist. I'm going to Chicago to see her portfolio and woo her."

Colm kept a carefully blank face, denying the scowl that wanted to seize his features. Max was passing off a goddamned veiled threat, and Colm wanted to knock him out for the way Sydney's lips fell open.

For a moment no one spoke. Then Colm said carefully, "What kind of work does this artist do?"

"Mostly abstract, but with an eroticism that reminds me of Sydney's earlier work. This one has that fresh, unsculpted element about her."

Colm braced his forearms on the table and stared at him. Was the man evil, or was he just that mindless of Sydney's feelings?

To her credit, she tilted her head and smiled. "When are you flying out?"

"Tomorrow." He sawed at his steak, then gestured at Colm with his fork as though he were a piece of furniture. "Do you feel comfortable enough being alone with him now to let me go that soon?"

Colm sat back, waiting for her to volley.

"That's not the point," Sydney said flatly. "I knew you were planning to go to Chicago and San Francisco, but this really is short notice. When did you find out you were leaving?"

Max took a bite of his food and chewed for much too long before he replied. "Only this morning, Sydney. I didn't want to interrupt your creative flow and pop the news on you. You and Colm appear to be working together in peace."

Her expression stayed neutral, but those two telltale red spots appeared on her cheeks. "And how long will you be gone?"

"Ten days, give or take. This artist is having a couple of small showings I want to attend."

She was quiet. Then she said, "I'm curious about her work. You'll have to e-mail me photos."

"I will." Max lifted his wineglass. "To hopeful new artists, and a potential client," he said, then took a long draught and smiled.

Sydney lightly sipped from her water glass, but Colm wadded his napkin and set it beside his plate. He was a whore, nothing better. He could take Max Beaudoin's money. But he didn't have to drink to his sick games.

Colm headed straight to his cabin after the miserable dinner, dialing the house in Silver Spring on his cell phone as he went. Amelia was sleeping again, so the nurse couldn't put the phone to her ear for him to talk to her. She slept so much. Beyond healing. Maybe it really was escape, a black hole where reality didn't exist— the reality Colm had given her.

The thought echoed in his brain as he climbed the steps to the cabin porch. He slammed the door hard behind him and strode straight to the shower, stripping as he went and leaving his clothing in a trail behind him. He felt so filthy. The shower beat hot on his shoulders, hot enough to sting his skin, and he let it, burning himself with its fire, nothing as hot as the hell he secreted away. He braced his palms on the shower wall and hung his head, breathing the steam in slow inhalations and cleansing away the mud clouding his conscience until the water turned cold.

When he climbed out, someone knocked at the cabin door. He wrapped a towel around his hips, not bothering to dry off whatsoever, and crossed the living room to answer it.

Sydney stood there in a paint-stained man's shirt and torn jeans, her blue eyes wide in the glow from the porch lights. Her gaze darted down his body and away before she said, "I didn't mean to drag you out of the shower."

"I was done." He fought the urge to shiver in the chilly night air and leaned a shoulder against the doorjamb, enjoying the sight of her a little too much. "What can I do for you?"

She hesitated. "I know it's late, but can you come pose for a while? I feel a sudden drive to work on your portrait."

"Let me get dressed." He backed up and opened the door wider. "Come in."

Glancing at the threshold as though it were the line between her feet and hell's fire, she shook her head. "I'll meet you in the studio."

"It'll just take a second. We'll walk over together."

But she backed off the porch, her arms wrapped around herself as though he were something menacing, as though she sensed the threat he was. And before he could say anything more, she'd disappeared into the darkness.

Sade wound serpentine vocals around Sydney's senses as she mixed colors on her palette, tan, more white, less burnt umber, a touch of crimson. Her hands were shaking. This wouldn't bode well for the portrait, but she didn't care. She needed to paint, to remember who she was—not the statue to Max's Pygmalion, not some ingénue anymore, but herself, the self she'd lost. Maybe Max was planning to replace her with the artist from Chicago. She knew him well enough to recognize the signs, and finally understood that the tension between them in the last few weeks had been leading up to the moment at dinner tonight when he mentioned his new client. Doubtless Sydney would never know the truth, but the mere suspicion fed the late-night drive she was experiencing to get something, anything, on canvas, to remind herself of the artist she was . . . and at long last to paint what she loved. Bodies in motion, love and emotion and faces of all kinds, ugly, beautiful, mesmerizing.

She would start with Colm, beauty personified. She would entangle him with other models in compositions of muscles and flesh and lithe limbs, and find her deepest desires again through the voyeurism of an artist's eyes.

Tonight's dinner didn't matter. Max's threats didn't, either. Nor Max.

Colm hardly made a sound when he entered the studio, closing the door softly behind him. She didn't look at him until he reached the platform, where he shucked his leather jacket, kicked off his shoes, and stripped off his long-sleeved T-shirt without asking her what she wanted for this session.

Sydney decided not to break the peace with unnecessary conversation. She worked a brush into her palette and added the gleam to his image's shoulders cast by the work light. His pectorals were firm, sculpted, his nipples hard from the draft in the studio. When he shivered, she ignored it and kept working. His expression was as set and determined as she felt tonight.

It wasn't enough, the shoulders, the chest. Setting aside her brush and palette, she stepped out from her workstation and approached him. "Brace your palms behind you and lean back on your arms."

A look she couldn't identify crossed his features but he obliged her, asking no questions. And with only her own pounding heart granting her courage, Sydney reached down and unfastened his fly, pushing the buttons through their corresponding holes with shaking fingers. His skin was hot against her knuckles. He smelled like shampoo and lime soap. He didn't ask why she was doing what she was doing.

She didn't offer an explanation.

On the last two buttons, he sat up and caught her hands. "Don't."

She felt herself flush. "You want to do it yourself?"

"No. It's just that I hurried to get here and I sort of . . . went commando."

"Commando?"

"No underwear."

The flutter in Sydney's stomach intensified. Her fingers flexed as she studied him and tried to think. What would the old Sydney do? Back away. She didn't want to back away. She wanted to jump off the precipice, drown in these feelings and ascend as someone new. She wanted to paint this night a different color.

"Commando doesn't bother me." She nudged aside the protective hand he'd rested on his fly and undid the last buttons. The hair of his groin was silky, darker than the hair on his head. She let her knuckles brush it in passing; she let his fly fall open naturally without pulling it wide to expose him. Appraising his entire position, she crooked one of his knees on the stage, angled the other to dangle off the side, and stepped back, squinting with an artist's eye. "Good."

When she returned to her easel and glanced at him, he was staring at her, his green eyes intense. Her gaze strayed to his fly. He was hard, darker, ruddier flesh obvious through the opening in his jeans, though not jutting out.

Sydney bit her lip and went to work. Sexual arousal wasn't uncommon with erotic art models. That was all he was. A model for her purpose.

The lighting wasn't right. She stopped and adjusted her lamp. "Turn your face to the left," she instructed. He did, but it wasn't right. She maneuvered the lamp again, then gave up and crossed to the platform to pose him again herself.

Gently grasping his chin, she turned his face aside. Her thumb accidently grazed his full bottom lip, and heat crept up her neck. After practically ripping open his jeans without his permission, it seemed silly to be embarrassed, but somehow touching his mouth felt more intimate.

"Sydney."

"What."

He caught her hand and to her astonishment lifted it back to his lips, laid a kiss on her paint-stained thumb, then her forefinger. And what was so very awful was that she let him; she simply stood there and watched him kiss her fingers one at a time, her body going fluid and hot and weak.

"Look at these colorful hands," he murmured, biting the knuckle on her ring finger. "A little rough, a lot talented."

She couldn't speak. For all its lack of invasiveness, his slow, thorough caress was the sexiest thing any man had ever done to her. When he reached her pinkie, he licked the tip, paint-stained and all. Her throat had gone dry; she didn't pull away. The proverbial question between man and woman hung there, a potent third party, until he voiced it. "What do you want?"

Sydney cleared her throat. "I'm not entirely sure."

"Then let's start right here, this moment, just you and me."

Her gaze shot to the door; she thought about locking it.

"Do you want this?" he asked, and without waiting, lifted her wrist to his mouth. Oh, God, his tongue found her pulse and traced its tender spot. Flicked. Soothed. She leaned into him; her hand found his thigh for balance and she felt his hardness. With a jolt, she withdrew from his grasp and stepped away.

"I want to finish this portrait, and the next one with you and the other models. I want to finish them both before you leave in ten days, and I want them to be flawless." Her delayed response to his question came too rushed, blatant defense against a force she couldn't truly fight. The words trembled at the end, the same way she trembled inside as she backed all the way to her easel and bumped into it like a dolt, nearly knocking the canvas to the floor.

Colm said nothing, just leaned back on his hands again and resumed the position she had arranged, those godforsaken jeans open at the fly, promising ecstasy.

"I want perfection," she repeated. And he was. He was seraphically beautiful, everything she'd ever wanted in a subject—in a man. She picked up her brush and made some brisk, gestural strokes on the canvas. Despite the declarations, this was the furthest thing from perfection she could create—this damned canvas quickly turning into a sloppy mess. This state of her life. But she could pretend. She could pretend everything slid across the surface in smooth, exquisite detail, that each of her days slid flawlessly into one another, that she didn't desire this man she'd known less than a week; that Max hadn't set Colm before her, all but served like a buffet dinner; and that she wasn't betraying Max's trust while not feeling guilty for it.

"Can we talk while you paint?" Colm's husky voice broke the silence, and Sydney startled.

"No," she said quickly.

"How long are you going to ignore what's happening here?"

She loaded her brush and globbed too much paint on the figure's neck. "Nothing's happening. Nothing's going to happen."

He was quiet for a moment. Then, "Dinner was a son of a bitch tonight."

The brush on the canvas went still, then resumed. Sydney knew what he referred to. "I'm not afraid of being replaced." Not anymore. Whatever Max could deliver at this point was nothing compared to the list of things she feared, starting with Colm.

"When was the last time he touched you?" he asked, as though the conversation were idle chitchat, as though he were asking about her ho-hum day and not framing a brutal observation of her fast-dissolving life.

She tried not to look at him and failed. He was holding his pose, his muscles taut, skin glowing in the spotlight.

"I'm starting to care about you." Colm didn't move, and yet his statement shook the room.

Care. More than *want.* Deadlier. Another way for her to fall before she'd even flown.

She swallowed the ache in her throat and applied more paint to the canvas, but this time mixed in too much crimson and turned the gleam on his shoulder a dusky pink. "Shit." Suddenly, all the anger from the last few weeks rose up like a dragon and breathed fire into her limbs, her veins, her brain, her heart. "Shit! Shit! I hate this!" She grabbed the canvas off the easel and threw it against the nearest wall, where it left a wet smudge of flesh tones before it hit the floor, facedown.

Ruined.

She hadn't planned to cry. Hadn't even known it was coming. But suddenly she was weeping, and when Colm said her name she turned away, rubbed her face with her hands to scrub away the weakness, but it was no use. It felt good to fall apart. She'd needed this far too long.

When she heard his bare feet on the wood floor, felt his hands on her shoulders, heard his soft, "Hey," she turned into his arms and let herself be held. Held against a bare chest, warm, smooth, lime-scented skin, and a fiercely beating heart. Life, beauty. Art. He was living art.

All the taut rage bled from her through her tears. Like a cloud-burst, it was over in minutes, but she stayed in his embrace, reveling in the way he stroked her hair and murmured indecipherable nothings of comfort against her temple. Max had never held her like this, even before the accident. Had he ever loved her as a person, a woman? Something more than as his novice, or a possession in his collection? She should be flattered, little Sydney Warren from Nowhere, Nebraska. A half-hysterical giggle rose in her chest. She should be destroyed. She was neither. Only distantly curious.

Who the hell was the man she'd spent four years trying and failing to know?

Somehow, in the course of a few days, she felt like she knew more about Colm—not the mundane details, but the essence of the canvas and its meaning—than she'd ever gleaned about Max.

Colm was a good man. It seeped from his embrace and into her bones, and she knew it as well as she knew her own soul.

Sydney couldn't have said when the drift of his hand over her head turned sensuous; maybe with the first shiver of pleasure it brought as his fingers combed her hair back from her cheek and smoothed it behind her ear, copying her own habitual gesture. She nestled in tighter to his chest, unfolding her arms where they'd been tucked against him like a bird afraid to spread its wings. They slid tentatively around his neck and then his cheek was on hers, prickly from a day of not shaving and deliciously warm. She wanted its mild scrape on her skin.

She wanted him.

"Syd," he said, his hand cupping her jaw. That was all. He was the only person who'd ever called her that, and she loved it. She had never been Syd until now.

He didn't swoop in and kiss her; if he had, she would have startled and flown away. But his mouth slid along her jaw, feathery, sinuous and dangerous enough for her knees to sag beneath her. He

would hold her up if she started to fall. She knew that about him.
Colm would catch a woman falling before him.

She couldn't look at him. She closed her eyes, tipped her head
back and in doing so, asked for what she truly wanted.

More.

CHAPTER EIGHT

As soon as the music box sound shattered the silence in its sickly sweet way, Colm knew.

Max was calling Sydney's cell phone, barreling between them once again with his passive-aggressive bullshit and mixed messages. Before Colm left this world, he'd have to know why in hell Max would hire him and then do his damnedest to get in the way. Despite whatever lies this guy had told himself, he didn't want Colm to succeed. Maybe he wanted to fool himself into thinking he and Sydney had something remaining to build on. Meanwhile she stood in the arms of another man and cried, and soft jazz vocals played in the background. Colm wanted to strip her naked, pull her to the floor, and bury himself deep inside her.

Sydney didn't seem to hear the phone; if she did, she ignored it. She tightened her arms around his neck and offered her mouth to him, tears still streaking her beautiful face.

And God, Colm wanted that mouth, the salt of those tears on his tongue. He nudged his nose against her damp cheek and took her exhale between his lips.

Mozart started a fresh round on her cell phone, insistent and discordant mixed with Sade's sinuous vocals echoing from the boom box. Sydney finally seemed to hear it and went still in his embrace.

"Don't," he whispered, but it was no use.

When she opened her eyes and looked at him, dazed, he sighed.

Flushed, she slid her arms from his neck, stepped back, and looked around for the phone, even though it sat right on the paint table where she usually kept it.

"Your worktable," he offered in a low voice, and she hurried there, grabbed it, and looked at the screen. He could tell by the way she bit her lip and shoved her hair behind her ear that his suspicion was correct—Max. Thank God the man was going to Chicago and leaving Colm to his work with the few days that remained.

Sydney's fingers trembled a little as she eased onto the barstool and dialed her cell phone. After another second, she said, "Hi. I was painting. What's up?" Pause. "He's right here. Do you want to talk to him?" Her blue eyes met Colm's across the six feet between them. "Okay, I'll tell him. No, that's fine, I was winding up for the night."

That understatement brought a rueful smile to Colm's face and he had to turn away. He went to the stage, grabbed his shirt, and pulled it on, grateful for the barrier against the studio's coolness, which had begun to seep into his muscles.

"I'll get up with you in the morning," Sydney was telling Max. "We'll have coffee before you leave for the airport."

Coffee. Not sex, not laughter, not intimacy. Coffee. Colm shook his head and tucked in his shirt.

When she hung up the call, she wiped her eyes on the sleeve of her paint smock and spoke in the same composed voice with which she'd addressed her boyfriend. "Max wants to see you at the house before you go to bed. He's leaving by dawn and needs to arrange early payment with you."

Just in case Colm could get her into bed and screw her all night. *Double the money.* He kept his head down and focused on buttoning his fly. He couldn't forget the way Sydney's fingers had unfastened it, pushing the buttons through their holes. The image sent a surge straight to his cock, and he immediately shifted his thoughts to the man in the wheelchair. A fresh chill stole his lust. "Maybe he shouldn't pay me before I've finished my work."

"Why not? Are you going to bail on me?"

When he looked up, she had leaned the ruined canvas against the wall and was on her knees, wiping paint from the floor with mineral spirits and a rag. The pungent smell rose up, reminding him of the artist she was and again, how much he desired her.

"What happened a few minutes ago was my fault," she went on, without giving him a chance to respond. "I want to thank you for putting up with me during my mini-nervous breakdown. It won't happen again." The words came wry and a little husky. She scrubbed harder. "I hope you'll forgive me for any untoward behavior I've exhibited."

He slid his hands in his front pockets and stood there, bemused. "*Untoward behavior?* Is that what you call it?"

"It was inappropriate." She reached for another rag. The paint on the concrete floor had mixed into a messy, rosy smear. "I fell apart, you were here, and I took advantage of that."

"Funny. I was thinking it was the real you coming out, and I kind of liked her. And I thought she might kind of like me, too."

Her head jerked up and she stared at him. "Well, I'm sorry for all of it." For a moment she held his gaze, then shook her head and returned to her task. "You should go to the house now. Max is heading to bed soon."

Colm didn't know why anger curdled the satisfaction that had lingered from their embrace. He wasn't supposed to care about either of these people or their twisted lives, and yet he reveled in Sydney as much as he despised Beaudoin.

He put on his loafers and jacket and headed for the door. It squeaked when he opened it, cold air rushing in to snatch his breath. "For what it's worth," he said, pausing on the threshold, "nothing about your behavior seemed inappropriate to me. Lonely? Yes. Frustrated and confused? All that and more. I'm glad I was here for your mini-breakdown. I'd like to be here every time it happens, and during your happier moments, too. Now that I've heard you cry, I'd like to hear you laugh, Sydney. I'd like to learn your smile."

She laid the rags on the worktable, then rubbed her hands on her jeans-clad thighs. "Your friend Garrett will be here at seven tomorrow, right?"

"That's what I told him."

"Good. I won't need you till then."

Colm nodded and didn't look back as he pulled the door shut behind him. There was no more reaching her tonight.

W ill you have a drink?" Beaudoin wheeled himself to a butler's cart and snatched up a crystal decanter of cognac.

"Sure." Colm stood in the middle of the library and looked around while he waited. Row after row of burgundy and gold-spined books, everything matching, balanced and just-so. *No John Grisham or Louis L'Amour here,* Colm thought wryly. Nothing in the massive, high-ceilinged room promised comfort, warmth, or satisfaction, not even the crackling flames in the fireplace. The space was a mirror reflection of Max: cold and completely unreadable.

Max rolled around with a snifter of brandy in one hand and maneuvered his way to Colm. "You're standing there like a soldier. Why not have a seat?"

Colm took the snifter and chose the nearest chair, a leather wingback with brass nailhead trim. "I know you paid Azure up front for the two weeks, so you don't want to see me about money. Why am I here?"

"Am I not allowed to ask you how things are progressing?" Max poured his own glass of brandy and returned. "After all, Sydney *is* mine."

Colm swallowed a curse along with a mouthful of brandy. He wanted to toss it back like a shot and then tell the guy to go screw himself. "If you say so," he said when he could talk around the burn in his throat.

"So?" Max wheeled closer, so close that the tips of his shoes nearly touched Colm's shins. He was in Colm's space in more ways than one. "How's it going with her?"

Colm held the man's steely eyes. "It's going."

"That's all?"

"It will go a lot better when you leave town."

"You think she'll be unfaithful to me."

"I don't know," Colm said. "I can't tell what she's thinking." He tried not to remember the way they'd stood in the studio, his cheek on hers, their mouths so close. How much did Max deserve to know? *All of it.* He was paying. Colm had nearly forgotten his own reason for being there.

"May I speak frankly?" He folded his arms and sat back to escape the man's close proximity.

Max seemed to take the hint. He wheeled back a few feet, swirled his brandy and gave it a sip. "All right."

"I don't think you want this thing to succeed."

The faint derision Max usually wore in Colm's presence faded a little. "Of course I don't."

"And yet you'll pay me double if I get her into bed."

"Only for exposing her as the whore she'll be if she falls prey."

Colm gritted his teeth. "Falling prey to a man who pays attention to her, keeps her company, and listens to what she has to say? You think that makes her a whore?"

"You have no idea what our lives are like in private, or how I meet her needs." Max wheeled away, headed for a refill.

"I know she feels hurt a lot. Earlier tonight, you threatened her with being replaced as an artist and maybe even as your lover." Anger knotted in his chest. "Does that inspire love in a woman like Sydney? Is she a masochist?"

"You tell me."

"I don't know her."

"Bullshit. I saw how she looked at you on Saturday morning when you walked into our house."

Colm's frown deepened as he sat forward, forearms on his knees. "She looks at everyone like that. She paints them in her mind. Hasn't she ever painted you?"

"That's not my thing." Max studied his drink. "I'm sure by now she has let you in more than you'll tell me. Those little sessions in the studio provide all kinds of opportunity for intimacy. Has she told you we've been distant for the last few months?"

"You mean in bed?"

Max opened his mouth, closed it, then shook his head and said quietly, "I'm a shell of what I used to be with her. Sydney's been very patient, but I can't stand the martyrdom, the good-natured tolerance. This . . . this invalid shit—" He whirled to face the fireplace. "I believe she will eventually leave me because of what I can't give her. Best to find out now than drag on for years."

Colm drained the rest of his brandy, determined to feel no pity for him. "You made a big mistake by threatening her like you did tonight."

"My replacing her is a very real possibility if she doesn't snap out of whatever phase she's been going through these past few weeks." Max's smooth tone returned. "Her work is losing its heat; she's losing interest in what has made her so wealthy."

"That's because what she really wants is to do portraiture."

"Portraits are a dime a dozen in this field. She won't get anywhere with it. And make no mistake about it, Hennessy, I will ruin her as an artist in this town if she fucks you. The new girl in Chicago is no threat, she's a fact. I'm merely thinking ahead."

Colm set his snifter on a nearby table and stood. "If it's that easy for you to move on, why don't you just let Sydney go?"

"Because I love her," Max said flatly. "Why else would I go to so much trouble to protect myself and what belongs to me?"

Colm almost laughed. Almost. "I don't understand you one goddamned bit. But as I said, that's not my job."

"No." Max's smirk returned. "However, you're serving a purpose. You have ten days to earn your extra money, and if you fail, well—this entire thing will be cash well spent for me either way."

Colm looked at him for a long moment before he opened the library door. "Thank you for the brandy."

"I won't see you again," Max said, wheeling too quickly toward him. Rushing, nearly, a vehicle out of control. "Leave your real home address with Hans so I can mail you your check for the extra funds. If necessary, of course."

It was Colm's turn to smile. "And who would I tell if I do accomplish what you're asking me to do? I can't imagine you'd take my word for it."

"Not usually." Max looked thoughtful, then drew a breath. "However, we're partners in this. And partners have to trust each other."

The fist squeezing Colm's throat tightened. "I hadn't thought of you as a partner."

"Oh, yes. You and I, partners in crime. But in the end, I won't need to ask you anything. I'll know it all simply by looking at Sydney's face."

Suddenly Colm couldn't stand another minute spent in the same room with him. "Is that all?"

"Leave your personal number, too, in case I have any questions."

"What kind of questions?"

The corner of Max's mouth curled up in reply.

Sickened, Colm stepped into the foyer and shut the door between them. He prayed the man was right—that their contact would be severed now. He never wanted to lay eyes on the son of a bitch again.

Sydney didn't see Colm on Wednesday during the day. When she walked across the yard to her studio, his black Ford Explorer was gone. That empty parking space did something funny to her insides—left them feeling empty, too. Throughout the day she took breaks from painting and stepped out onto the studio porch to watch for him, but by nightfall he hadn't yet returned. What if he didn't show up for their appointment with the other models tonight? What if he'd truly had enough and had taken off permanently?

Frustration held a tight grip on her chest by the time the studio door squeaked open. Her heart gave a hopeful leap, but it wasn't Colm. A tall, tawny-haired man stepped into the room, and instantly Sydney jolted off the barstool.

"Hi." His smile faded as he took in her defensive stance. "Sydney, right? I'm Garrett."

Garrett. A friend of Colm's, someone he liked and trusted. And she trusted Colm. But where the hell was he?

She took a breath, tried to laugh at herself for being so nervous, and failed. "Hi, Garrett. It's a pleasure." She forced herself to meet him halfway across the studio. "Colm has told me a lot about you."

He grinned. "I'm scared to ask."

"Nothing too incriminating. Thanks so much for accommodating me, by the way. I know it was short notice."

They clasped hands. His palm was warm and dry; he offered a friendly squeeze and didn't linger, which helped put her at ease. Relaxing a little, she took a second glance at him and found him to be all-American attractive with wavy, light brown hair and blue eyes that could make a girl feel warm in her skin. Nothing like the flutter Colm set to life in her stomach every time she looked at him, though.

Nothing like Colm.

He nodded at the platform. "Is that where the magic happens?"

"I hope so. Colm had the day off," she added. "I'm waiting for him and the other model, Cherise, to get here before I explain what I'm envisioning tonight." She started toward the coffeemaker. "Do you like French roast?"

When he hesitated, she glanced over her shoulder at him and had to smile at the disappointment on his face. "You prefer something a little stronger?"

"It might help relax things."

Good point.

He gave an approving nod when she withdrew a fresh bottle of Shiraz from the weathered cabinet. She poured him a paper cup full and one for herself. Colm was now five minutes late.

"Here's to your dream ménage à trois," Garrett said, his smile disappearing behind his cup. He drank his wine in one swallow, so she poured him more, and then he wandered over to her workstation and picked up a tube of paint. "Oils?"

"Acrylics. It forces me to work fast."

"Colm said you were really talented."

She waved a hand. "Oh, I think that's all subjective."

"And his subjective opinion, Sydney, is that you hang the moon."

She didn't know what to say. Relief battled with bemusement when the door swung open and Colm stepped into the studio.

"Hey." He sounded breathless, as though he'd jogged to get there. He brought the crisp, fragrant autumn into the room with him. Sydney had the ridiculous urge to shoo Garrett away and put Colm alone on the platform, where she would capture him anew on canvas just as he was, in his jeans and jacket, flushed and a little ruffled from the November wind. And when his gaze collided with hers, electricity buzzed through her limbs.

"Wine?" she asked him, snatching up a paper cup. "We're relaxing before we begin."

Colm stopped beside his friend and grasped his hand in a brief shake. "Relaxing, huh? Your influence?"

Garrett grinned. "Of course."

Sydney handed Colm his cup then left the men to talk while she alternately readied her workstation and sipped her wine. She'd never felt self-conscious with models before, but suddenly she couldn't quite envision the men entangled with beautiful Cherise, or how it would feel to witness the unquestionable sensuality of the night ahead. A thread of anticipation went through her at the idea of watching Colm in action with other people, hints of what he looked like when he touched a woman in carnal need. Slow warmth seeped through her at the idea, compliments of wayward arousal and wine drunk too quickly.

Cherise, of course, ran late. When she half stumbled through the door, Sydney glanced at her watch and raised her eyebrows.

"Sorry, I'm so sorry. My GPS broke and I was sure I could find this place without it. This neighborhood is way the hell out here!" She hopped off the ramp and slid out of her fitted leather coat, exposing a body clad in a tight chartreuse sweater and even tighter jeans. "Are these guys my victims for the night?"

"We are, thank God." Garrett approached her and took her hand. When a pleased flush reddened her cheeks, he upped the ante and lifted her knuckles to his lips. "I'd hoped you be gorgeous."

She flashed him a saucy smile.

Colm rolled his eyes at Sydney from behind his cup and she bit back a laugh. She cleared her throat and offered Cherise the obligatory Shiraz, which, to Sydney's surprise, the girl politely waved away.

"I feel more sensuous in my skin when I'm smoking weed," she explained.

Sydney sighed. "I don't have any weed."

"No big deal," Cherise said with a shrug. "I can fly sober."

Garrett's grin widened, but Colm didn't react. He was watching Sydney with an intensity that made her stomach feel light and fluttery. The sexual tension in the room sent galvanized thrills through her nerves. "Let's get started."

"Naked right away?" Garrett asked.

"Yes. There's a changing room over there and robes for everyone." She wasn't one bit surprised when all three models began to strip right there.

Cherise's nude body emerged first, lithe, ivory, and flawless. Immediately the girl wrapped her arms around her breasts and shivered. "It's kind of cold in here."

"It'll warm up," Garrett murmured, but Sydney grabbed the space heater she'd asked Hans to drop off and aimed it in the direction of the stage.

Colm was the last to finish undressing. He seemed unusually quiet as he folded his clothing and set it on a nearby chair then joined the other two on the stage.

She hadn't seen him fully nude more than once, and if she thought it had affected her before, now the sight of him bolted through her. The easy, fluid way he moved, the muscles shifting beneath his skin . . . she wanted to stare; she wanted to revel in his beauty; in the beauty of the three models standing so unabashedly naked before her.

Cherise was long-legged and sleek, almost too thin, but lissome in a way that would read beautifully on canvas. Garrett's physique was slimmer than Colm's, his muscles defined by nature but not with that same sculpted quality that spoke of exercise discipline. Where Colm's chest was smooth, his complexion more olive, his friend was fair-skinned and had just a sprinkle of brown hair on his chest. And Colm—even his stance while he waited for instructions was graceful, and again Sydney thought of demigods emerging, all muscle and smooth flesh, from slabs of marble.

It was time to stop ogling. Rubbing her hands together to warm them, she approached the platform, where she adjusted the yards of black brocade on which they would pose. "Okay, Cherise, I need you to sit in the middle, Garrett beside you and Colm on your knees behind them."

Once they were positioned, she hopped up on the stage, moved to Garrett, and drew his arm around Cherise. "One hand on her left breast," she told him. "Open your lips against her cheek like you're about to kiss it, but not quite. More a breath of a kiss."

She tilted Cherise's head away from him and drew her long

brown hair over one slim shoulder. So beautiful. Already Sydney was excited about this canvas's potential. "Give me ecstasy," she told the girl. Cherise closed her eyes and immediately affected a look of such rapture, Sydney thought of the climb to orgasm.

At last she moved behind Colm, where she stopped. She didn't know how she could put her hands on his naked skin without going weak and foolish. "Shift away from them just a little, as though you're beginning to separate from the unit. Slide your right arm around Garrett and rest your hand on his opposite biceps, like you're about to turn him toward you, to take him with you." She drew a breath and adjusted his warm, muscled arm across Garrett's chest, vaguely aware how tense he seemed as his fingers found his friend's opposite shoulder and curved around it. Despite Colm's apparent discomfort, Garrett was obviously someone Colm trusted. Sydney decided to take advantage of that.

"Now, put your lips on his bare shoulder," she told him low, kneeling beside him. "And breathe. Can you do that?"

They were so close he could have just as easily put his lips on hers. He locked eyes with her, hesitated, then finally turned his head and dropped his mouth to Garrett's smooth shoulder, his lashes sliding closed.

Garrett shivered. "Yowza."

"Shut up," Colm gritted out.

"This is going to look so hot," Cherise added.

Colm lifted his head slightly, said something under his breath that made Garrett burst out laughing, but they settled quickly back into position. The exchange lightened the mood though, and Sydney smiled to herself. It was beguiling to see Colm interact with a friend, someone from his other life, which she knew so little about.

With his heated attention momentarily aimed in a different direction, her focus honed in on the canvas and she picked up her charcoal to sketch. Slowly the figures took shape, entwined, like willows twisting in a tempest. Sexual electricity bounced between the models, heedless of gender, singing only of sensuality and beauty. And Sydney wasn't left out. Every time she took in the whole, exquisite picture they made, arousal engulfed her, the voyeur.

Cherise was right. This was definitely going to be hot.

CHAPTER NINE

Colm had never touched another man's thigh, nor wanted to. Of course, he had never dreamed of being a prostitute, either. He had never dreamed of being here, tangled up with Garrett and some Barbie doll named Cherise. He had never dreamed of Sydney, or the twisted emotions he was experiencing tonight.

Garrett shifted Colm's hand aside to scratch his thigh, then slapped it back into place. "Sorry. Itch."

They'd been at it nearly three hours except for brief breaks. For this particular pose, Colm's hand was much too close to his friend's genitals for comfort, but fortunately Garrett had avoided a hard-on most of the night, with the exception of any particularly intimate contact with Cherise. Then he sported his arousal without a blink.

"I might offer her a freebie," he told Colm during their last break.

"More sex," Colm said wryly. "That's just what you need." In truth, on the previous two breaks, Cherise had cozied up to Colm a little too closely for him to give his friend the thumbs-up. For all Garrett's swagger, when it came to women outside the club, his ego was an eggshell. Fortunately, Sydney had mostly paired Garrett with the girl whenever they changed positions, leaving Colm curiously separate, more and more with each new pose, as though he were a spurned lover and stood alone.

As ten o'clock crept around, Sydney set down her brush and grabbed a camera from the cabinet. "I think it's time to call it a night. Mind if I take a few photos?"

They held the pose for a few shots, and then she dismissed them. Colm climbed off the platform and pulled on his boxer-briefs and jeans. Jesus, his muscles were tight. Not necessarily from holding the pose for so long, but from watching Sydney, from wanting her, from suppressing the arousal that kept creeping up as he read her passion while she painted. It was, he realized, the only time her barriers crumbled and exposed the wildness within.

After Cherise finished dressing, she threw her arms around Sydney, who startled, but then hugged her back. "Thanks for the job." Cherise said. "I hope you'll use me another time."

"I will." Sydney gave her a confident smile. "You held those poses as skillfully as anyone I've ever worked with."

Garrett was next on Cherise's attack list. While he was slipping into his jacket, she gave him a long embrace, snuggling into his arms. "You are so, *so* hot."

He just laughed.

"I'll see you around," she said, and kissed him straight on the lips, her fingers curling into his lapels to hold him close.

He grinned when she backed away. "On that promising note, I think I'll take off." He thanked Sydney, saluted Colm, and headed outside, a gust of frigid air whirling through the door as it closed behind him.

When Colm grabbed his leather jacket and started to follow, Cherise caught his arm. "Wait." She drew a piece of paper from her purse. "You got a pen?"

He didn't need to ask why.

"I have plenty," Sydney said in a dry tone without glancing up from capping her paint tubes. "Look on my table."

Colm waited, vaguely disconcerted, as Cherise picked a pen from the metal can on the worktable, then jotted something down and returned to hand it to him. "Can you read that? It's sloppy."

Her phone number, followed by 'Call me,' was scrawled in bubble writing that reminded him of high school.

"I can read it. Thanks." He smiled, tucked it in his jacket pocket, and glanced in Sydney's direction, but she had disappeared into the bathroom and he could hear her rinsing her brushes.

Cherise should have said good-bye then, but she didn't seem to understand social cues. She stood waiting, her big brown eyes expectant on his face.

The practiced male prostitute in him kicked into play. He let his fingers trail along her angora-covered forearm down to her hand, which he gently squeezed. "Listen, I need to catch Garrett before he's gone, but I'll be in touch."

"'Kay," she said softly, and he could feel her gaze burning his back as he escaped the studio.

Garrett had reached the end of the long driveway and had one foot in the driver's side of his Audi when Colm caught up with him.

"I won't see you for a few days, but I appreciate you showing up tonight and making this thing easy on me."

Garrett smiled. "No problem. You know I love this shit."

"I think Sydney's happy with the start on her portrait, even though it might not be what she truly wants to paint."

Garrett nodded and looked at Colm a long moment before he said, "That's important to you, isn't it? Her happiness."

Colm shrugged, keeping a neutral expression in the glow from the driveway lanterns. "She's a job."

"If you say so."

Out of nowhere, anger swooped in. "I said she's a job. That's it."

Garrett waved a hand. "Okay, I hear you. You don't need to be defensive with me, James. And hey, the fact that you are indicates—"

"It indicates how important it is that I keep my eye on the end result, which is double the money if I can get this woman into bed. Double the money to help me keep Amelia in good care. That's what every part of this indicates. So mind your own goddamned business."

Garrett gave a single nod and started his car, his expression stony in the glow from the dashboard.

"Jesus . . ." Colm looked skyward. How had he ended up in this place at this moment, hurting all the people around him, even Garrett? "Look, I'm an asshole. But you need to understand—"

"I do understand."

"No." Colm shook his head. "This isn't just any job."

"Even though a minute ago you said it was."

"There are things you don't know."

"James." Garrett laid one forearm across the steering wheel and shifted to stare at Colm. "I don't need to know much to figure this whole thing out. You're not exactly immune to her. That's a mortal sin at Avalon, and once it happens, it's hard to untangle. What's it been, five days?"

With nine to go. *Shit.*

Garrett went on. "I'm just being the devil's advocate here, and I'd count on you to do the same for me if I was in your shoes. You know there's always the possibility that we could be exposed through something like this if it gets out of hand. Azure will fire your ass at the very least. You need this job and all the others connected to the club. So do I. So get this thing over and get out of here."

He was right. Garrett was always right. The anger and desperation tightening Colm's chest loosened its hold and he rubbed his
hands over his face. "I hear you. And I'll rein it in. No one's getting
exposed except me—and Beaudoin—for the bastards we are, and
that won't be until I leave Sydney in the dirt."

"You're not a bastard," his friend sighed. "You're an asshole."

"I'm the worst kind."

Pulling on his seat belt, Garrett offered him a faint smile. "Then
we all are. But you can be king." Just like that, the tension snuffed
itself out. "Now give me Cherise's digits, you slut. I know she gave
them to you. She looked at you like a hungry dog all night."

Colm handed over the slip of paper. "You really never are fucked
out, are you?"

"A total impossibility." Garrett shifted gears and the headlights
flashed on the manicured hedges bracketing the driveway. "I'll see
you in a week or so, buddy. Good luck."

Colm walked slowly back to the studio to get his jacket, rubbing
his arms as he went. Damn, it was cold. After a day of working on his house in Silver Spring and visiting with his sister, all he
wanted was a warm bed and a dreamless sleep. No more posing, no
Garrett, no Cherise. Only Sydney, but that was an improbability
tonight after the phone number fiasco. His mind was so tired. He
needed to call home, talk to the nurse about a change in schedule,
and then fall into bed.

"Colm." The sultry voice came from nowhere as he reached the
porch, and he paused before he spotted her sauntering toward him.
Cherise again.

When she reached him, she tilted her head and eyed him in a
feral way that both amused and exasperated him.

A wry smile curved his mouth. "I thought I said goodnight to you."

"What are you doing tonight?"

"Going to sleep," he said. "You?"

"Having a drink with you, if you've got something in your cabin."

He wanted to laugh. Cherise was sex on sticks, and any man would be crazy to turn her down. But even if Colm hadn't been working, even if he didn't have a job that kept him from being an average man without a cellar of secrets, he wouldn't have said yes. He wanted only Sydney. Christ, he really might be in trouble here. Somehow he needed to slow down the game while speeding it up.

"You don't look legal to drink," he told Cherise.

"I'm twenty-four." She drew herself up to her full height, almost as tall as he. "Come on, one drink."

He pictured Sydney at her easel, her brows lowered in concentration, the way she caught her lip between her teeth as she worked, the tension in her slender body as her electric blue eyes shifted with lightning speed between her canvas and her subjects.

"I can't tonight," he said. "But thanks."

"Maybe another time?"

He tried to conjure another smile and couldn't. "I don't think so."

She looked at him in the glow from the studio porch light. "I think you find me attractive but don't want to admit it."

"I have no problem admitting you're gorgeous."

"Are you gay?" she demanded.

"No."

"Then at least kiss me goodnight." And rising on tiptoe, she slid her arms around his waist and pressed her mouth to his.

Her lips were soft and she tasted good, like Fruit Stripe gum. When her tongue tangled with his, he grasped her shoulders and set her away from him. "Whoa."

"For real?" She smiled; she knew her effect on men. Sydney didn't. Sydney had no idea how beautiful she was, how fragile and yet strong she seemed. He wanted inside her so badly, suddenly he couldn't even meet Cherise's eyes.

"Let me walk you to your car." He started toward her ancient Ford Bronco and finally, reluctantly, she followed. When they reached the vehicle, she climbed in and he shut the door for her before she could launch another attack.

She rolled down the window. "Sure I can't change your mind?"

"It's hard to say no to you."

That brought another smile to her bewildered expression. God, she was gorgeous, yet clichéd, simply another just-bloomed flower in the basket of beauty to which he'd grown immune.

"Well, maybe I'll see you around. I model all over town." The subtle pout of her bottom lip was meant to entice, but he said nothing in response.

She gave him a last long look, sighed, and revved her motor. He stood in the driveway and watched her red taillights wink and disappear. When he turned back toward the studio, the windows were dark. Sydney had obviously locked up for the night and slipped out the back while he was screwing around. Jesus, had she seen the kiss Cherise laid on him?

A fresh wave of determination burned off his exhaustion. He needed to get this thing rolling tonight. Max was gone, the pall that hung over the estate with his presence had lifted, and all Colm could think about was replacing the memory of Cherise's mouth with Sydney's. He headed toward the mansion to find her, his purpose burning with every step.

CHAPTER TEN

Sydney took her time walking to the neighborhood park. It was only a half-mile away, and she always enjoyed strolling there at night when families were tucked in their houses. Like a wayward voyeur, she loved the ones where the curtains weren't yet closed for the evening, where the sight of everyday people living everyday lives painted itself in golden light.

Now, though, she hardly saw any of it. Her heart was in her stomach, and she couldn't admit why, only that it had something to do with Colm hooking up with Cherise. He'd proved Sydney right—that she needed to fly free of men for a long, long time, no weights pulling at her when she spread her wings. Why should she be surprised?

She reached the park, its silence and chill washing over her in fresh, cleansing waves. She thought about swinging on a swing— such a silly thing, and pure magic. But the merry-go-round beckoned her and seemed to suit her life better. One big, fat circle, around and around.

Tucking her coat beneath her backside so she wouldn't freeze on the cold metal, she seated herself on its edge and cast off with her foot. She rotated toward the streetlight, toward the winding road that led to the house . . . and that was when she saw him. A shadow, tall, graceful, walking in that easy, level way that had become familiar to her much too quickly. Sensing his purpose, she lightly dragged her foot in the sand and created a mini-moat around herself before she slowed and stopped the merry-go-round. Then she tucked her legs beneath her and waited.

Colm crossed the lawn and stopped at the edge of the circle where the grass had worn away. His eyes glittered in the glow of the playground night lights like a nocturnal creature. Sometimes she really did think he could read her secrets.

"You weren't in the studio when I came back," he said.

"I wasn't?" She didn't smile as she gazed up at him.

He set his hands on his hips and looked away toward the street, his eyes following a passing car.

Sydney set herself rotating again with the push of a sneaker. "How did you know where to find me?"

He shrugged as she circled past him. "I asked Hans."

"Ah, yes. Hans knows everything. Even my hiding places."

"He said you hadn't come into the house, and that sometimes you come over here."

"Hmm. I think he likes you too much to mind his own beeswax."

Silence again. She made two rotations on the merry-go-round and had nearly passed him again when he stopped the ride with his foot.

She studied his clothing. He was still wearing the same brown Doc Martens oxfords, jeans, a long-sleeved maroon T-shirt advertising some restaurant in Virginia Beach, and his open leather jacket over that. She'd seen every inch of him naked tonight, and yet for some reason his appearance in that nondescript outfit seared her just as much. As always, her mind slid a paintbrush across the canvas, capturing him, half shadow and half man. How ironic, and frustrating, that in the few days she'd had him standing before her as a model, she hadn't even finished a single sketch of him.

He shifted his weight and shoved his hands in his jacket pockets. "I sent Cherise home."

Warmth curled through her veins, but she kept an impassive expression. "That's nice." Then, because she couldn't help herself, "I thought you might have a date."

"No," he said.

He was probably planning to get with her later. But if Colm was the gentleman he seemed and did take Cherise out for a real date instead of a late-night booty call, where would they go? To a midnight movie, then home to his place in the city? She tried to envision his bedroom and came up with an imperfect image of an unmade bed with wrinkled sheets, khaki walls, books or magazines scattered on the floor by the bedside table. An empty beer bottle on the windowsill. Condoms in the bedside table drawer.

She wanted him, but he could never know what she was thinking, sitting here before him while her existence, her life as she knew it, dangled dangerously close to the edge of destruction.

"What are you doing, Sydney?" His voice came gentle, as though he read her mind. "Here? Alone?"

She swallowed and looked past him at the empty swings swaying gently in the cold night. "Thinking about my secrets," she said finally. "I have a lot of them."

"I know."

He knew because in a mere five days, he'd looked into her and torn off her defenses in slow, bleeding strips. She rubbed a hand across her eyes and tried not to meet his gaze. He was deadly.

His foot, braced on the edge of the merry-go-round, gently

swayed the steel structure on its axis, back and forth, while it squeaked like a cranky child. "I have them, too, Syd."

The diminutive nickname sounded sweet to her ears. His scent floated on the breeze, warm skin and lime.

And out of nowhere, slicing brutally through her desire, welled an unbidden wave of tears.

"I'm a really damaged person, Colm."

He didn't comment on the choked quality of her voice. He lowered his foot and held out his hand. When she took it, she thought he meant to help her climb off the merry-go-round, but instead he urged her to scoot back on its diamond-plated expanse. "Lie down on your back."

Her brows lowered, but she did as he instructed, bracing herself on her elbows so she could read his intentions. The metal seeped cold through her coat, chilling her butt and spine, and she felt awkward with her legs dangling off the side.

"Put your feet up so they don't touch the ground," he told her. When she obliged, he moved to lie beside her, separated from her only by the steel handlebar. He braced one foot on the platform and used the other to push the merry-go-round into rotation again.

After a moment, Sydney glanced at him. He didn't look back, so she watched his profile, so finely sculpted against the glow from the playground lights. He had one arm tucked behind his head, his gaze fixed on the sky. The moon was high, an ivory crescent sliver, the shadow of its dark side a blacker promise than the night could offer. She finally laid back, too, and let her head rest uneasily on the metal platform. The stars radiated in all their glory, so many they looked like pinpricks on the surface of heaven. She thought of a long-ago man named Greg, first her mother's lover and then her own. Rage squeezed her throat again. Rage and shame and grief for lost innocence.

Colm's foot pushed them a little faster. Now the stars blinked and blurred. A silken breeze raised goose bumps on her naked arms beneath her coat sleeves, dried the moisture trickling from the corners of her eyes and down her temples.

"Truth or dare?" he said.

Shock and amusement assailed her at the same time. "Really?"

"Really."

"Do I have to do this?"

"You're chicken."

"I'm not chicken." She sighed. "Truth."

He thought for a moment. "What's the worst thing you ever did as a kid?"

So many things. Too many to count. She searched for something safe, circumvented the greatest sins of her life. "When I was fourteen, my mother went out of town and made the mistake of letting me stay by myself for a night. I took the car and drove it around the city."

"Did you get busted?"

"No. She never knew the difference."

She sensed his amusement but didn't check for his smile. The last time he'd smiled at her, in the midst of something Garrett had said earlier tonight, a spear of desire had caught her right in the stomach. Then he'd laughed, and the sound of his laughter, warm and genuine to her ears, suited him perfectly. Every part of him was designed in the image of something so much more beautiful than anything she'd known.

If he smiled again, she would reach for him.

"Truth or dare?" she asked instead.

"Truth."

"Same question you asked me. Worst thing you did as a kid."

"There's a long and distinguished list." He considered, then said,

"I broke into my high school on a dare and got caught. Arrested. My parents let me rot in jail for twenty-four hours before they bailed me out. My cellmate puked on me."

Sydney pressed her lips together to keep in the laughter that pushed through her sadness. "He just . . . walked up to you and *blaaaah*?"

"Yeah. A big, threatening guy who didn't like scrawny kids with smart mouths. I tried to disappear into the bench."

"Did you think he was going to hit you?"

"Absolutely. His fists were the size of hams. But then he puked on me instead."

She laughed and rolled her head to look at him. "I bet you smelled like a rose the next day."

"Jeez." He shuddered. "My dad wouldn't let me in the car. He made me walk home from the jail. Three miles."

Now she really laughed, one arm flung over her head and the other falling across her stomach to keep from coming apart. She didn't remember the last time she'd genuinely laughed.

She stopped when he said, "Truth or dare, Syd? Any girl with guts would choose a dare now."

But she didn't trust him enough. She didn't know how. "Whatever. Truth."

"What's your biggest regret?"

Her mind went blank. She didn't want to think about any of it. She had to swallow before she could reply. "That I ran away from home at seventeen and never went back." She didn't give him a chance to ask about it. "Your turn."

His fingers curled around the metal bars on either side of his legs, and he changed feet, hooking his other heel on the edge of the merry-go-round. "Truth."

"*Your* biggest regret in life. What's good for the goose . . ."

He didn't speak for so long, she poked his arm. "Come on. Spill it."

"My wife died in an accident."

Sydney turned her head to look at him, but all she could see was his profile silhouetted against the golden lights they passed.

"I was driving," he said.

"Colm." When she sat up, he reached for her hand.

"We're still playing the game." His voice came low, unemotional, even as he slid his fingers between hers and squeezed her hand. "Truth or dare?"

"I'm so sorry. Colm. I'm sorry." She met his eyes when the merry-go-round rotated out of shadow again, and withdrew her hand from his warmth. "I can't do this. It's not right, not after what you just told me."

"Truth or dare?" he repeated, the words coming harder now, insistent.

She blinked once, then again, her stomach aching and hollow. "Truth."

"Tell me why you're so afraid. Of men. Of me."

Her own regret and misery paled before his confession. But she couldn't block the memories, or stop the fresh tears, a river of them now, as she released a breath, and with it, the darkest truth she could muster. "It's ironic, really, my fear, considering what I've done . . . but . . ."

"But?" he prompted gently.

"But I had an affair with my mother's boyfriend when I was sixteen."

The merry-go-round stopped abruptly under his direction.

She drew a shuddering breath, tangled in feelings of horror and sympathy for the secret he'd shared with her, and the deepest shame for her own. "I was an angsty, multi-pierced teenager who looked like trouble. The guys my mom brought home—they liked to come after me, but she never believed me when I tried to tell her. And then she started dating Greg, and he was different. He actually listened to me and talked to me when she ignored me. He acted like he cared."

The tightness in her throat threatened to choke off the words. Why in God's name was she admitting any of this to Colm? And why did it matter that he would likely find her as disgusting as she still found herself fourteen years later?

Fresh tears squeezed through her lashes as the teenager in her rose up and finished the story she couldn't bring herself to speak. "This whole thing went on for a few weeks behind my mom's back, but eventually she put two and two together. It wasn't until she kicked him out that I started thinking maybe . . . maybe it wasn't okay that a forty-year-old man had wanted to be with someone as young as me."

She drew a shuddering breath and hung her head. "Then I hated him, but my mother hated me more. So I ran away. Came to D.C. After a few years of waiting tables and living with college students, I met Max at a party where I was a waitress. He had such a mental force, and at the same time he gave me the sense that he would be my family—that I would finally have a family if I trusted him. He believed in me. So I—"

She couldn't finish; she was too sick inside. Slowly Colm sat up beside her, but he didn't touch her. He gave the merry-go-round another push with his foot. The cold breeze gently lifted free the strands of hair that had stuck to her damp cheeks.

She wiped her eyes on her shoulder and finally found her voice. "I'm sorry."

"Don't be," he said quietly. "It's just a game."

She swallowed. She didn't want his pity. She wanted him. His realness. His rawness. His honesty. "Truth or dare?" she managed to ask, and prayed he'd tell her something else that would lift them both from the darkness.

Grasping the bar overhead, he ducked his head to look at her as they passed into shadow again. "Dare," he said. And before she could draw another breath, he leaned in and kissed her.

To his astonishment, she didn't kiss back. Damn it, her mouth didn't move one bit, not even when he angled his head and slid the tip of his tongue across the soft seam of her lips. He could taste the sweet saltiness of tears and went hard just that easily. He tried again, licked her top lip, then her bottom, but while her mouth quivered, she didn't invite him in. Finally, he eased back and met her eyes, which shone liquid with tears.

"Why did you do that?" she whispered.

"You dared me."

"No." She shook her head. "No."

"Didn't you?" He lifted a hand to brush the unkempt hair back from her temple. He loved her like this, so broken and imperfect. He breathed in her scent, flowers and fruit. "Just like last night in the studio, we're alone here. You have tears in your eyes. I want to kiss them away. I want to kiss you, again and again."

"You can't." She put up a hand and climbed off the merry-go-round before he could act on his words. "Not last night, not now, not ever."

He leaped up and followed her.

"Why?" he asked, catching her elbow.

"You know why."

"I wouldn't hurt you."

Self-loathing ate into his conscience. He thought of Amelia and kept talking. "There's this thing between us, Sydney. From the start. It's keeping me up at night." A truth, but not enough to banish the mortal sin of the lie he offered her every day. And now that he knew the pain she carried from her past . . .

Wretch.

He lowered his voice, heard the same husky tone emerge from his throat that he used on his clients at Avalon. "You know what I think about when I lie awake?"

"Don't say it."

Don't say it. Let her out of this trap, let her run free.

Amelia would go to a nursing home when the money stopped coming in.

"I think about touching you . . ." He traced the curve of Sydney's eyebrow with a single finger and she shivered, her face upturned to him, asking for his kiss, yet ready to turn it aside again.

"I think about tasting you"—he leaned to murmur in her ear—"and making you cry out with pleasure . . . "

"I said don't." She drew back and wiped her eyes on the sleeve of her wool coat. "Even if this were the passion of a lifetime, Colm, it's not going to work. Do you honestly think I'd go bounding into an affair with the man Max hired to model for my next show? He's trying to help me."

"Hell of a way to do that," Colm said shortly.

"But I do think he is, in his own messed-up way. So I won't betray him. He and I . . . it's ending, but not until I can do it right. We've gone too many miles together."

He didn't answer. The half-decent being still alive inside him wanted to lay down the truth about her beloved Max.

"I'm sorry," he told her as he rose from the merry-go-round. "I won't touch you again until you ask me."

She gave a dry laugh. "You really think I will? Come on, Colm."

"Let me see you home safely and I'll leave you alone." More lies. Even though it was dark, he imagined he could see the doubt die in her eyes and knew she trusted him to do just that. The hustler in him knew this wasn't over. She was gullible. He would have her under his hands and mouth, twist her and mold her into exactly what he wanted.

Exactly like Max Beaudoin had for four years—only Colm would do it in nine days.

CHAPTER ELEVEN

Sydney couldn't sleep.

Four hours after she and Colm shared a tension-choked walk home, she kicked free of the binding covers and climbed out of bed. The wood floor creaked under her feet loud enough to wake the dead, but not even a phantom would be interested in her sleeplessness.

Downstairs, she flipped on the kitchen light and blinked in its high fluorescent glare. The room was cavernous. Who needed such a big kitchen? Three people lived in this house. She, Max, and Hans. Three. The kitchen would never know the sounds of children, either. Once upon a time Sydney had believed she could change Max's mind—change him. But the subject of children, the impasse they'd reached, had ceased to even matter with his accident, like a child in its own right the way it took her attention, her time, her devotion, every cell of her soul.

Now, again and at last, the relationship was over. When he came home from Chicago, she would tell him good-bye. As friends, if he would allow it, but no more so-called lover, and no more puppet master. It was all she knew for certain in her existence on this damned planet.

Sleep tonight was a fickle friend. She headed back upstairs to dress.

When she stepped outside and drew the massive front door closed behind her, the world outside was hers. Wind rifled through the dried autumnal canopy overhead as she swung her flashlight along the path to the studio. Somewhere in the distance a dog barked.

Beyond the trees, Colm's cabin windows glowed golden and muted, reminding her of one of those clichéd, mass-produced prints that somehow still appealed to her haggard artist's heart. His cabin looked warm and welcoming.

Sydney changed direction at the last minute, away from the studio and toward Colm. The fallen leaves crunched beneath her tennis shoes as she approached the small guest cabin and slowed to see if she could spot him through the open curtains. The TV was on. His bare feet were braced on the coffee table in front of it, his ankles hemmed by pale blue pajama bottoms. Although she couldn't see all of him, she knew he was slumped down on the sofa so that the back cushions caught the nape of his neck, one hand resting on his flat stomach. Even from the porch steps, she could hear the low murmur of his voice, the conversation indecipherable but the tone low, intimate. He was obviously on the phone, talking to a friend. At this inappropriate hour, a very special friend. Someone uncomplicated who deserved such intimate attention, not a woman entangled in a mess with Max Beaudoin.

Feeling like a fool, she backed away and headed for the studio. Inside, she jacked up the heat, set the canvas of the ménage against the wall, and uncovered Colm's portrait, then put it on the easel to look at it. It could still be salvaged from the other night. She played with her brushes, trying to decide if she wanted to work on it now, while night waned and dawn threatened, and a few yards away, Colm was the only other person awake in the world.

Then she remembered the way the champagne had made her feel the night of her last show—that she could do anything, even stand under a beautiful man's piercing regard and discuss genitalia. Hers.

A new bottle of Shiraz in the cabinet, via Hans, would have to do.

Soon she was settled down with a plastic cup of wine and a fresh palette of paint. She put on some Joan Baez, poured herself more wine, organized her supply area . . . poured herself more wine, changed her mind about working on Colm's portrait, tried to stretch a canvas and felt too silly and loose-muscled all of a sudden to deal with hammer and nails.

By the time the bottle was three-quarters empty, she sat perched on the barstool again, staring at the portrait. She did need to fix the smudges from where she'd thrown it on the floor. The part that wasn't ruined looked just like him, especially the eyes and the collarbones. Collarbones? The thought made her smile. She stopped abruptly when the room tilted a little. His lips looked good, too, but there was no way to capture their resilience in two dimensions. They were so soft, and God, did the man know how to kiss, with sinuous tongue, with soft invasion, which meant he probably did everything else with the same thoroughness and care.

He shouldn't have kissed her earlier. She certainly hadn't given him a signal to do so. Had she? Maybe she should ask him. After all, he was awake. Maybe she should come clean and tell him that he was creating all sorts of problems for her, and by God, if anyone was going to rock her boat, it would be her own damned self, not some man. Men were pain-in-the-ass wolves, thieves, and liars, and she could hardly tolerate them.

Well, some of them.

She turned off her work light, shut off Joan Baez, and headed out of the studio without bothering to lock it.

The guesthouse porch light was still on, but the windows were dim. It didn't stop her. One knock, two, the second one significantly sharper, and then Colm answered the door. She'd obviously awakened him. His short hair stood in spikes and he squinted at her in the amber porch light glow. "Here to play truth or dare again?" He glanced at his watch. "At four a.m.?"

Sydney swayed and grabbed the side of a porch rocking chair, which instantly listed her sideways. When he caught her elbow and straightened her, she shook him off. "I'm here to say . . . to tell you off." God, she sounded tipsy. Deep down, the part of her that wasn't buzzed completely panicked. What was she doing?

"I have a few things to say," she continued, sounding less confident with every slightly slurred word. "Some truth and some other stuff."

His mouth twitched. "Okay. Do you want to do this inside, or out here on the porch where it's freezing?" He glanced at her breasts in her thin sweater, and she instantly went hot all over. She would not look down to see if her nipples were as perky as he'd implied.

She looked down. They were.

"Inside, if you don't mind."

The living room with its fifties hunting lodge décor set a cozier scene than she remembered from the couple of times she'd been in the guest cottage. Hans had decorated it and lived there a brief time while the big house was being built three years ago. The man had a surprising eye for creating atmosphere with his hunter green and gold plaids, the red chenille sofa and maple tables.

The only light in the room was a small hurricane reading lamp beside the sofa and the flickering glow from the fireplace. Much too

intimate, she decided, and turned to leave . . . just in time to see
Colm shut the door and lean his back against it.

"Have a seat," he said.

"No, thank you. I'd rather stand." But the floor rolled beneath
her, so she perched carefully on the sofa arm. "I have things to say."

"I'm ready." He pressed his palm against his abdomen, that muscled, six-pack sculpture Sydney would never, ever touch, or caress,
or lick. Especially no licking, even though she knew his flesh would
be tough and smooth under her tongue.

She waved a hand. "You shouldn't have done that . . . that thing
at the playground."

His smile widened. "What thing, Boss?"

"Don't call me that."

He sobered and looked at her, the fire's dancing glow reflected
in his eyes. "What thing, Syd?"

As if he didn't know. She hated when he spoke to her quietly and
softly. It made her go all light and funny inside. "You know what
thing. The kiss."

Colm pushed away from the door and came to sit a proper distance from her, on one of the old-fashioned rocking recliners. It
squeaked under his weight when he leaned his forearms on his knees
and said, "I know. It was an unfair thing to do, and I apologize."

She opened her mouth to argue and realized there was nothing
to contradict, so she stared at the fire rather than the flames in his
green, green eyes. "Does that mean you wish you hadn't done it?"

He didn't reply, just sat there and watched her.

"Say something," she ordered, and finally he straightened, but
before he could speak, a wave of nausea brought burning wine into
her throat. She swallowed a few times but it didn't help. God, she
was going to throw up. She leaped to her feet and bolted for the
hallway. "Bathroom!"

She didn't wait for his directions. The first door she opened was a closet.

"End of the hall on the right," he said calmly, and she made it to the toilet just in time.

Sydney had heaved the last of that godforsaken wine when she became aware of his bare feet to her right, then his long, strong legs in those low-slung pajama bottoms, then the rest of him. Damn, she hadn't shut the door.

"You can't be in here," she groaned.

"Oh, but I can. This is my cabin for eight more days." She sensed him move, heard the sound of the water splashing in the sink, then jolted as something cool and damp touched her nape.

"Just a washcloth," he said.

It did feel good. "Go away."

A gentle hand settled on her back. "Think you're done?"

"I'm definitely empty."

"Why did you drink all that wine?" Damn that voice. Soft and low, soft and low. The way he would kiss her body if she let him.

She quickly flushed the toilet and got to her feet with his hand at her elbow to help. "I'm confused. About stuff. Not about you, of course."

"Of course not." He opened a drawer in the vanity and withdrew a toothbrush and toothpaste. "Brushing my teeth always helps me feel better after I puke my guts out."

A warm flush seeped from her cheeks to her ears. "I did not."

"Did too." He paused in the doorway. "Come to the kitchen when you're done."

She didn't want to go to the kitchen, she wanted to run like hell for home. Why was she here again? Oh, yes. Because she couldn't stay away. And she was tipsy. And he was a magnet and apparently she was a shaky paperclip sculpture like the one on Max's desk in the library. All tangled, clingy pieces and confusion.

She brushed her teeth, and he was right, it did make her feel better. When she stopped in the kitchen doorway, Colm swung open the fridge, reached inside, and handed her an ice-cold sports drink.

"To replace the electrolytes you lost. Now hold out your other hand."

She obeyed, and he dropped two aspirin in her palm. "For the thundering headache you're going to have if you don't take these."

Obediently she took the pills, then he handed her a piece of fluffy, delectable smelling bread. "Plain white bread."

She preferred whole grain.

"This stuff is glue in your gut," she said flatly, but took a reluctant bite. Oh, it was soft and so delicious in that starchy, loaded-with-preservatives way she remembered from childhood.

A faint smile tugged at his mouth. "I'm so sorry I don't have brioche or croissants, Your Highness. Eat the whole thing or your stomach will hate you in the morning."

She stood in sulky silence and finished the bread. Then he led her by the hand, unresisting, to a darkened room near the living room.

When Sydney saw the queen-sized bed, she immediately stepped backward and bumped into him. "Are you kidding?"

"No," he said, "and you've got a dirty mind."

"I can't spend the night here."

"Why not?"

"How will it look?"

"To who? Hans? I don't think he'll rat you out."

"He told you I was at the playground," she said. "He's the enemy. He cannot be trusted."

Colm studied her. "Maybe he's the only one you *can* trust." Then, "Are you going to sleep or not?"

While she stood there, dancing a mental jig of indecision, he went to the closet and pulled out a couple of blankets and a pillow. "I'll wake you up in a couple of hours so you won't have to take the walk of shame back to your house in the blazing sun."

"But . . . I can't take your bed." She sat down on the edge and closed her eyes. "Where will you sleep?"

"Sofa, remember? You're fading fast. Lie down." He slipped her unlaced Keds from her feet and helped her stretch out.

"I'll only lie here a minute," she said, without opening her eyes.

"Uh-huh."

The weight of a blanket settled over her, scented with cedar and so soft and warm. She snuggled into it and drifted off, but not before feeling him push the hair away from her face. No one had tucked her in since she was a kid. Months had passed since anyone had touched her so tenderly. Sure, she'd feel embarrassed later. But for now . . . oh, it was sweet. He was sweet.

She slept.

Sydney awoke at daybreak with a bitchy little headache and what felt like a mouthful of cotton. The floorboards creaked under her as she crept to the bathroom, where she found he'd left her a fresh washcloth, her toothbrush, and mouthwash. *Nice birthday present,* she thought. *Happy birthday to me.*

She scrubbed her teeth and swished, wiped her face, drank a glass of water, and felt human again. She vaguely remembered Colm saying he'd wake her before sunrise, but when she peeked into the living room and saw him still asleep in the sliver of golden dawn peeking through the curtains, his long form cramped up on the too-small sofa, she couldn't blame him for sleeping through his promise. All she wanted was to climb back into his cozy bed and snooze till noon.

Max was out of town. Hans wouldn't tell. She already knew the valet had her best interests at heart. Before she went back to bed, though, she had to get a good long look at Colm.

She crept closer, her footsteps muffled on the living room's braided rug. He slept on his right side, still bare-chested, his pajama bottoms slid low on his hip. Even utterly relaxed, his body remained hard and sculpted. *Art at rest,* she mused, her gaze taking in the bulge of his biceps, which pillowed his head, the other arm folded over his stomach. Not an ounce of fat on him.

A wave of chill bumps spread through her, raising the fine hairs on her arms. The fire had died with the night, and a stark cold that reminded her of her mother's house in Nebraska pervaded the room. Moving gingerly so as not to wake him, she drew up the blanket he'd kicked aside and tucked it around him. It didn't look like enough. She headed back to the bedroom, grabbed her own blanket, and returned to spread that over him, too.

Then she studied his profile, the long lashes resting on his cheeks, the perfect, uninteresting nose, those soft lips and stubborn chin. What would it be like to wake up every morning with such a man beside her? She'd slept alone so long, she could hardly remember what it felt like not to be an island in her bed. Even in the old days, Max hadn't been a cuddler; he liked his space, and so Sydney had often awakened hugging her side of the bed to keep from rolling into him in the middle of the night. What would Colm be like? No doubt a lot of women knew. His wife. God. The one who'd died in the accident.

Her eyes shot to his face again, and she wondered what it had been like between them before the car wreck. Sydney pictured a smart, witty brunette, no doubt with a bod to die for, someone capable of keeping up with him. They would have been the golden couple, turning heads wherever they went. How did he live with her loss? The crinkles around his eyes weren't all from smiling. Grief did the same damage. She couldn't imagine him crying. If a man like him cried in front of her, she would cry harder. She couldn't stand the thought of him grieving.

Suddenly Sydney felt like a Peeping Tom, peeking into his life as he slept unaware. Half-ashamed, she crept back to his room and this time slid beneath the sheets. They smelled so good, so clean and masculine. She buried her face in his pillow and inhaled the scent of his skin, then hugged the softness to her breasts and rested her cheek against it. She would doze a little longer, just a few minutes more.

When she woke again, late-morning daylight poured through the half-open curtains. The clock read ten thirty. Colm was sitting on the edge of the bed watching her.

She scrambled to a sitting position. "What are you doing?"

"Watching you sleep." He was dressed in a pair of jeans and an unbuttoned, untucked shirt. His hair was damp from the shower and the scent of Irish Spring and shampoo tickled her senses.

Despite the knowledge that he'd been watching her, she didn't feel violated. She wanted him to look at her. She wanted to strip off her clothing and let him see all of her, naked and shivering and wanting. Naturally she said, "You have no right to do that."

"Yes, I do," he replied. "You're in my bed. I slept like hell on the sofa because of you."

Her eyes dropped to his mouth, to the vague smile curling the corners.

He brushed the hair back from her cheek. "Keep looking at me like that and you're going to get yourself kissed."

She should have averted her eyes. Said something. Ended it right there. Instead she leaned forward to taste him.

He drew in a sharp breath at the first touch of her lips, and for a moment they both froze, mouths so close they nearly breathed for each other. Then she grasped the open edges of his shirt, pulled him to meet her, and tentatively brushed her lips against his again. Again. Again. She heard him swallow and she scooted closer, one leg sliding across his thighs and the other behind his backside, so they fit like puzzle pieces. She drew back enough to search his gaze and found his lashes lowered as he stared at her lips.

"Sydney," he whispered. "Don't do this unless you mean it."

"I mean it." She slid her fingers into his damp hair and opened her mouth over his, and this time he came to life and took her face in his hands, holding her as his tongue dipped between her lips and tangled with hers. Back and forth, thrust, retreat, while she felt herself go soft and wet, and thought she'd never been kissed like this in her life, that she'd never known such want. Beneath her leg he was hard, and she loved it, she wanted more, to feel that beautiful, perfect part of him in her hands, to caress and stroke until he lost all his confident control.

They explored each other's mouths for what seemed like forever, tilting their heads this way and that, bumping noses and coming at each other a different way until he groaned and held her still and took control. He tasted like mint and warm, wet heat, his tongue silky as it stroked hers. He stopped only to kiss the corners of her lips, her cheek, her chin, then her mouth again, probing and hungry.

Only when his hands slid away from her jaw and moved down to cup her breasts through her sweater, only when piercing pleasure darted to the wanting place between her legs, did she put a palm to his chest and push him back.

Instantly he straightened, flushed and tousled from desire and her gripping fingers.

Oh God. What had she done? "I'm not thinking straight."

"I like the way you're thinking."

But she shook her head and untangled herself from him. Grabbing her pants from the floor, she thrust one leg in, then hopped to get her foot through the material, humiliated and excited, refusing to look at him, because if she did, he would win. She would drop to her knees before him, slide her palms up his hard thighs, and take him, then beg him to put his hands on her everywhere, his mouth and tongue on her flesh, his fingers inside her.

If Colm knew what she was thinking, he didn't show it. His mouth had thinned to a grim line. He grabbed up her paint-stained tennis shoes and tossed them to her one at a time. She was surprised he didn't wing them at her head.

"And here," he added, throwing her the bra she'd left draped over the night table, "you might need this in case someone's watching your walk of shame and runs to call Max."

"It's not a walk of shame."

He uttered a humorless laugh and leaned back on the bed. "All the girls say that."

Face burning, she wadded the bra in her hand and headed to the living room. He didn't follow. When she reached the door, she hesitated. Hollering a belated thanks for letting her stay, for taking care of her while she puked, for being so good as he always was . . . it would have seemed patronizing, so she said nothing. She slipped out and ran for the house, regret burning deep in her chest.

CHAPTER TWELVE

A fiasco. A failure like none he'd known since Azure's invention of Colm Hennessy. So which side of him was falling for Sydney Warren, she who was no more than an unknowing customer and the victim of the greatest deception in which he'd ever taken part?

One hour after she'd left his cabin, Colm shoved a hand through his hair and stood barefoot on the guesthouse porch, watching for Sydney to make her way from the big house to her studio. No sign of her. She was probably already there working. There might be no further interaction between them today, no steps toward seduction after all; his lust had chased her off.

Nothing was sexier than a woman he could barely keep his hands off of reaching for him, taking him by surprise, laying her lips on his, digging her fingers into his shoulders and inviting him between her legs. All he'd had to do was ease her back on the pillows, kiss her when she tried to renege, sway her into her own much-needed compliance with hands and mouth.

Why hadn't he? Why couldn't he read her when she was ready

for the next step? Instead, he and his lack of savvy had all but helped her out the door, watching the extra funds disappear with her.

He drained his mug, went back inside for his shoes, then headed for the studio. As he'd guessed he would, he found her there, her head bent over her palette as she mixed colors and prepared herself for an everyday session with him, as though they hadn't stood on the precipice of sex only hours before.

By God, if she could fake it, he could, too. It was his job. He drew a breath, determined anew, and stepped quietly through the door, letting his gaze sweep over her slender frame and well-curved ass, letting his desire for her flow through him, no playacting, but the real thing, the true role of his lifetime. But he would follow Max's path to damnation.

"Day six," he said softly, a reminder to himself more than a greeting.

Sydney's head jerked around and she uttered a breathless laugh. "Oh! The door didn't squeak. You scared me to death."

"Sorry." He closed it behind him.

Today's choice of music was Coldplay. The vague melancholia that seemed an inherent part of her persona made him smile. She was an artist through and through. And despite her current cheerfulness, she didn't easily let go of things. Humiliation radiated from her across the studio, and he knew damn well she was thinking about what had happened on his bed that morning.

The room was chilly, the air scented with fresh paint. "How's the ménage picture?" he asked, knowing better than to broach the subject of the latest kiss.

"It's coming."

When he sauntered down the ramp to take a look at it, she stepped in front of it, her cheeks flushing a faint pink. "I'm taking a break from the ménage right now. Working on something else."

He spied a naked shoulder and knew it was his portrait, and that she felt like she'd been caught doing something taboo. A smile threatened to creep across his lips. "Need me to pose?"

"Yes." She paused. "No. Oh, hell, I don't know."

Without another word, he headed to the stage, crossed his arms to grab the hem of his Henley shirt and drew it up and off, taking his T-shirt with it.

Sydney set the space heater close to the platform and returned to sit at her easel. They fell into a silent partnership as she resumed painting, she with her blue eyes darting between his form and the canvas, he standing in the simple pose she favored, drinking in her features.

"Tilt your head a little more to the left," she said at one point.

He followed her direction. He was stiff from last night's ménage pose, but he held perfectly still. "I'm curious about something."

"What's that?" Her attention dropped to his abdomen, then lower, and up again to meet his gaze.

"Posing for the ménage last night. It wasn't what I'd thought it would be."

She dabbed her brush in paint and applied it to the canvas. "What did you think it would be?"

"More of a threesome. But you kept me separate from Garrett and Cherise by several feet during most of the poses."

"Not most of them. Just some."

He didn't reply. He was baiting her, and waited while she slowly swirled her brush in water.

"I was trying to tell a story," she said finally, straightening. "One of a woman who's with one man, but also of a second lover who would do anything to please her, if only the woman would reach for him."

"Does she reach for him after your story ends?"

She glanced at him, then at the neglected ménage canvas leaning against the wall. "I think . . . she doesn't know what to do."

Colm climbed off the platform and wandered over to her workstation to study the painting she'd set aside. "She's looking at me. The rejected lover."

She turned to stare at it. "You're—he's—not rejected."

"Then what is he?"

"Forbidden."

He moved closer to her from behind until his lips were nearly against her ear, and she didn't shy away. She sat with her back ramrod straight, but her breathing came fast and strident, the way it had that morning when she decided to kiss him.

"He's forbidden because she feels trapped by her situation?" he asked, the words touching her silver hoop earring.

"Because . . . because she's waiting, and I have no idea for what."

A near-confession. The time was now. Colm's fingers gently swept her hair behind her ear and he nuzzled her cheek, her earring, waiting for her to turn her head and meet his mouth.

"You're going to kiss me," she said in a low voice.

"You're right," he said. "Ask me to."

"Ask *me* to, damn you."

"Kiss me."

She swiveled on her barstool to face him and nearly leaped to reach his lips, her knees bracketing his hips. He caught her around the waist and opened his mouth over hers, kissing her until she whimpered, until her palms wandered restlessly over his naked back, then his naked chest. He slid his hands under her thick hoodie and filled them with her breasts, and she didn't stop him. She opened her knees wider, he pressed closer, pelvis to pelvis, and she touched her tongue to his, withdrew and thrust, teased and tangled with him until he slid his fingers into her hair to hold her head, to hold her still and devour her.

The sound of Mozart rang from the worktable, and the world shattered.

"Don't," he whispered, nipping her chin, her throat. "Damn it, Syd, don't answer it."

"I have to. You don't understand what I—"

"You're right." He released her. "I don't get it."

Mozart played on like a sick joke.

She swung away from him and picked up the phone. "Max."

Colm stalked to the cabinet, withdrew a bottle of water and guzzled it, then paced an agitated distance beyond the stage as he tried not to listen to the conversation and hated every word that reached his ears.

Sydney sounded falsely cheerful as she asked Max something about the new artist's shows and how well the woman had been received. Then she said, "I'm working right now, but can I count on you to be home within a week?"

Her head lowered, a wave of blond hair shielding her profile as she cradled the phone close and listened. "Okay," she said finally. "I'll look for the photos tonight in my e-mail."

After that, the conversation was polite, strained. Colm felt like he was eavesdropping on the end of a relationship. It promised double the money, but it didn't help the ache in his chest or the hard-on in his jeans.

When she hung up, he returned to the platform, but she cleared her throat and climbed off the barstool. "I think we should stop."

"Tired?" he asked grimly, snatching up both his shirts. "Because I sure as hell am." The practiced gigolo in him had disappeared again, fickle bastard, and he was acting like a high schooler with blue balls.

She sighed and stuck her hands in the pockets of her hoodie. "Can we start over?"

That stopped him. He shoved his arms through his T-shirt sleeves and slowly pulled the hem down over his stomach. "What are you asking?"

"For your friendship."

"For my . . . ?" He burst out laughing. Hell, he hadn't seen that one coming. "Sure." He drew on the second shirt, pushed the sleeves to his elbows, and met her in the middle of the room. "What do you really want, Sydney? Don't lie to me. I know dishonesty when I see it."

Her cheeks were flushed, her lips swollen from his kiss. All he had to do was slip an arm around her waist and pull her against him, and it would be over. He took a step closer and started to do just that, when she swallowed and said, "I want pizza."

Colm stilled. "Are you serious?"

"Why? Did you have lunch yet?"

She was completely serious. And slamming doors faster than he could open them. His hands flexed at his sides. *Screw this.* "I'm not hungry."

"You're off until tomorrow," she said flatly. "I've lost the desire to work today."

"We're wasting time," he gritted out.

"I don't care! It's my call, and I say I'm not in the mood."

Colm closed his eyes and tried to compose himself. "Fine. I'm going into the city."

"Fine."

They were both breathing fast. The mental echo of time ticking away burned a hole in him. Another afternoon off when she didn't want him near. And God help him, he had to have her.

First, though, he had to get away from her before he ruined everything again, leaped at her and took her down like a lion with a wayward gazelle. He stalked to the door and without turning around said, "Enjoy your pizza."

"I will," she shot back.

He stepped out of the studio and closed the door too firmly behind him.

L ong time no see." The woman in the wheelchair studied Colm carefully as he found a seat on the patio and took one of her hands. "When are you coming home to stay?"

Colm reached to brush back the dark hair from her forehead and smiled into her eyes. "Soon. Isn't it too cold out here for you?"

"I love the fresh air, even though I have to fight the nurses to get my way."

"And you win."

"Every time."

In the dappled sunlight, Amelia looked so much like her old self—if not for the frail frame of her body, which could no longer support her. She'd been an athlete once, played soccer in high school, then became an avid bicyclist in her early twenties. She had lived with spirit and wild, reckless joy. And Colm's mistake, his inability to see the world beyond his own emotions, had—in the blink of an eye—cost her all that and more.

Yet she'd never shown the slightest sign of blaming him. Right now he wished she would.

They talked for a while, casual conversation about nothing in particular, where Colm gave little away and Amelia sat there with no secrets. She'd never kept secrets, even as a kid. Colm was the dark one. When they lapsed into companionable silence, he took note of the freshly fallen leaves and branches on his lawn. His brick bungalow in Silver Spring needed attention.

No, Sydney needed attention. But right now it was his sister's turn, and with her he could breathe again.

Birds tweeted and played tag overhead; the early afternoon sun offered bone-soothing warmth from a sky the shade of Sydney's eyes. Everything seemed bucolic, if not for the wheelchair, and Amelia's nurse lingering just inside the kitchen's door.

"So what's going on, Amie?" he asked, as though everything were normal, as though she wasn't a quadriplegic and he a prostitute, both of them having left precious normalcy in the wreckage three years ago.

"I've been busy," she said. "You know, running marathons and stuff."

"Not funny."

"Sorry." She paused. "I talked to someone today. You'll never believe who."

An odd foreboding crept along his nerves. "The president of the United States?"

"That was yesterday."

He smiled. "I don't know. Who?"

"Roger."

Instantly he stiffened. Roger Hatch. The wealthy, useless coward who'd put a ring on Amelia's finger when she was a wild beauty, then broke every promise when Amelia broke every bone. Unable to deal with the changes in her, Hatch had left her six months after the accident, and Colm had thought it would kill her. Her grief— Christ. Even now, he wanted to wrap his hands around Hatch's neck and squeeze.

"Did you tell him to go screw himself?" he demanded.

"He's coming over for a visit tonight, James."

Colm shot to his feet. "You've got to be kidding me."

"I think he's changed. He sounded so different on the phone. He—"

"Someone who abandons people doesn't change, Amelia. I can't believe you'd—"

"Shut up!" Her cheeks had gone pink, her thin shoulders tight. "Stop talking. I don't want to hear it. I'm allowed to have a life, and my own friends."

"And I'm allowed to say when I think your taste in 'friends' sucks!"

"No, you're not, you asshole!"

Colm's jaw dropped. "*I'm* the asshole? Hatch is the asshole."

Before she could fire back, the French door opened and Jane, the nurse, stuck her head out. "You two okay?"

"We're fine," Amelia said without hesitation. "Just having a little sibling scrap."

Jane harrumphed and shot Colm a warning glance. "Don't scare the neighbors."

"Shut the door, Jane," he snapped.

She made another scolding sound, but did as he'd told her.

In the silence, Amie blew into the oral mechanism that controlled the chair and wheeled around to look at him. "I don't want to fight with you."

"Then tell that son of a bitch not to come sniffing around. He's not welcome in my house."

"James, just . . . please. Let's not do this." Tears shone in her eyes. "I don't want us to be mad at each other."

Ah, Christ. He couldn't stand to see her cry. But he couldn't help himself. "He'd better pray I don't run into him."

"Stop! Please stop. Let's talk about something else. The Virginia project. Tell me about it."

Her desperation pierced his anger. He drew a deep breath and reached to adjust the blanket the nurse had wrapped around her, mainly to give himself something to do short of punching the nearest brick wall. "It'll end next Friday, and then I'll be home."

"Are you having any life at all?" she tried again with a note of forced cheer.

He was so agitated, he couldn't think straight. *Jesus—Roger Hatch?* Amelia had been so devastated when the man called off the wedding. More than losing the use of her limbs, it seemed, losing Hatch had shattered her. What did he want with Amelia after three years? He was made of money; he could have any woman he wanted. Even before her injuries, Colm had never thought her relationship with Hatch was anything more than a walk on the wild side for him. The straitlaced bastard had shocked the hell out of Colm when he'd put a ring on Amelia's finger a few weeks before the accident.

"James?" She was watching him with such anxiety, he finally swallowed his anger.

"It's a life," he said.

"A good one?"

Colm wanted to laugh. He moved away from her and paced the patio, dumped gathered water from the drain plate of a potted plant, and didn't speak for a long time. Then he exhaled, and his frustration folded in on itself, shifting him back to Sydney, to what he had to do. "It's a pain in the ass."

"What's her name?"

Jesus, his sister was as bad as Azure with her intuition. How did she know there was a woman?

Amelia's long lashes blinked. She was waiting for him to spill it, and he wished he could. He wanted to tell her everything, to fall down on his knees in front of her and beg her forgiveness, beg her permission to continue on the road to damnation he'd carved from the stony terrain his life had become.

"Her name," she repeated, dark eyes filled with humor now instead of anxiety.

"Isn't it getting colder out here?" He zipped his jacket and reached for her wheelchair handles.

"James," she said with as much acid as she could muster, "stop. Come down here."

With a sigh, he knelt by her chair. The flagstone dug into his knees through his jeans, and he deserved the pain. He should be bleeding outside as well as in. "There's nothing to say. She's no one I should be involved with."

"Why not?"

"She's too good." If Amelia knew how good, she would hate Colm as much as he hated himself.

Amelia released a huff of laughter. "When a man says a woman's too good for him, she'd better believe him."

"It's almost over, and then none of it will matter anymore."

"Except you look damned miserable."

"It's just the job," he said grimly.

"Liar." But when he gave her a hard look that said he was finished with the subject, she smirked. "What's so bad about the job?"

"I don't know. The guy I'm working for, to begin with." He rose and leaned down to kiss her forehead. "I need to get going."

"You don't want me to do your tarot cards today?"

Hell, no. Amelia had always believed in that crap, and usually Colm humored her, but lately he wasn't in the mood to have anyone read his insides. "Not today."

"You've got more darkness around you than usual," she said. "Sit back down and let me read your aura."

"Jesus, Amie."

"Then your palm. Let me do that. I've been studying up on the methods—"

The nurse rescued him when she came out of the house and with a bright smile announced, "Time for a bath, Amelia."

"Saved from the crazy woman," Colm muttered, and darted aside when his sister lurched her chair at him.

"You two are worse than my kids," Jane said. "Are you staying for dinner, James?"

"Not tonight. I have some work to do in the city." He walked slowly alongside Amelia as the nurse pushed her toward the house, pulling dead leaves off plants as he went. "I'm sorry I'm gone so much right now. Take care of her, Jane."

"You know I always do."

He paused at the doors and lifted Amelia's hand, studying the thin veins beneath her translucent skin. "I'm sorry I yelled at you."

"You didn't yell. You spoke sharply. And you worry too much."

He looked at her for a long time, then kissed her knuckles and laid her hand gently in her lap. "Be careful, Amie."

"I will. It's just a visit, nothing more. And I could use a little male company, because yours doesn't count." She winked at him. "Love you, James."

At that moment, he could barely stand to hear it. He let himself out through the gate, once again bent on his mission of lies.

CHAPTER THIRTEEN

Sydney's pulse picked up speed when Colm walked in at nine o'clock sharp the next morning and headed straight for the platform. "Did you have a nice afternoon off yesterday?" she asked with a smile, determined to return them to a place of camaraderie where no kissing, groping, or arguing had occurred.

"I did," he said politely.

"Where did you go?"

"I went to see my sister."

"I didn't know she lived close by." When he didn't say anything, she added, "So how is she?"

"She's fine." He shrugged out of his jacket and stripped off his shirt, found his pose without her guidance.

The boom box sat silent as she began to paint; no Sade or Coldplay this time. She and Colm didn't talk, but things weren't tense between them now; he seemed to understand she needed quiet—maybe he did, too—and she was grateful for once that he might know her so well.

They worked for hours, their only communication relayed with their eyes. When they were done, she threw a cloth over the canvas and approached the platform. "Thank you."

He stretched and released a long breath. "Am I finished?"

"I don't know. Do you mind if you are?"

"You're the boss," he said as he rose from the edge of the platform.

"So we're back to that."

He picked up his jacket and looked at her. "You know we're not. But friendship isn't a viable alternative anymore, Syd. Every minute I sit in here with you and know your eyes are on me, I want you more."

She swallowed, her pulse thrumming a rhythm of insanity. Before she could tell him she felt the same, that this was the most thrilling and horrible thing she'd ever experienced, he said, "I'm going for a run. Want to come?"

She gave a mirthless laugh. "I haven't jogged a day in my life."

"I'll go slow. Go change and meet me at the cabin in fifteen minutes."

They ran in the same fragile peace as they had worked in the studio. Sydney tried not to look at him too many times in the afternoon's golden light as their feet hit the soft carpet of the abandoned horse trails that wound through the estate's acreage. She listened to the rhythmic sound of his breathing, to the hammer of her own heartbeat, to twigs snapping underfoot and the call of birds overhead.

When they reached a rushing creek, they stopped. Sydney was winded but tried to control her panting until Colm gave her a knowing look. Then she burst into breathless laughter. "I am so bad at this."

"You're doing great," he said with a mild smile. "Want to rest before we run back?"

"Do we have to run back? Can't we just stroll? Briskly?"

It was his turn to laugh. "No way."

"You're cruel and inhuman."

They sat on a fallen log, where the dampness of the wet, soft wood seeped into their running clothes. It felt good to Sydney's heated skin, distracted her from the scent of him, perspiration and hot, clean male.

"When I found this place for the first time, I fell in love with it," she said, gazing around at the blaze of dying foliage, the crystalline rush of water over mossy stones. Every time she came here, it was like seeing the enchanted spot for the first time. "It's so peaceful."

He leaned his forearms on his knees and studied her. "You belong in Max's world. The big house, the fancy cars, the money." She would have argued, but he added, "And you belong here in the woods, right in this moment, all damp and flushed, with your hair sticking up a little." He smoothed a wave of blond hair behind her ear. "You're beautiful. More beautiful than anything in this place, Sydney. You surpass it all."

Her mouth had fallen open somewhere around "all damp and flushed." "Oh. Thanks." She sounded brainless, but what did a woman say in response to things she'd always wanted to hear?

"Happy birthday," he said, and her pulse took off on a mad race. She thought no one remembered. She couldn't believe he had.

Colm took her chilled fingers in his. "I have a surprise for you, if you're the kind of person who likes surprises. Otherwise I'll tell you what it is and you can say yes or no."

She hesitated. She loved surprises and hadn't known many of them in her lifetime, but it was so hard to trust this man sitting beside her, looking at her so intently, waiting for her answer.

What the hell.

"Surprise me," she said at last.

His smile was the sweetest reward. "Dress nice," he told her, helping her to her feet. "I'll pick you up in an hour."

She gaped at him. A mere hour to dress, primp, and recover from this hellish thing called jogging? "Only an hour?"

"You'd better run fast, then." He took off into the woods, and with a laughing groan, she hauled herself up and sprinted after him into the shadows.

She wore a basic black dress that fell above her knee and simple faux pearls she had bought herself. The strand of pearls Max had given her was safely tucked away, waiting to be returned when she saw him again.

In typical last-minute fashion, Max called to make sure his annual bouquet of roses had arrived. Sydney hadn't even noticed where Hans had left them. She thanked him and felt a little put off when he cut the conversation short, but her curiosity about Colm's surprise soon banished any of the old rejection she felt in Max's presence.

When Colm came to retrieve her, he rang the doorbell, and she paused at the top of the staircase, nervous as though this was her first date all over again. She listened to him greet Hans, heard the two men laugh. Max never talked to Hans. In so few days, Colm had painted Max in a dull light, but what did it matter? After tonight—a benign evening, the sensible woman in her had decided—there'd be nothing more between her and Colm. Desire could be controlled; love couldn't, and right now she was deeply in like. Tonight his company would be a lovely gift, something she'd long needed, but that was all, no matter how enticing he was.

And he was. He wore his usual leather coat and plaid scarf over a gray button-down shirt and dark slacks, and she thought she'd never seen a more handsome man.

When she finally got her pulse under control and started down the stairs, he stopped midsentence in his conversation with Hans and watched her descend. "You look amazing." The low declaration slipped from him as though he couldn't stop it.

"Thank you. So do you." She couldn't stop her own words of truth, either.

When she broke the look between them, he smoothly recovered and glanced at Hans. "Don't you think she's beautiful tonight, Hans?"

"Yes," Hans said with a faint smile. "But then, I've always thought so." He handed Colm Sydney's coat as though he knew it wasn't his place to help her slide into it, then discreetly left them alone in the marble-tiled foyer.

Colm held the black ankle-length coat for her, his hands lingering on her shoulders when she slipped it on. "Thank you," she murmured, for so much more than the gentlemanly gesture—for making her feel talented, lovely, feminine, desirable. She would never know anything more than his touch on her shoulders, or the useless kisses they'd shared, but he was the person who'd helped open the cage to set her free.

She didn't know where he could possibly take her in fancy dress so early in the evening, but it indicated a long night ahead, and she was glad for it. They drove into Alexandria in his black Ford Explorer, and this time there was little silence between them. They talked music, sports, politics, religion—some of which Sydney normally avoided, but now she craved to know what he thought, how his mind worked.

The topic of Max didn't come up. He didn't belong in the narrow space between her and Colm. In her mind this was the beginning of good-bye. She could give herself, and Colm, this one evening, this camaraderie and pleasant conversation, the sweet minutes ticking off until they parted ways.

He maneuvered the SUV through rush hour traffic and found a miraculous spot on King Street in Old Town. When he came around and opened her door, she gave him a hard look. "Where are we going?"

He nodded down the crowded street. "Around here somewhere." He took her hand, his fingers laced through hers as she stepped onto the sidewalk. So intimate a gesture, so presumptuous, but she loved it. They strolled in peaceful quiet, passed a family of noisy tourists, laughed as a toddler broke away from the group and smacked into Colm's legs.

"Whoa, partner." He gently re-guided the little boy toward his family, and Sydney wanted to weep for all Colm was. If she'd met him four years ago instead of Max, she would have—no, she wouldn't have been smart and seasoned enough to look beyond his beauty. She would have run from him, and it was hard not to do so now.

They walked on, and when a damp wind caught Sydney and stole her breath, he tucked her hand in the crook of his arm. "Cold?"

No, she was warm all over. Filled with joy and regret. Everything in the world spun around her. "Well, maybe a little."

"Good, because we're here."

She hadn't been tracking their path, and now she looked up to see a nineteenth-century factory building with a modern facade. The sign over the broad glass doors read *Artist Co-op*. The last time she was here, she'd been a lost girl, a waitress at a TGI Friday's, miles away from Max and Colm and the life that now entangled her. "I love this place. It's been years."

"There's an artist I want you to see."

She held tighter to his arm. "Really? Someone you know?"

"Not personally, but he has a space here where he shows his work. I've observed him and he's impressive."

The building's interior was set up like a mall, with studios on

each side of the long, wide corridor, glassed in so visitors could ob-
serve the works in progress. Colm once again slipped his fingers
through Sydney's and they walked up a few doors until they reached
one with *Philip Franklin* scrawled across the glass.

The artist was arranging a space with an olive green backdrop
and a narrow wingback chair draped in black when they walked in.
He looked up and straightened, his gray handlebar moustache
nearly hiding his broad grin. "You're right on time."

Sydney glanced at Colm. "We have an appointment?"

"That's right."

The artist, rubbing his hands together as if to warm them, motioned to the wingback chair. "If you'll sit, Sydney, we can begin."

Warm with self-consciousness and delight, she laid her purse on
a nearby table and seated herself. The artist came forward to adjust
her arms so they curved, languid, in her lap, one hand turned
palm-up to keep her from appearing too stiff.

"Don't be nervous," Colm said, watching from near the easel. "I
think you've wanted to do this, Syd. To see what it's like from the
other side of things."

The knot of bittersweet emotion she'd harbored all evening
nearly blocked her reply. "I've never been a model before," she
managed.

"Then it's time. Breathe," he added with a faint hint of irony, an
echo of what she'd murmured in his ear when helping him pose for
the ménage à trois session.

Philip Franklin stood back and gave a nod of satisfaction at her
position, then glanced at Colm. "Does this work for you?"

"In every way, except for one last thing. May I?" He approached
Sydney and, crooking a finger beneath her chin, tilted her face up
and just slightly away from the light. She would be half-illuminated,
half in shadow—*Sydney in Real Life*. His fingertips trailed along her

jaw, more caress than direction, stroking her heart into overdrive. Then he stepped back and went to lean against the wall beyond the easel, ready to watch.

The session lasted one hour, during which Sydney sat in obedient stillness, even though her neck began to ache and her shoulders went stiff. How in God's name Colm sat so long for the sake of art she didn't know, but she would never again feel agitated with a model for any restless shift of position. And even if she had to sit paralyzed all night, she was determined to honor him for one of the most exquisite gifts she'd ever received.

There was little conversation among the three of them, only the soft sound of Debussy playing from a stereo near the easel. Try as Sydney might to keep her gaze straight ahead, it kept drifting back to Colm, to travel the long, graceful form of him leaning so casually against the wall, arms folded over his chest. To settle, again and again, on the shuttered green eyes that never strayed from her face.

"Eyes right here," the artist reminded her a few times, always with a patient grin. Then finally, "Are you newlyweds?"

Sydney's mouth fell open, but before she could deny it, he waved pastel-stained fingers. "Ah, I've changed my mind. Look at your husband as you please, Sydney. Your face softens just right when you do."

"My husband?" Her face blazed. "Oh . . ."

Colm raised his brows as if waiting to hear what she would say. For a moment her gaze darted between his face and the artist's; then she relaxed and flashed Philip an embarrassed smile. "Okay, then." And returning her attention to Colm as instructed, she found him smiling, his lashes lowered to hide anything else he might be feeling.

When the session ended, she stood and stretched, suddenly self-conscious as the artist signed his work and turned it for her and Colm to evaluate.

The woman in the pastel drawing was Sydney Warren . . . and someone else. A woman lost in love.

"Perfect," Colm said.

N ight had fallen when they drove from Old Town Alexandria toward the highway.

"Are you hungry?" Colm asked, flicking the turn signal as they slowed at an intersection.

She wasn't hungry. Her stomach was twisted into knots, that old, sweet mixture of excitement and anticipation like a first date all over again. And regret. Always, always regret with this man. "I don't think so."

His gaze shot to her over the console and back to the road. "You won't let me take you to dinner?"

She swallowed and shook her head, craving the wrong thing, loathing the right. "It's getting late, Colm, and . . . I can't."

"I see." He didn't sound irritated, only curious as he steered the SUV onto Route 9 and accelerated. "Have you had enough of my company?"

"There's no such thing."

He smiled a little. "Then it's because you're afraid of me."

"No, I'm afraid of me."

"Well, then." He checked his rearview mirror and changed lanes. "I guess I can't argue with that."

They drifted into languid quiet. She loved the easy way he steered the vehicle, one-handed, the other loosely looped around the gearshift. She loved the faint golden glow of the dashboard on his features, which grew more stern with concentration. She loved that she couldn't quite read his thoughts as he fiddled with the stereo and filled the Explorer's interior with the mellow sound of Norah Jones.

Colm turned on the seat warmers, and Sydney finally settled in for the hour-long drive to the estate. They didn't speak much, but the peace between them soothed her. He was a man who didn't need to fill the air with anything but sensuous, lazy jazz.

When they pulled into the estate's driveway and parked, the harvest moon hung high in the night. He turned off the motor and for a long time they merely sat there, looking at the sky through the windshield.

Then she glanced down at the tube she carried containing the portrait. "How did you know?"

He turned his head to look at her.

"How did you know this would mean more to me than anything?" she said.

"I know you," he said simply.

"I'm see-through, aren't I?"

Colm gave a soft laugh. "No, you're a brick fortress."

"Then . . . ?"

"Don't ask me how I know you. I just do. That's all."

A sigh wisped through her as she turned the tube in her hands. Then she said, "Thank you."

"You're welcome."

Quiet fell anew, rife with unspoken desire and the forbidden possibilities that draped the evening. And all the while he watched her, his eyes glittering in the darkness.

Finally she cleared her throat. "You don't have to walk me to the house."

Humor touched the corners of his mouth. "Why not? Think Hans will be watching when I kiss the hell out of you?"

"Hans wouldn't . . ." She faded off. "Colm, that's not okay."

"I know it's not. Come here anyway."

She couldn't help herself. One kiss—the end of an enchanted

night. She leaned across the console and immediately his mouth was on hers, warm, avid, soft. One hand cupped the back of her head while his tongue dipped inside her mouth and stroked.

God, the man kissed like no other. Instantly, hot, liquid desire flowed through her, and she kissed him back, no holds barred.

The rushed sound of their breathing filled the Explorer's interior. Colm shucked off his jacket and came back to her, hungrier than before, and foolish woman, she welcomed him, straining to meet him. Leather creaked. The console dug into Sydney's stomach. Colm banged his hip on the steering wheel and cursed.

He tore his mouth from hers and framed her face with his hands. "We're steaming up the car windows. Wait there." He climbed out and slammed the driver's door, then came around to her side, where he drew her out of the vehicle, shut her door, and turned so that his back was against the cold SUV and pulled her to him. "Right here," he spoke against her temple, sliding his arms inside her coat and around her.

When he grasped her hips and pulled them flush against him, a sound of surprise whimpered out of her. She could feel every bit of him—his chest, his abs, the shamelessly hard and formidable part of him beneath the placket of his pants.

Sydney needed to stop. This wasn't part of the plan. Flying free of Max and her old life? Yes. Falling utterly and completely for Colm Hennessy in a week? Never. She opened her mouth to tell him . . . *no* . . . *don't* . . . and what came out was, "Oh, God. Colm."

Whirling them so her backside was against the car, he pushed her coat off her shoulders so it fell around her elbows, leaving her shivering not from the cold, but from the incredible heat flowing through her veins. He slid his hand down, rucked up her dress and caught her right thigh, lifted her leg so it hugged his hip, and shifted closer. Close enough that if they had been naked, he'd be inside her now. Close enough that soon she would never forgive herself for the reawakening of her old weakness, her loss of character and integrity.

Colm was hot, hard against the hungering center of her. She gripped his firm backside to draw him closer until he groaned some unintelligible encouragement and rubbed against her.

Hands off his ass, the voice of reason ordered.

She quickly relocated her palms to his chest. Beneath her right hand came the fierce pounding of his heart and its stutter when she whispered, "Colm. Enough."

His mouth curled into a humorless smile as he slid his hand from her thigh. "No?"

"No more." She pressed her forehead to his shoulder. "In another time, another place . . ."

"Except we're here and now."

"Colm."

"Okay then," he whispered, but she was the first to let go.

He got her portrait from inside the Explorer and tucked her back into her coat, straightened it while she stood paralyzed with un-slaked desire. The night was over, the sweetness fading, the cold pervading.

As he backed away, he flashed her a grin. "'Night, Birthday Girl."

"'Night." And hugging her portrait to her heart, she stood there and watched him stroll across the lawn to his cabin, the moonlight shining a halo on his head and shoulders.

CHAPTER FOURTEEN

I t was time to stop the game.

He stood beneath the hot beat of the water and showered off a sleepless night as the realization rolled through him yet again. Time to admit defeat and ride out the remaining week with the single, clinging shred of decency left in him—the one part of him that cared more for Sydney than made sense. What did losing the extra money Max had promised really matter? It hadn't existed in the beginning. Colm would still be walking away with the payment he'd counted on since the beginning. Win or lose, he had his cut, and it wasn't exactly modest for two weeks' work with no real effort involved.

Ah, who was he kidding? It was more effort, more torture, than he'd ever experienced. His heart ached in a way he couldn't explain. His body ached in a way he could. And the worst of it was that Sydney made him want to start from scratch and remake himself, regain what he used to be. He laughed at the futility of it and cut off the water hard enough to make the pipes knock inside the wall.

When he slipped into the studio an hour later, Sydney wasn't there yet. He wandered around, examining her supplies, noting for the first time the orderliness amid the paint-splattered cans and containers lined on the table and simple wall shelves. He sat on her barstool, whirled around a few times, looked at the brushes staggered in an old latex paint can, at the blank canvases stacked in a corner, at the half-finished ones leaned in another. He breathed deep and knew he would never again encounter the scent of mineral spirits and oils and acrylics without remembering a somber, leggy blonde with the bluest eyes he'd ever seen.

The studio door opened. He spun on the barstool and found Sydney on the ramp, watching him with an unreadable expression.

"Hi," he said.

She wandered down to where he sat and stopped a couple of feet away. He thought she would speak, but she just looked at him, her blue eyes wide and uncertain.

His brows drew down. "What's wrong?"

"Max's flight arrives this afternoon. He's coming home early."

Colm swiveled away, toward the easel, where his portrait sat half covered with a stained cloth. "Does it matter? We still have a few days left."

At her indrawn breath, he closed his eyes. *Here it comes.*

"Colm, I'm letting you go."

Colm, it's over. Colm, go back to your life and lose me forever.

"Why?" he asked finally, toying with the edge of the cloth covering his portrait. "Why let me go early when you still have several canvases to do before your next show?"

"I can take photos of you today, before Max gets home, and work from those. I think I've got you enough in my head to easily summon your image."

"Yeah?" A rueful grin tugged at the edges of his mouth. "That goes both ways."

Silence fell between them, and then she said, "It's nothing personal."

"Bullshit, Sydney."

Her face flushed. "I beg your pardon?"

"I said bullshit. This is nothing *but* personal." Anger rushed up and squeezed his throat, more emotion than he'd allowed himself to display with her yet. "I think we've come to know each other well enough in the last few days to avoid the tiptoe crap. So don't try to save my feelings, or your own, by selling short what this is really about."

She pressed a hand to her throat and moved past him to straighten a portrait hanging on the wall. "You're still getting paid."

"Don't."

"But—"

"Jesus, Sydney, just be quiet." He pushed a hand through his hair and hopped off the barstool. The whore in him was banished, the man in him fully alive and fighting for the truth. "We know what this is. If we keep on, we're going to sleep together. You and I both know it."

"So you have to leave."

"Sydney." He grasped her hand and drew her closer. "Listen to me. I know you're loyal to Max. It's one of the things that makes me desire you—that you want to stay honest until the bitter end with him. Your honesty puts me to shame. But Jesus . . . don't cut ties with me, too, before we can figure out what this could be between us."

What this could be between us? Nothing. A joke. But he couldn't stop himself from fighting for what he couldn't have, even as she bit her lip and pulled away.

"You can't be part of the plan, Colm. It just won't work."

He squinted at her. "What plan?"

"The one where I learn to have relationships without a bunch of baggage attached. As much as I want you—and I do, God, you know I do!—I can't start a new life out from under Max's shadow by jumping into a relationship with you. You can't argue with me on this. I won't listen."

Colm sighed and hung his head, pinching the bridge of his nose. In that moment, that excruciating, gut-wrenching moment, it didn't matter that he'd been a whore hired to deceive her. It didn't matter that she was fighting old ghosts to spread her wings. If he made love with her, that's what it would be. Love. God help him.

Everything in him reached for her, but he squelched the urge to touch her again and instead wandered over to sit on the edge of the platform, his pulse racing. "You want me gone when Max gets here?"

"I think that would be best."

"We still have a few hours."

She glanced at the clock on the wall. "His flight gets in at four. He'll be home by six."

"Then will you do something for me?"

Sydney licked her lips and nodded.

"Will you finish the portrait of me on your easel?"

A reluctant smile formed on her lips. "Okay. Why?"

He shrugged and dug a faint smile of his own from the black pit of his heart. "Just so I feel like you finished something based on a live model. Remember, Syd, your work comes alive . . ."

"When I have a live model." She released a breath and her shoulders relaxed a little. "Take off your shirt."

She had no idea the storm roiling within him as he stood, tugged the hem of his shirt from his jeans, and drew it up and over his head. When he tossed the garment aside, she was watching him, not with an artist's eye, but a woman's.

She was his just that easily, and he couldn't stop the seduction, not when he himself was so utterly seduced. Choosing his words carefully, he said, "How do you want me?"

"Sitting on the edge of the stage . . . lean back on your elbows." She paused. "And unbutton your jeans."

His gaze never left her face as he propped himself on one elbow and flicked his fingers down his fly.

"No commando this time, I see," she said.

"I can take off my underwear if you want it like last time."

To his surprise, she nodded. "You can use the dressing room."

She had to know him better than that. Standing before her unabashed, he shucked off his jeans, stepped out of them, then slid his fingers inside the waistband of his gray boxer-briefs and pushed those down, too. He had stood before a thousand women with an erection, but this time seemed different. His arousal went so deep it ached in his marrow, as though he could take her a million times and it would never be enough.

Sydney seated herself on her barstool as he pulled his jeans back on without buttoning them, tucked himself in carefully, and positioned himself as requested on the platform. They worked in silence for a long time, their eyes meeting across the few feet between them every time she looked at him to check the details. The sexual tension built in him, layer upon layer until he broke a sweat and wanted to explode.

At last she laid aside her brush and palette, and adjusted the work lamp so that the light shone differently on the right side of his face. His pulse quickened when she approached him and without explaining herself as usual, gently took his chin in hand and tilted his head a little more to the left.

Then her hand skipped featherlike down his chest, his abdomen, to his fly, and she spread the sides wider so that his cock threatened to burst through the opening.

"Like this." Her voice emerged husky.

He wondered if she was as wet as he was hard.

Before she could walk away, he grasped her hand and drew it to his lower abdomen, where the muscles jumped beneath the heat of her palm. "A few hours, Sydney. It's all we have left. Touch me."

The indecision on her face killed him. He was her demon, her temptation, threatening to ruin her integrity at last, and she was wavering. Colm gritted his teeth, torn between remorse and the steely sense of what he craved.

When he released her hand, it stayed where he'd placed it. Her fingertips moved, glided over his stomach, a light tickle that brought a groan to his throat, one he suppressed. She was like a skittish doe, waiting for sustenance from an outstretched hand. A single sound would have her bounding away, although the silence seemed louder, limning the incredible tension that stretched razor-tight between them.

Her fingers swept his chest, traced his pecs, his nipples, his sternum and throat. He swallowed beneath her touch, and nearly jumped when she touched his bottom lip with a single fingertip. He wanted to lunge up and grab her, pull her down, and strip the paint-splattered yoga pants right off her long legs, but he forced himself to lie still, to subject himself to her slow, light exploration.

"You're incredible." She straightened and spoke at last, her voice low. He hadn't heard it like that before—a little desperate, hoarse with passion. "Don't do this to me."

"Then will you do it to me?" He caught her hand and returned it to his abdomen, and within his jeans grew painfully harder. Maybe she would pull away, but all he knew was how much he craved the feel of her fingers on his flesh.

Sydney's tawny brows drew down as she studied the sight of her own hand on his skin. And then she moved. Her fingers glided into the opening of his fly, slid through the dark hair there, and lightly touched him.

Colm shuddered. Reaching down, he shoved his jeans to his hips, freeing himself so that he rose hard and hot, demanding more.

"Oh," she whispered.

Who knew what that meant? Shock? Approval? He shifted, resisting the urge to beg, and drew her hand back to his erection. For a long time—forever—her hand didn't move, just rested lightly on his throbbing flesh. Then with an indrawn breath, she enclosed him in her slightly rough, paint-stained fingers, and pleasure rocketed through him. He pushed into her grip, once, twice, until she picked up the rhythm and stroked him, base to tip, her thumb finding the sensitive underside of his erection.

Colm's hand closed over hers. Watching her through his lashes, he guided her touch up and down, his breath coming hard and fast.

He knew only too well how to time his own orgasms, but this was Sydney.

Sydney.

Just that fast, after a mere week of wanting her so badly, the climax built low in his belly, tightened his muscles, rushing, rushing—

And like an untried teenager, he arched against the platform, pushed into her hand one last time and shuddered to climax.

S ydney didn't want it to end, but Colm finally shivered, halting her fingers on his flesh. His chest rose and fell like a bellows, but she was panting just as hard. She throbbed everywhere as much as if she had been the one to come. His pleasure was more spellbinding than any artwork she'd ever seen, and she wanted to revel in it, to spend hours in bed with him, to learn his body by touch and taste and mold every inch of him with her hands.

The vague scent of his release rose to her senses and woke her from her trance. "Let me get you a towel."

He didn't say anything, just raised himself on his elbows and watched her, his expression dark as she backed away.

The silence between them filled her with uncertainty . . . and then came the remorse. She would have touched Colm, would have taken him in her hand, even if she hadn't planned to break it off with Max. She couldn't help herself. This entire last week had been a slow descent into infidelity and the ever-cursed poor decisions for which she hated herself.

My mother was right. She was bound to repeat her mistakes over and over.

As she drew a towel from a shelf near her easel and brought it to Colm, the implications of what they'd just done left her doubting her ability to speak.

He did it for her. He wiped his stomach and chest, tucked himself into his jeans, and sat up to look at her. "Hey. Come here."

When she stepped closer, he caught her fingers. "You okay?"

"Yeah," she said. "You?"

"I'm okay." He hesitated, his thumb whisking over the back of her hand. "What are you thinking?"

"Nothing," she said. "I'm just confused."

"Well, I'm not. I want inside you, Sydney. Right here on the platform. I want to come inside you, not in your hand."

She shook her head and stepped away from him, unsure of where to flee. He was deadly. The memory of his groan at the height of pleasure played through her mind, and fire blazed inside her everywhere, from the aching place between her legs to her throat, her cheeks. "I've done a lot of bad things in my life. And now I've done it again."

"Don't say that. What you did has been building between us for days, and I wanted it even more than you." He rose to his feet, adjusted himself in his jeans, and reached for his shirt. "I can't leave without asking you again. Let me make love with you. We both need it. We have the time."

She resisted the urge to glance at the clock, her heart pounding. "I can't. I'm sorry."

"Because of Max."

She looked away.

"Watch out for him, Syd," he said quietly. "He'll fight for you, and it'll be through manipulation."

"I'll ignore it. None of it matters now except taking care of myself."

"And you think I would keep you from doing that."

She rubbed her hands over her face. Her cheeks were so hot. She was hot all over. "Our timing was bad. I never expected you."

"I never expected you, either." He started for the door, struggling into his shirt as he went.

Her dream was leaving the room. But God, it had been sweet. "Colm."

Colm turned to look at her.

When she reached him, she slid a hand into the thick, short hair at his nape and drew his mouth down to hers. For a long time they kissed, lips softly caressing, their breathing stalled and hearts thrumming.

Her words were choked when she finally broke away. "Pack your things and leave right away, before . . . before I . . ."

"Before you what?"

"Before I follow my usual path and fall. It can't happen, Colm."

While she stood there, watching in desperation, he pulled the door open and took a final glance at her over his shoulder. The sad smile he wore tugged at some place deep inside her, where bad things happened to people who didn't deserve them, and the world tilted in favor of unfairness and confusion.

"Jesus, Syd," he said softly, resting his cheek against the edge of the door. "I didn't think it would be this hard to say good-bye."

She couldn't speak without crying, so she didn't speak at all.

And then he was gone.

CHAPTER FIFTEEN

Sitting in motionless bumper-to-bumper traffic an hour later, Colm rubbed his bottom lip and stared at the minivan in front of him. A sticker of five cartoon stick figures in descending size graced the corner of the rear window: mother, father, two boys, and a girl. Lower down, a bumper sticker proclaimed, *My child is an honor student at St. Bernadette Academy.*

He felt like he'd just swept in on a UFO.

An hour ago, Sydney's hands had been on him. Not too soft, but not abrading. Firm grasp and easy slide. He replayed it over and over, his entire body throbbing again as though he'd never known release at her hands. He wanted her.

He missed her.

Coldplay sang from the radio about trying to fix someone. It reminded him of Sydney. He snapped it off and sighed, watching the minivan with the stick-figure family change lanes and inch out of sight. As usual, he was in the slow lane. Damned Washington traffic.

At home, he found Amelia in the living room, watching talk shows.

"Hi!" Her big green eyes studied him as he set down his overnight bag and her smile faded. "What's wrong?"

He sat on the closest chair, the weight of his mistakes curving his shoulders. "I lost the job a few days early."

"Oh, Colm."

"I still got paid, but it feels all wrong."

"Hold my hand." When he grasped her fingers, she said, "I'm so sorry. I know how much you love your work."

He wanted to laugh; he wanted to cry even more. He couldn't stand the lies any longer. He couldn't think about what the truth would do to his sister, either. Out of his power, it clawed its way up his chest to his throat. "Amie. There's something I need to tell you."

Those long lashes blinked. "What is it?" His hesitation stretched on until she added, "Hello?"

He wobbled on the edge of destruction . . . so close . . . and then, miraculously, swallowed the truth. It curdled his stomach, but the sense of relief was greater than the pain. What good was confessing now? Hurting her now? Ah, God, why the hell had he agreed to swallow Max's bait in the first place?

"I'm having a rough day. Tell me something that won't make me feel like crap."

She laughed. "Want me to say something nice to you?"

"Yeah." He stroked her hand, the feel of her cool skin the only thing that grounded him. "Butter me up."

"Something nice. Let me think." Then, "I'm so proud of you." Admiration shone in her eyes. His sister. His best friend. She loved him and was proud of him for deeds he'd accomplished a million years ago, deeds that had been erased by lies and prostitution. Maybe he'd started out wanting to help her, to take care of her, but now he was too far gone. He embodied the world he inhabited. He told women what they wanted to hear, touched them when he didn't want them, whispered lies in their ears, took their money. He lived an untruth every single day.

When he didn't respond, Amelia's eyebrows drew down. "Want to tell me what happened?"

"I don't know." He shook his head. "I do know. I engaged in completely unprofessional behavior."

"Ah." She compressed her lips as if to hold back a smile. "You got fired for romancing someone."

"In a matter of speaking."

"Does this chick feel something for you, too?"

"Yeah." The ache in his chest expanded, a mixture of exultation and agony. One week of knowing Sydney had totally turned his life inside out. What kind of fool was he, laying his entire existence— and Amelia's—on the line with useless feelings for a woman he hardly knew?

"Well," Amelia said. "You're gorgeous and amazing. You do great things. She's a fool to let you go."

He forced himself to smile back and lifted her hand to kiss it. "Thanks, Amie. I feel like a new man."

"You're full of shit."

Colm laughed and got to his feet. "I've got to run some errands, but I'll be back tonight."

"Late as usual?" she sighed.

"Not tonight. I'll see you for dinner."

Azure was in her office when he reached Avalon.

"I'm done," he told her, sinking into the brocade chair across from her desk. "Sydney Warren was a lost cause." So, apparently, was his common sense, and worst of all, his heart. He had to pull it together, or Azure would see right through him.

She stared at him with those cold blue eyes, her fists propped beneath her chin. "It doesn't really matter, I suppose," she said finally. "The pay is the same whether you win or lose. Most companions wouldn't have been paid for services unrendered. You do know how lucky you are?"

Dread tweaked the back of his neck. She was just winding up; he could feel it coming. His gaze wandered to the painting behind her desk while he waited in the thundering silence, an Impressionist church landscape whose artist he didn't recognize. *God, just get this over with.*

Never one to disappoint, Azure said, "What I want to know is why you failed to seduce her. That should always be in your power."

"I told you from the beginning. She's completely devoted to Beaudoin."

Azure sat back and sighed. "You're lying."

He glanced at the painting again. The church's spires rose against a rosy setting sun, beckoning. *Come all ye sinners . . .*

"There's a look in your eyes I've never seen before, Colm. Do you have feelings for her?"

He gave a humorless laugh. "After a week?"

"You fell in love."

"I don't even know what that is."

"Convince me."

He forced his hands to relax on the armrests and searched for the safest admission. "Let's say I liked her."

Azure's gaze never wavered from his face. "And did you want her?"

"Every day."

She leaned forward again. "Fool. I thought I could trust you."

"I thought you could, too." He got to his feet, maintaining a cool demeanor even though his heart was hammering. He couldn't play games about this. Not about Sydney, and not about his job. "Am I fired, Azure?"

She thought for a long moment, steepling her fingers against her lips. "Is it over with her?"

"It's over."

"Are you going to get back to the old Colm who could handle three women a night?"

How could he? Everything was different now.

Just lie.

"I can't wait," he said, meeting the challenge of her gaze with a stoic one of his own.

"Then you still have a place here." She rose, glided around her desk, and caught his face in her hands. "Colm."

Jesus, what more did she want? He was back in her grip, ready to work. What else would she demand of him?

His jaw tightened as her fingers traced his eyebrows, his nose, his mouth. Then she said, "Lovely. Tell Maria to write you a new schedule. And one last thing."

His eyes dropped to her full, red-painted lips. She wasn't smiling anymore. "What's that?"

"Don't ever try to bullshit a bullshitter. One chance is all you get, darling. Don't lie to me again."

Darkness had just fallen, bringing with it a colder wind than Sydney had felt all year, when the lights of Max's limousine flashed across the front of the house. She was sitting on the brick steps in a leather jacket and gloves, a scarf looped around her neck. Inside the foyer closet, her packed luggage was stashed to give her a chance to talk to Max first. After finding an apartment in the city, she would arrange a moving company to get what little furniture she'd acquired over the past few years.

The limousine's black finish shone like glass as the car pulled around to the entry. The chauffeur promptly climbed out, retrieved Max's chair from the trunk, and brought it around to transfer him into it. Max refused a specially equipped van for such purposes. He liked things the old-fashioned way. He liked his employees to work for their money.

"What are you doing out here in the cold?" Max gave her a curious smile as he wheeled himself toward the ramp, the wind catching at his cashmere scarf. She'd bought it for him last Christmas. It matched the deep gray of his eyes.

She rose and waited for him at the top of the ramp. "Just needing some fresh air."

"You look like you're going somewhere." He reached her and took her hand as she bent to brush her lips against his cheek. As he rolled behind her into the house, he added, "Are you going somewhere, Sydney?"

She wouldn't lie to him. "Yes, Max."

Halting in the black-and-white tiled foyer, he drew a breath and said, "Are you leaving me?"

Tears burned her eyes. He looked so small and twisted in his wheelchair, suddenly. "Yes, Max."

Hans appeared through the dining room and met the chauffeur at the front door for Max's luggage. "Welcome home, Mr. Beaudoin."

"Thank you, Hans." Max cast him an unreadable smile. "Did you know, Hans, that Sydney is leaving us?"

The valet's expression never changed. "I did not, sir. I'm sorry to hear it." He glanced at Sydney but said nothing more, just hoisted the leather carry-on and garment bag and headed upstairs.

When he was out of earshot, Sydney said, "Why don't we go into the library and talk?"

Max inclined his head and wheeled in front of her, throwing open the double doors when they reached the massive room. The interior was chilled and dark. He turned on a single reading lamp and then pivoted his chair so he could meet her eyes. The glimpse of a broken man was gone. His posture had straightened, his gaze glittering in a way that reminded Sydney of shards of granite.

"Are you having an affair?" he demanded.

She didn't answer right away. She thought about the last week, the days and nights of mixed sweetness and agony. Through all of it, Max had never been further from her life. Whatever she'd been through with Colm belonged in the sacred, female part of her mind and couldn't be retrieved except on those long, lonely nights that no doubt lay ahead. Whatever had been between them, it was her history, her truth, for her only.

"This is about you and me, Max," she said. "I'm sure you must have seen this moment coming."

"Not at all." He wheeled toward the butler's cart and the Baccarat crystal decanters sparkling in the dim light. "Will you have a drink?"

"No, thank you."

"Then do you mind if I do?"

Sydney shook her head and crossed her arms over her breasts, lingering near the door. She didn't want to drag this out, but he appeared to be settling in for a long winter's nap.

"How about we ask Hans to light a fire for us while we talk?" he said.

"No." She backed up until her spine hit the door. "Max, I can't stay."

"You want me to ask why you're leaving."

"I feel I owe you an explanation if you haven't figured it out for yourself."

"Then by all means . . ." He gestured with his snifter of brandy, sloshing some of it on the Persian rug.

Her arms tightened as she hugged herself. "You stopped loving me awhile ago."

"Not true."

"Then you stopped showing me you did. Whatever happened, something integral changed between us, something I needed and missed."

He sighed. "Go on."

"In this time I realized a couple of things. One is that our relationship no longer made me happy. The other is that I don't want to do erotic art anymore, but portraiture."

"You'll never make it," he snapped so quickly her eyes widened.

Then ire crawled through her. "Oh, really."

He smiled a little. "I'm not being unkind, Sydney. Take this as professional advice. Your talent lies in erotic art. You've made yourself a wealthy woman in that genre. Don't mess with it if it ain't broke."

The crass saying splashed like acid across her nerves. "My life is 'broke,' Max, and has been for a while. I plan to fix it. And while I'm so very grateful to you for your knowledge and direction in the past few years, you, too, have benefited from my success. We were a good team for a while. Now it's time for me to move on, and you to do the same."

He rolled back to the butler's cart and poured himself another brandy. When he pivoted to face her, he said, "So you're leaving because I wasn't demonstrative enough and you want to do a different kind of art. Kind of silly, don't you think?"

"Don't patronize me." She gritted her teeth and forced herself to drop her arms, to straighten, to meet his thundercloud eyes. For all his outward coolness, the expression in his gaze roiled with outrage. "I'm done talking about this. I'm going into the city to a hotel room, but I'll be back in the next few days to get my things."

"Are we parting as friends?"

"That's up to you." She opened the door and stopped at the threshold. "We've been through a lot together, Max. I'd hate to part as anything else."

Although the right half of his face was lost in shadow, she could see his pleasant expression fade. His mouth tightened, his chin nudging upward. "Is it the wheelchair, then? The handicap? The fact that I don't—I won't—"

He knew right where to stab. "No, Max. It never has been. I would have loved you forever if you would have loved me the same."

"I did. I do."

"Please." She rubbed the aching place between her brows. "I'm packed and ready to leave. It's over. My mind is made up."

"Who will agent your career?"

"Right now? Me."

She started to pull the door up behind her, but he blurted, "One last thing."

She waited, her heart pounding.

"Are you seeing Hennessy?"

"No." The truth came easily. Colm had opened the symbolic door for her, but she wouldn't be running through it and into his arms. The realization was agony, but it was her reality, the one she wanted to embrace. "Is that all?" she asked.

"Come and kiss me good-bye, then."

Reluctance slowing her approach, she crossed to where he sat and leaned down to kiss his cheek.

"My mouth," he whispered. "Sydney. Kiss my mouth. One last time."

Swallowing a surge of reticence, she did as he asked, and his lips caught hers, avid, hungry, his hand sliding up to cup the back of her neck.

Sydney pulled back, her pulse surging with anger and regret. "It's too late."

She didn't say good-bye, nor did he. She rushed out of the library and found Hans waiting for her in the foyer to help load her luggage into her sedan.

When she drove away, she took a final glance in her rearview mirror. The mansion's myriad windows glowed warmly, as though happiness dwelled there. Only the solitary figure silhouetted in the library window told the whole, sad truth.

On Monday, Colm went back to work. Azure scheduled him for only one client, a punishment, he supposed, for the feelings he couldn't quite hide. He was changed, but he would still do the job, lay low until the storm passed.

Then, thank God, the client canceled her late-afternoon appointment, and Colm was free.

At home, he frowned at the silver Audi sitting in the driveway as he swung in and parked. Virginia tags. He didn't recognize the car.

Jane met him at the front door.

"You're home early," she said, sounding a little breathless as she took the bouquet of flowers he'd bought for Amelia.

"Canceled appointment." He hung his coat in the front closet. "Whose car is that?"

When the nurse hesitated, he turned to look at her. Then it washed over him. That son of a bitch Hatch was here.

"Where is he?" He didn't wait for her answer, just stalked past her and glanced room to room until he came to the dining room French doors.

He squeezed the knob hard enough to bruise his hand and stared through the panes. Roger was tucking a blanket around Amelia's lap, talking too quietly for Colm to hear anything but the low tone of his voice. Whatever he'd said made her laugh . . . and her green eyes sparkled . . . and the cold flushed her cheeks, and joy softened her features . . .

And Colm wanted to kill Roger Hatch.

"I know it's none of my business," Jane said behind Colm, "but she seems so happy when he comes around—"

"You're right, Jane," he said flatly, staring through the panes. "It's none of your business." He hardly sensed her surprised silence until the tread of her footsteps moving into the kitchen woke him. Then the sound of his own too-harsh words echoed around him. He ran a hand over his face and released a long, painful sigh. "Jane."

He found her standing at the sink, jamming rose stems into a florist's vase and muttering to herself.

"Hey." He put a hand on her broad back. "I'm sorry I snapped at you, but you don't know the whole story."

She whirled to face him. "Of course I do!" When his brows went up, she said, "What do you think Amelia and I do with our hours together? I probably know more about her than you ever could! I don't care that you're her brother. You don't know what she's missing, her dreams, her hopes that she refuses to let go of, the ones that feed her spirit—"

Ah, Christ. He pinched the bridge of his nose. "Roger Hatch can't be one of those things."

"Oh, but he can. And I know it's not my place to say so, but don't stop me now because I'm on a roll. That man has been here nearly every evening for dinner for the last week, and no one could convince

me he's not in love with her. He's so careful of her, such a good lis-
tener, such a kind man. James, can't you support her making a go
with him again?"

"If he breaks her heart again, there'll be no picking up the pieces.
There'll be nothing left of her." He stared out the kitchen window
at the couple on the patio, at Hatch sitting so close to Amelia and
yet both of them restrained, as though they were courting in another century. "That man is not welcome in my house."

"Then go tell him yourself. But remember it'll be you breaking
Amelia's heart this time, not Roger Hatch." She set the vase down
on the counter and briskly dried her hands. "My shift is over. I'm
going home. Molly will be here any minute to replace me."

Colm followed her to the door and retrieved her coat from the
closet while she grabbed her purse from a console drawer. "You
think I'm a real jerk, don't you?"

She hardly looked at him as she stepped out onto the front landing, the chilled wind ruffling her short silver curls. "I think you love
your sister and would do anything for her. Look at the hours you
work, at all the nights you come in late and exhausted. I know you
want the very best for Amelia. But you've got her on a tether, James.
Maybe you haven't realized it before, but she needs a life." She patted his cheek, then said, "Be honest with yourself, honey. Maybe
what you're really wondering is, who would want her?"

He swallowed, unable to deny it. "Not just anyone can take on
the job of being her provider, her family."

"You haven't given anyone else the chance to try."

Before he could reply, Molly's small car pulled behind Jane's sedan on the street. Jane swung around to look at Colm one last time
before she started down the steps. "And what about your life? Where
is it? What do you do besides work?"

"Okay," he growled. "Now you really are barking up a forbidden tree."

She laughed a little and reached to squeeze his hand, then waved to the younger nurse climbing out of the car.

Back inside, Colm came face-to-face with Roger as the tall, red-haired man pushed Amelia's wheelchair down the hallway toward her bedroom.

Amelia went pale. "James, what are you doing here?"

"I live here," he said more calmly than he felt.

Molly came behind with a brisk step and took the chair handles from Roger. "I can manage from here," she sang, and before Amelia could protest, had whisked her safely into her bedroom, away from the two men staring each other down.

"It's been a long time," Roger said, his arms relaxed at his sides.

Colm jammed his hands in his pockets to keep from punching the other man's well-bred nose down his throat. "Long enough to change your character?"

Roger blew out a sigh and glanced down the hall. "I know I'm not welcome here."

"You're right, and for all the reasons you're thinking."

"I'm making it up to her," Roger said. "I might have to spend the rest of my life trying, but—"

Colm grabbed his arm and directed him none-too-gently into the living room, out of Amelia's earshot. "What does she have that you want, Hatch? Why are you even here?"

"I still love her." His face reddened. "You think I'm lying?"

"I think you want something."

"Yeah, that's right. *Her*."

They were both breathing hard now, and Colm moved away to regain control of his emotions before he spoke again. "Get this straight.

I don't trust you. I don't want you here. But if it's what Amelia wants, then I'll try my best not to kick your ass onto the street."

"Thanks so much," Roger said mildly. "Look, James—"

"Stay the hell out of my way," Colm interrupted. "If I think you're bringing anything less than a smile to her face, we're going to have a serious problem."

Molly appeared in the hallway and gave the men a tentative smile.

"Tell Amelia I'll call her tomorrow," Roger told the nurse, and without another word to Colm, let himself out the front door and closed it quietly behind him.

Colm heard the sound of the wheelchair's electric motor but didn't turn to look at his sister until she spoke.

"Did you kick him out?"

"Not quite," he said. "He ran off all by himself."

"Thank you, then."

"Don't thank me for this," he replied, his shoulders stiff. "Just keep him away from me."

"James."

"What are you thinking, Amie?" He whirled to look at her, hands clenched. "If this doesn't work out, do you have any idea what it could do to your recovery? You've been making great strides. Why would you—"

"I want a life."

"You'll have less of one than ever if he leaves you again." She just stared at him, refusing to argue, so he finally threw up his hands and muttered, "I'm going out."

Colm drove aimlessly until he found himself in downtown D.C. for the second time that day, parking a block from Avalon. He'd been so happy to get away earlier, but now he felt drawn back to that world, to his quiet room, to the escape of pleasure, even if it wouldn't be his own tonight.

He tried not to think of Sydney as he used his key to open the employees' door at the back of the building and stepped into warm, perfumed dimness. This was his world.

"Back so soon?" Azure's secretary said with a curious smile when he stepped into her office.

"I forgot to check my mail." A lame excuse, but he didn't owe anyone explanations.

She handed him a small stack. No thank-you notes this time, not that he deserved them. He'd been on automatic pilot even before he met Sydney, and he didn't know how to jumpstart himself again.

"We have two last-minute requests from clients," she said. "The first one could be here in thirty minutes. Would you be interested?"

Hell, no. But something in him needed to work, to prove to himself that he hadn't been ruined in one paltry week. He took the stairs two at a time and changed into the casual attire Azure favored for the companions, khakis and a white button-down shirt. Then he paced the room, waiting for the first dreaded phone call.

His client arrived, a repeat customer he hadn't seen in a while. He didn't make conversation. He pushed her up against the wall and kissed her, feeling nothing, fleeing to a place in his mind where only Sydney existed, only the last few days, only a non-reality that had ended too soon.

The woman's touch was too brusque. Her perfume was all wrong. The color of her hair and eyes. The texture of her skin. But somewhere along the way, this had become his life.

His own private hell.

CHAPTER SIXTEEN

Trembling from the cold, Sydney made a mad dash into the gallery and shook off the rain. She'd forgotten her umbrella and her hair hung heavy and damp on the back of her neck. So much for the sleek image she'd once cultivated as an erotic artist. Fortunately the focus wouldn't be on her; she was only one of several artists whose work was being displayed tonight.

Three weeks ago, when the gallery curator had called and asked her to participate in the show with one of her erotic paintings, she'd only hesitated a moment. She needed the continued exposure. No doubt Max would be there. They hadn't spoken since their breakup, but she was determined there'd be no animosity on her part. As he'd suggested, she would exist on a distant but congenial level with him, and tonight, at long last, was her final foray into erotic art. Two threads of her life neatly tied in little bows . . . so why did she feel so uneasy?

Naturally Max was the first person to spot her standing in the entry, and he wheeled forward to greet her, his gray eyes alight with enthusiasm. "You look relatively drowned," he said with an easy smile.

She slid out of her coat and smoothed her wet hair back from her face. "Do I need repairing?"

"No. You're always beautiful. Just go like this . . ." He smoothed his fingers under his eyes and she followed suit, wiping away the mascara that had smudged beneath her lashes.

"Thanks."

"I like the dress and pearls," he said.

She glanced down at the navy, slim-fitting wrap dress. The pearls weren't the ones he'd given her; she'd left those for him in the mansion foyer the night she moved out. Suddenly she became hyper-aware of herself, and that the camaraderie between them was shifting into something that made her step back. She didn't like the proprietary way he looked at her.

"I'm going to grab a quick snack," she said, and skirted around him to head for the buffet table.

Thirty minutes later, patrons filled the gallery to bursting. People had shown up despite the icy rain, milling about and chattering at a noise level that made Sydney's ears ache. She stood in the general vicinity of her work, answering questions and offering smiles of greeting. The familiar faces provided a surprising sense of comfort, glimpses of her old life that gave her a vague pang of sentimentality.

She also noticed Max's new novice, the one he'd hired from Chicago. The little redhead was a talented erotic artist and perfect for him, appearing to hang on his every word, wide-eyed and anxious to please. Not so very long ago, that had been Sydney, but oh, how old she felt now. How jaded.

Once or twice she imagined she saw a tall, handsome man with a black-haired companion standing among the crowd, but when she blinked, they were gone.

She glanced at the ménage à trois painting behind her. Colm in all his stunning beauty stared back at her, his green gaze as direct on canvas as it had been in person. Memories of the night she met him slipped undeterred through her force field, the way they'd stood beside each other and gazed at her erotic paintings, and how very much she'd wanted to disappear into a crack in the ground when he'd studied each one so carefully.

The urge to laugh tightened her chest at the recollection of mixed emotions she'd experienced that night. Her work hadn't been soft enough for his taste. *It's not quite accurate,* he'd said. *A woman's flesh is softer.* Other than the few useless kisses they'd shared, he would never get the chance to find out how soft she really was, especially in his presence. He had stolen the starch right out of her spine and molded her into someone new, someone she liked.

She smiled sadly to herself and turned to accept a glass of champagne from a server when she saw him. Colm. For real.

Not with Azure, but with someone else. A woman about his age, ash blond, slim and attractive, but with the odd, slightly-off features of someone who'd had too much cosmetic surgery.

As if feeling himself observed, Colm glanced around, and then his eyes collided with Sydney's through the crowd. He looked at her forever, a dark frown playing across his features before his companion said something and he glanced down at her, breaking the connection.

A spear of agony went straight through Sydney. After three weeks the sight of him shouldn't hurt so much, but it did. It squeezed her throat and made her want to weep.

Pulse racing, she finally averted her gaze and looked around, desperate for a friendly face. She spotted an elderly Georgetown socialite to whom she'd sold several paintings in the past, and they chatted briefly, Sydney hiding the tremble of her hands behind her back. When the socialite bid her good-bye, Sydney swallowed and looked back toward Colm. He had moved to a different painting, one dangerously close to hers, his petite date clinging to his arm as though he held her afloat.

The woman wasn't studying the works of art; she seemed more fascinated with the crowd, craning her neck and pageant waving to people she apparently knew. Colm wore an expression of mild pain, his gaze volleying between Sydney and the ménage painting, but whenever his date spoke to him, he nodded or smiled at the comments she made behind her hand, and the irrational shrew in Sydney wanted to clobber him.

Then the woman's attention locked onto Sydney's painting and for a moment she simply stared at it. Instantly Sydney knew—the blonde had recognized Colm as one of the models in the work. She pointed at the ménage and tugged at his arm. A subtle sigh lifted and lowered his chest as he allowed her to tug him toward the painting.

Panicked, Sydney stepped away from her station, nearly bumped into a waiter with a tray of canapés, and took off for the restroom. She made no excuses for herself. She'd reverted to a hapless teenager whose heart was breaking at the sight of her high school crush with another girl.

Once in the ladies' room, she braced her hands on the vanity and dragged in deep, gulping breaths. Her heart beat like a tympani in her throat. How was she going to get away from the reception? She'd promised the curator to spare a mere two hours to discuss her work with attendees. God, she needed to grow up.

She splashed cool water on her face, patted dry with a handful of paper towels, and was just heading out the door when someone pushed in from the other side. Before she could excuse herself, her words froze in her throat.

Colm's date let the door swing closed behind her and gave a light laugh. "I nearly mowed you over. So sorry."

"That's okay." Sydney tried to sidle by, but the woman touched her arm.

"Can you wait just a second? I followed you in here because I saw the painting of the ménage à trois. My friend was one of your models."

Her friend. Why was every female in Colm's dating life "a friend"?

"Wonderful," Sydney hedged, her cheeks warming. She resisted the urge to bulldoze through the woman's blockade and run for her life.

"It's Colm Hennessy," the woman went on. "He's here with me tonight. Did you see him?"

"I'm afraid I missed him." Sydney's gaze slid toward the door. All she wanted was to get out of there, out of the gallery.

"We both love the painting," the woman was saying. "Colm has the nicest things to say about your work."

"He's too kind." The rain outside wouldn't be so bad. She would walk in it, let its icy drops cool her heated face, if only she could escape.

But the woman braced an arm against the opposite doorjamb, effectively blocking Sydney from slipping by. "So you know Colm from where?" she asked, her hooded brown gaze sliding down to Sydney's nude strappy heels and back before she smirked and tilted her head. "Azure?"

Surprise jolted through her. This woman knew Azure, too? "Azure Elan introduced him, yes. I needed a professional art model, and Colm was excellent."

"Colm's excellent at everything he does." The sly humor on the woman's lips slid away, and she extended her hand. "I'm Myrna Shea. It's Sydney Warren, right?"

"Right." Sydney clasped Myrna's hand, thought about the woman touching Colm with those manicured fingertips, and once again felt a deep pang in her stomach. Suddenly, she couldn't play the politesse game one more minute. "It's so nice to chat with you, Myrna, but I have to get back to greet patrons. Thank you for attending the show."

"My pleasure. It was Colm's idea. He knows how I love these things."

No doubt.

"In case you don't run into him," Myrna said, "I'll tell Colm I caught up with you."

"Please do." Sydney slid by and out the door, her eyes sweeping the milling crowd for the curator. She didn't see him, but all of a sudden Max was there, and strangely, relief at his familiar face seized her.

He took her hand. "You're flushed. Are you sick?"

"I think I might be getting there. I'm going to slip out."

He squeezed her hand, but as his eyes slid away from her and fixed beyond her shoulder, they narrowed and a scowl twisted his features. Sydney knew exactly who he'd spotted and fought the urge to roll her eyes.

"Max—"

Pulling her back down, he spoke against her ear. "Hennessy is here."

"Is he?" She made a show of glancing around, purposefully avoiding Colm's gaze, which burned into her over the heads of three men studying her canvas. "He's probably here to see the painting. After all, he was the model."

"Be sure to give him my best when you talk to him again."

Sydney ignored that. "It looks like your new artist is a success, Max. Congratulations."

She smiled a little and straightened. "Take care, Max."

"I'll be in touch."

They wouldn't have much to discuss. She forcibly withdrew her hand from his and went to retrieve her coat. Then keeping her attention fixed on nothing in particular, she maneuvered her way through the crowd and out into the blessed, frigid, lonely night.

On Thanksgiving night, Colm's nightmares returned. Maybe it was the fact that Roger had taken Amelia out for dinner, handling her wheelchair and all her needs by himself. Despite the fact that it was a family day, Colm had to work early, but he sped out of Avalon the minute he was done, anxious to get to the house and be sure Amelia was there in one piece.

At home, everything was dim and silent. Colm wandered around Amelia's room, the sight of her empty bed haunting something deep inside. He did a load of laundry, drank a beer, checked his cell phone fifty times, and finally propped up in bed with a book and waited for his sister to get home. The hour grew later, though, and his frustration mounted. At ten o'clock, he berated himself for not demanding Hatch's cell number when the man had taken down Colm's. Where the hell were they?

At eleven o'clock he drifted off, despite his determination to wait up for her return.

And that was when the nightmares began. The squeal of brakes, the world spinning out of control, his hands gripping the wheel, trying to stop the inevitable collision with the bridge's barrier . . . Jill's scream as the side of the car met concrete and the world exploded.

Amelia's scream.

Colm bolted up in bed and swung his legs over the side, trembling so hard the mattress squeaked. The cold sweat had dried on his forehead, but he couldn't shake the sounds. He couldn't shake the reality of the agony he had caused.

After a moment, he gained control of himself and glanced at the clock. One a.m. He rose, opened his bedroom door, and glanced down the short, dark hall. Thank God the light was on in Amelia's room. *Roger Hatch had better not be in there with her.*

He moved quietly to her door and peeked in. For once she was truly alone; the nurses had the night off to celebrate with their families. Roger was probably holed up in his luxury penthouse across town. How did the man manage to get her into the house so smoothly and quietly, back into bed, and all without waking Colm?

Maybe Hatch was better about dealing with Amelia than Colm had thought.

Amelia must have been dozing, but her eyes popped open when she heard his soft knock. "What are you doing up?" she asked, turning her head to look at the clock hanging above the closet.

"Bad dreams."

"Come in."

He sat on the edge of her bed, careful not to sink the mattress and cause her to roll. "How was it? Did you eat enough turkey?"

"Oh my God, yes. We had a great time. The restaurant was a beautiful old mill, and the food was amazing." Her smile faltered as she gazed at him. "I'm sorry you were alone."

She had no idea he'd left for work at five o'clock, and that being alone was something he definitely hadn't been.

"It didn't bother me," he said. "Other than worrying about you. How are you feeling after all that running around with . . ." He couldn't quite speak Hatch's name.

"Fine. Great."

Colm couldn't help himself. "Did he have an assistant or someone help you back home and into bed?"

"Nope. He did it all by his lonesome. You were dead asleep, so we were very quiet." She smiled. "Admit it. You're impressed, aren't you?"

Colm just scowled.

Her green eyes studied him for a moment before she said, "And you? How are you feeling, James?"

He lowered his head, ran a hand over his face. "Amelia, I don't understand you."

"What do you mean?"

"I don't understand how you don't blame me for . . ." To his horror, he choked up. For a long time he didn't speak, struggling to regain his composure. Then, "You have to hate me sometimes. You have to."

"I never hate you." She ducked her head to meet his gaze. "You do that enough for both of us."

He swallowed and looked away.

"It wasn't your fault, James," she said. "When are you going to stop blaming yourself? The roads were wet—"

"I was going too fast."

"I don't believe that. I was there, remember? I knew how fast you were going. The same as everyone else on the road."

"I wasn't watching when the lanes narrowed. I was too busy yelling at Jill."

She gave him a hard look. "And that's what this boils down to, isn't it? You can't live with the idea that some stupid fight with your wife, who could be a real bitch on wheels, was the last thing you remember before we skidded and hit the bridge. You think you caused the accident because of that fight."

"I don't think. I know."

"You're wrong. It just happened. That's why they call them accidents."

He closed his eyes. When he opened them, Amelia was still watching him.

"My life's been no romp through the poppy fields," she said with a sad smile. "But I don't think it's anywhere near the torture yours is. How long are you going to punish yourself?"

He shrugged and looked away. It was either that, or crumple.

Amelia gave a slow nod. "I see. So let me ask you. The woman you met on that job a few weeks ago—was she a chance at happiness? Did you let it slide because as with everything, you thought you don't deserve better than loneliness? James, look at me."

At the mention of Sydney, he raised his eyes to hers and found her face soft with compassion.

"Your sadness is mine," she said. "How can I be happy if you're miserable?"

He sat there a long time and held her limp hand, his thumb brushing over her knuckles. Then he drew a breath. "It was lonely here without you tonight."

"I wish you'd have come to dinner with us instead of skulking around in your secret world."

A faint smile tugged at his mouth. "Is that what I do? Skulk around?"

"You're full of secrets, weirdo."

They both laughed. Then he said, "How weird would it be if I just stretched out right here next to you for a little while?"

"There's plenty of room. Grab a blanket."

In a million years he'd never thought he would find himself sleeping on his sister's bed, craving comfort. He found a blanket on a nearby chair and crawled gingerly onto the hospital bed beside her, crooking an elbow beneath his head for a pillow. They spoke no more. Her warmth, her easy presence, lulled him. Finally, finally he slept, dreamless at last.

CHAPTER SEVENTEEN

Snow fell soft on Sydney's shoulders, brushing her face and the back of her neck as she dragged the Christmas tree down the sidewalk and left a path of pine needles and streaked concrete behind her. She should have driven, but the tree lot was only two blocks away . . . and she loved winter . . . and the light snow . . . But now it fell harder, gathering in her collar, and the population of pedestrians on the sidewalk thinned. She walked a little faster and wished she'd been a little smarter.

Getting a Christmas tree alone was cold and depressing.

It was only midafternoon, but the wind had picked up and she shivered beneath her down jacket. Determination set her jaw. If it hadn't been December twenty-third, she wouldn't have bothered picking up a tree. As relieved as she was to be independent of Max, Thanksgiving spent alone had been a miserable experience last month, and she was determined not to endure such a magic-less holiday again. She would get this darn six-foot tree to the warehouse apartments where she lived and up the steep, narrow staircase to her third-floor loft.

She glanced over her shoulder to check the condition of the tree as she arrived at her building. A little worse for the wear, but it had been dragged over curbs and pavement. She could face the bad side to the window.

When she turned back to start up the entry stairs, a ghost stood before her. A tall, arresting phantom from another life, one she'd never imagined she'd encounter again.

"Hi, Sydney."

She sucked in a breath and just stared at him. Colm stood with his hands in the pockets of his leather coat, the snow floating down to dust his shoulders and neatly shorn brown hair. The strands still held streaks of the golden sun as it always had. The cold flushed his clean-shaven cheeks, and he looked so healthy and strong, she imagined crawling into his arms and curling up inside his coat, next to his steady, thrumming heart.

For a moment her old life came rocketing back, and nonsensical fear seized her. For a moment she thought about dropping the tree and racing past him, up the stairs and into the lonely warmth of her loft, but then courage took over. She couldn't just stand there and stare. Finally she approached him, dragging her Christmas burden with one hand as though it was the easiest task in the world.

They were alone on the sidewalk. Everyone else—smarter than they—had scurried off to warm homes.

"Is this your place?" he asked, and oh, his voice was a welcome sound, washing over her with its husky sweetness.

She nodded, not trusting herself to make decent conversation.

He leaned around her and examined the tree. "Can I help you with that?"

"No, but thank you."

"Please?"

She bit her lip. "The elevator has been broken since yesterday, so we'll have to walk up."

"I don't mind."

With that muscular shape of his, he didn't exactly look like the climb would exhaust him.

She half smiled. "Thanks. I'll get one end."

He caught the trunk, while she took the soft-needled top. Together they maneuvered it through the wide double doors and into the lobby, where she dropped her part of the tree. "Stop for a minute."

He set down his end.

So many questions whirled in her mind, she hardly knew where to start. The fact that he stood in her world again, looking so damned delectable and polished, made her stomach turn circles and her chest go tight. She couldn't wrap her mind around this dreamlike moment.

"What are you doing here?" she asked, her voice emerging hoarse. "This isn't a coincidence, running into you on a snowy street the day before Christmas Eve."

"No. That would be like a bad movie." He stared at his gloves and flexed his fingers as though he didn't know what to say. Then he met her eyes, and the look in his green gaze sent heat shimmering all the way to her feet. "I wanted to see you."

"Why?"

His mouth twitched at the question. "Do I have to have a reason?"

"Well, yes."

"Seeing you at the gallery opening last month . . . we couldn't really talk—"

"You were on a date with someone else."

His brows drew down. "And you were with Max."

"I wasn't with him. He was there because he had clients in the show."

"I saw the look on his face when you talked to him. He's still in love with you."

"Well, it's over with him. And why do I owe you an explanation?"

"You don't. And I don't owe you one, either."

They glared at each other like a couple of petulant kids.

"What does it matter?" she finally said. "Colm—"

"You're right." He drew a breath. "I'm not here to bicker. I'm here because we left things unfinished and I want to settle it, not under duress like before, but in a peaceful way."

How did he plan to do that? The only thing left undone between them was making love. She couldn't—wouldn't. Yet the memory of the feel of his flesh, of him climaxing under her fingers, shot through her mind. He was probably thinking the same thing. She had to shift her eyes from his, they were so intense. As before, they stripped her defenses and made her feel hot and naked at the same time.

"How did you find me?" she asked. "I'm still unlisted."

When he didn't answer right away, she squinted at him. "Who told you where to find me?"

"Hans."

She shook her head. "How does he even know these things? I never gave him my address. The only person who has it is Max, and it would be among his things, which means Hans had to dig through those things to . . . and he would never . . . oh. Apparently, yes he would!"

Colm smiled a little and shrugged. "I consider him a friend."

"Yeah? Well, he's a villainous character." With a sigh, Sydney bent to pick up her end of the tree and waited for him to do the same. "I'm up three more flights. Have I thanked you yet for doing this?"

"You thanked me."

They made it to the third floor, where she dug her keys from the pocket of her jacket and fit them into the locks, all four of them.

"This isn't the safest neighborhood," he said behind her shoulder, sounding concerned and not one bit winded.

"It's up-and-coming, and besides, I like all the space I have." She spoke like a petulant child in response to his unwarranted protectiveness, but damn it, she didn't know how to act. The unexpected sight of him standing in the snowfall had turned her inside out, and every moment with him close at hand left her knees more watery and her resolve weaker. Would he try anything? If he did, could she control herself after all these weeks of aching for him?

She swung open the door, and he dragged the tree over the threshold by himself.

"This way," she said, leading him into the wide-open space. "Let me help you."

"I've got it."

She showed him into the living room area, where he laid the pine down near the multipaned factory windows. When he straightened, he slipped off his gloves, studying her all the while. She wanted to stare back, to gulp in the sight of him. Instead she looked at her coffee table and noticed the dust on the corners.

"You look good," he said, drawing her attention back.

Glancing down at her gray jacket and jeans, she fought down a wave of self-consciousness and shoved her hands into her back pockets. "So do you."

And oh, *good* was such a ridiculous understatement. He was wearing khaki cargo pants, brown Doc Martens, and a cream-colored sweater beneath his open coat. The scent of some kind of sandal-wood aftershave brushed her senses, not overpowering but subtly delicious. Sydney wanted to gulp in big breaths of his fragrance, it was so poignantly familiar.

"Are you happy?" he asked, tilting his head to regard her with speculative green eyes.

Leave it to him to go straight for the kill.

"I'm getting there." Her chin lifted. "Are you?"

"Define *happy*."

She moved a little closer, stopped to take off her jacket and hold it against her chest, blocking the pull that tugged at her solar plexus. After a moment of staring at him, and him staring back, her face went hot and she turned away, headed for the galley kitchen. "Would you like something warm to drink? I can put on coffee or mix some hot chocolate—"

He caught up with her. His hand closed around her upper arm and gently turned her to face him. "I don't want anything to drink."

"Then what?"

Bad question.

That ever-subtle smile made a welcome appearance. "Let me put the tree up for you. I know it can't be easy to do it alone."

Such a simple request. Her nod came before she could stop it. "I'll take your coat."

When he slid out of it and handed it to her, she resisted the urge to bury her nose in it and breathe in. And when she turned from hanging their coats in the closet near the kitchen, she stopped in her steps and stared. Beneath his ivory crewneck sweater, a tan T-shirt peeked above the sweater collar. She remembered that T-shirt. She remembered how he would stroll into her studio and strip it off. It was easy to picture it now—the particular way he would cross his arms in front of him and grab the hem, his naked torso emerging as he pulled the garment up and over his head.

In all her thirty years, Sydney had never known a more handsome man.

"I'm going to look at your canvases first," he told her, heading toward the area where she painted. "If I have your permission."

"Of course."

Hugging herself, she followed and kept a respectful distance to allow him space to examine each new piece. The portrait of Colm wasn't there. In her hurry to get out of Max's house, she'd left it behind, and lately, missing it, she'd begun to think it wasn't so accidental that she had forgotten it. She'd been so determined to get on with her life, she'd shoved the memory of Colm into the past with everything else dark and hurtful.

He didn't deserve that. He'd been a bright spark, an awakening light.

While she watched him, he stopped before the Philip Franklin pastel, which was framed and hung over her worktable. He looked at it a long moment, his thoughts unreadable, then turned to regard the large canvases leaning in a line against the wall.

"The portraits are actually auction pieces from charity events, waiting for pickup," she told him.

Colm cast her a look of surprise. "So you donate your services?"

She nodded. "It makes me feel good."

"And your work is more vibrant than ever. Are you working from live models?"

"No. Just photos right now until I gain some confidence."

"Good," she thought he said.

Her brows lowered. "What did you say?"

"Nothing."

She cleared her throat. "I haven't sold much since . . . since Max, but the last show helped, and I'm living off my savings for now and trying to establish myself in portraiture circles. Business is starting to build."

"That didn't take long, but then I'm not surprised." He glanced at her, then back at the paintings. "I love them," he said finally. "But this one most of all."

He motioned to a newer version of the ménage à trois he had never seen, for she had only started it a week after moving into the loft. In this monochromatic rendering, Colm was kneeling beside an entangled Garrett and Cherise, his back turned to them but holding Cherise's hand behind him, as if unable to release her.

"You know," he added, leaning to take a better look at the life-sized painting, "Cherise looks like you here." He moved closer, squinting at it. "A lot like you."

Heat crept up her neck to burn her ears. She'd never noticed before, but he was right. The only thing that looked like Cherise was the dark, shoulder-length hair. Everything else was Sydney, even the breasts, which weren't as full as the other woman's. And the way she was twisted away from Garrett and clinging to Colm's hand . . .

She nearly choked on realization. How had she painted herself into this work and not have recognized it before now?

Thank God Colm had moved on to look at the next picture. All she could think to say was, "I really need some coffee. Sure I can't persuade you?"

Colm's mouth twitched, then he took another sweeping look at the paintings and nodded. "Maybe after I put the tree up. Is the ménage for sale?"

"No," she said quickly. The piece was too risqué to auction at the charities. And anyway . . . she wanted to keep it. Colm was in it.

And apparently Sydney was, too.

He tucked his hands in his pockets. "How about I get started with the tree?"

While he went to work, she put on the pot of coffee and some soft Christmas music. Bing Crosby sang sweet and low on the stereo, and the snowy gloom beyond the factory windows seeped into darkness. She moved around the loft, turning on more lights, sending golden warmth descending on her home.

For the first time since she moved in weeks ago, everything felt right: Colm kneeling to secure a fragrant pine in its stand while Christmas music limned the air; the scent of coffee drifting from the kitchen; the gilded light warming them. Sydney even turned on the gas fireplace. It wasn't her intention to set an intimate atmosphere. She would have done the same even if he hadn't been there, but it all just fit together with his presence, and she wanted to please him. He pleased her even now . . . and she knew so little about him. After tonight, she might never see him again.

"Are you still modeling?" She leaned against the wall between the studio and living room, letting the curiosity rise in her untethered at last.

"Mostly."

"For art students again?"

"Right."

Art students like beautiful, sexy Cherise Ford, who'd made it no secret she wanted Colm. Sydney blinked and banished the image of him in bed with some hot young painter. "What else do you do?" she asked, cupping her mug in both hands to warm them.

"Different things. I keep busy."

She didn't know if he was being intentionally vague, but she had nothing to lose, and damn it, she was curious. She straightened away from the wall and wandered into the living room. "I'd like to know more about you, Colm."

"Oh, yeah?" He leaned his head to peer through the branches at what he was doing. "Ask me anything."

"Well . . . do you have a degree?"

The Christmas tree listed to the right, and he straightened it again. "I have my master's in architecture. I used to design houses and civic buildings. Then the economy went bust and so did my work."

A frisson of surprise went through her. "Wow. Why didn't I know this before?"

"We never got around to that part of things." He switched hands, using one to hold the trunk and the other to work the screws of the stand. "How about you? Did you graduate from college?"

"No. I never even started." She blew on her coffee. "I'd like to go to school eventually. Study art history, maybe." Silence fell between them, then she asked, "So you're only modeling now?"

His eyes flicked to her, then away. "The pay's not bad."

"Oh. Of course." Embarrassment made her shift where she stood. "I'm being incredibly nosy."

"It's okay." He finally stopped and looked at her. "I'm sorry I didn't tell you more during our week together, Syd. I wanted us to be closer, but we didn't have much time."

Yet she'd had time enough to slide her hand inside his jeans and bring him to orgasm. Liars, both of them. They knew how close they'd really grown.

Sydney finally went to fix him a cup of coffee. With each creeping minute, she dreaded his leaving more. He seemed to belong in the wide-open, lonely space. He filled the loft with his warm presence, with the pretty sight he made down on his knees, maneuvering the tree into the stubborn stand.

And she wanted him. She had forever, it seemed.

When the tree was secured, he found a box of string lights and began settling multicolored strands among the branches, artfully pushing the flashing ones close to the trunk so the tree came alive with a million sparkles.

It took a good half hour, and then he was done. The beauty of that tree, even without its ornaments, made Sydney want to cry. She'd never had a real Christmas as a child. Her mother was an atheist and eschewed anything that spoke of a higher power. The trees she'd shared with Max were designer trees, created by professionals he hired to decorate the house with bows and pheasant feathers and Swarovski ornaments. Now, with her very own tree, Sydney went overboard, but Colm was there to help, to share it with her, and against her will, tears of gratitude stung her eyes.

If he noticed, he didn't say anything. Holding his mug, he sat on the white shag area rug with his back against the sofa, one long leg stretched out and the other knee bent, the picture of relaxation. She was a fool to think he belonged there, but he did . . . and she couldn't stop the mental images of spending not just this precious time, but the entire night with him. He would make love to her. More than once. She would open herself to him and let him take and take until she had nothing more to give, and then she'd give more.

There was so much unsaid between them, so much undone.

"I know it's getting late," Sydney hedged, buying time as she eyed the box of ornaments near the kitchen, "but would you like to help me hang decorations on the tree, too?"

Colm glanced at his watch and rose to his feet. "Why not?"

They worked in companionable silence. Hanging the mercury glass ornaments together held an odd intimacy and felt like a task married couples performed.

Colm took his job very seriously. More than once he moved an ornament he'd placed in an unsatisfactory spot.

"It doesn't have to be perfect," she said with a laugh, peeking through the sparkling branches at him.

"I want you to be happy."

"I am."

He didn't look at her, just kept hanging red, silver, and gold glass balls on the midsection of the tree. There was a method to his madness—larger ornaments on the bottom, graduating to smaller ones on the higher section. He was a brilliant, if mildly obsessive-compulsive, tree-decorator.

At the end, she handed him the tinsel star she'd bought at an antique store and he placed it atop the highest point. Then they backed up to survey their work.

Sydney had never seen a more radiant tree. With all its charming kitsch and shine, it sparkled like a universe of multicolored stars, and she wanted to hug it, to hug him. The magic of the holidays flowed through her and filled her with sentimentality as corny as her decorations.

The lump in her throat grew as she turned to face him. "Thank you, Colm. Thank you."

He nodded, his expression solemn as his gaze wandered over her features. "Merry Christmas, Syd."

"Merry Christmas." Her eyelids slid closed when he leaned forward and pressed his lips to her forehead.

Then, to her eternal disappointment, he crossed to the closet, retrieved his jacket, and said, "I have to go."

Where? Where are you going on a snow-choked night like tonight?

"Did we settle what you wanted to resolve?" she asked as she followed him to the door. She already knew the answer, but she wanted him to say it.

Amusement curved his mouth. "Not quite."

"What do you want, then?"

Colm's smile faded. "You know what I want."

After Max, after years of being under a man's thumb, what did

she truly have left to give? She and Colm had built up too much between them for sex to be the only answer.

She offered him something less than what he desired. "Let me
give you my cell number."

"I have it," he said, slipping on his gloves. "Hans, remember?"

Sydney didn't know whether to hug Hans or strangle him.

"I'll call you," Colm added as they stepped out into the hall.

"I'd like that." *We could hang out,* she almost added, and nearly
laughed out loud at her ridiculousness. *Hang out, Sydney?* he would
say. *Really?* And as before, he'd be the one to laugh.

She trailed him to the landing, her heart aching with every
pulse. What was right and wrong anymore? He was no longer a fan-
tasy, or a temptation, but the real deal, standing there and waiting
for her to finally, finally reach for him.

Colm descended one stair before he stopped and gave her a long
look. "There's one more thing."

Hope surged in her chest anew. "What's that?"

He frowned, looked down at the ground then back at her. He
seemed to be having trouble formulating the words. Finally he said,
"Once in a while you and I move in the same circles. The art opening, for example."

"I know." Sydney resisted the urge to add, *And it stings like a bitch
to run into you.*

"People talk," he went on. "They talk about things they don't
understand."

"Like what?"

He looked so troubled suddenly, she moved to the staircase,
where she stood close enough for the scent of his leather coat to rise
between them.

"Do you mean people like your date at the show a few weeks ago?"
she asked. "She cornered me in the bathroom to talk about you."

A sigh escaped him. "I won't ask what she said."

"She said a lot of nothing. Made a few suggestive comments complete with eyebrow-waggling. And she referred to you as her 'friend.'"

Colm burst out laughing, then quickly sobered at the look she gave him. "I'm sorry. It must have been pretty awkward."

"Are you and she—?" She shivered and put up a hand. "God, please don't acknowledge that. I don't know what's wrong with me tonight."

He grasped her hand in his gloved one and lifted it to his lips, kissed the tips of her fingers. "That makes two of us."

It took her a moment to speak again. "Is she really your friend, this woman?"

He shrugged.

"What is a friend to you, Colm?"

"Someone I care about," he said, his thumb whisking across her knuckles.

"Was I a 'friend' to you? Like Azure? And that woman in the restroom? If you speak of me, will you give a casual shrug and say, 'She was a friend'?"

"No."

"No?" Confused grief squeezed her throat. "Why not?"

"Because you were so much more."

She couldn't think of a response that wouldn't emerge with a rush of tears, so she did the next, most natural thing. She leaned forward and caught his mouth in a gentle, clinging kiss. Nothing deeper, although everything female in her screamed for his tongue, his hands, the feel of his naked skin.

When she straightened, he stroked her cheek with a leather-clad finger and offered her a faint smile. "Does that answer your question?"

"Yes. Thank you."

"You're welcome." He took another step down and looked back at her. "Goodnight, Sydney."

"Goodnight, Colm."

She stood at the top of the stairs and watched him descend until he disappeared and the door three stories down clanged shut, snow swirling in the rush of air. And then she stood there long minutes more, the sound of her aching heart thudding in her ears.

CHAPTER EIGHTEEN

Amelia was drowsing when Colm snuck into her room on bare feet. The floor creaked beneath his weight and she opened her eyes. "Is it Santa?" she exclaimed, her voice foggy with sleep. "Why, no! It's my brother wearing hideous plaid pajama bottoms!"

He tugged at his shirt. "And a Muppets T-shirt in your honor."

"Thanks for thinking of me."

He laughed and leaned down to brush his lips against her cheek. "Santa came in the middle of the night and left all your presents at the foot of the bed. Should I start delivering?"

"You know it."

He pulled up the chair beside her bed and held up a silver and gold-wrapped box.

"Give it a little shake," she instructed, and he obliged, as they'd done as children. The Bose headphones inside thudded around.

"Tear into it," she said with a big grin, so he did as ordered. Paper flew and landed around his feet as they went through gift after gift. The pièce de résistance was a computer designed for her disabilities, a replacement for the one she'd recently worn out.

"You're officially glutted," he said at last, when they were finished and loot covered her bed.

"And where are your presents?"

"I left them in the living room." He didn't want to tell her he had nothing. What did he need? His real present was the day off from Avalon. Sometimes Azure seemed surprisingly benevolent. The pleasure club had a wide non-Christian clientele, and she could have put every companion to work if she'd chosen. Instead she excused them all for twenty-four hours.

As Colm gathered up all the wadded wrapping paper and shoved it into a garbage bag, he envisioned Azure wandering her opulent apartment on the top floor of the Avalon complex, all alone . . . or was she? Her life was such a secret, the companions didn't even bother to guess at the details. Not even the ones who slept with her on a regular basis knew anything.

"What are your plans today?" Amelia asked, her gaze following him while he picked up the trash.

"To be home." And what would she do? Lie there, or hang around in her wheelchair. She had a few friends who would come by to see her today, maybe even Hatch, but mostly she was alone, and Colm wouldn't leave her that way.

Yet even now, his self-indulgent brain shifted to Sydney. He wanted to tear across town, race up the three flights to her loft, burst through the four locks, and take her. Two nights ago they'd danced around it. He knew she wanted him still. He'd read the stealthy glances she shot his way when she thought he didn't notice, and he'd done the same, his eyes wandering over her slim, graceful form as she moved through the kitchen fixing coffee and quietly humming along to Bing Crosby.

"There's somewhere else you'd like to be." Amelia's observation brought him back to her. "Or someone else you'd like to see."

Colm shook his head. He was a damned fine liar when the situation called for it, even in his personal life. Little white lies, lies of omission, flat-out lies that could tear people apart if they knew the truth about him.

The only one he couldn't fool was his twin.

"Maybe there's someone else *I'd* like to see," she added cryptically, and of course he knew. Still, he demanded, "Who?"

Couldn't Roger guess her heart was as fragile now as her body?

Before he could assail her with more questions, Molly the nurse chose that moment to tap lightly on the doorframe. "Merry Christmas." She laid a silver-wrapped gift in Colm's hands. "This is for Amie, if you'll open it. And, Colm, I made you cookies. They're in the kitchen."

He gave her a hug, slipped her an envelope with a large tip to ring in the holiday, and then sat down to open his sister's gift for her. Inside the box was a blue downy blanket Amelia instantly loved. She chatted with Molly as the woman prepared to lift her into her chair.

"Let me lift you this time and give Molly a break," Colm said, but Molly simply smiled and drew back the blankets.

"Go be where you really want to be," Amelia ordered.

He studied her green eyes, avoiding the sight of her pale, wasted legs momentarily exposed. "I want to be here." To watch over her. To stand as a wall between her and anything that could damage her eggshell heart.

"I won't be alone, James."

His jaw tightened, but she went on. "A few people will come by. And then I have Molly the rest of the day, and then Jane will be here. We're going to celebrate, right, Molly?"

"You know it," the nurse said.

Colm grabbed up the trash bag and stopped in the doorway. "I'm going to take this out."

"Don't come back," Amelia said. "Go do what you need to do."

"Don't boss me around," he told her. "You and I are watching *A Christmas Story* as soon as Molly wheels you out into the living room."

"Suit yourself," Amelia said. "I hope you can bear my choice of company when he gets here." And then he couldn't see her face anymore, only the back of her pillow-ruffled dark hair as Molly shifted her into her chair.

Sydney was curled up on her sofa with a cup of hot chocolate, gazing at her crystalline Christmas tree, when her cell phone rang. At this late hour on Christmas night, it had to be Max. She'd changed his ringtone back to a generic ring, and after checking the screen, she saw his name and hit Decline. The peace in her home was as soft, thick, and quiet as the snowy world outside.

When the phone rang again a few minutes later, she muted Dean Martin on the stereo and sighed. It would only be Max again—this year's holiday must be lonely for him, now that the lavish parties were over and all his friends were home with their families or traveling the globe. With a sting of compassion, she grabbed it off the table without looking at it. "Hello?"

"Sydney," said a low male voice.

Surprised delight shivered through her. "Colm?"

"Did I wake you?"

"No. I was just sitting here looking at the tree."

"Are you alone?"

"Yes," she said. "Are you?" *Dumb question.* What was it about him that made her trip over her own feet?

"I am." His tone was deep, a little sleepy and hushed to suit the hour . . . and the intimacy that instantly sprang between them.

"It's so good to hear from you," she said, as though they hadn't spoken two days ago. As though the long, empty hours without him had stretched into years.

"How are you?" he asked, just as inanely.

She had to think about that. The most benign yet truthful answer was, "Sleepless."

"Me, too."

She let her eyelids drift closed and swallowed hard.

"Syd?"

"Yes?"

"Truth or dare?"

She groaned and dropped her head to her hand. "Oh God. For real?"

He laughed. "You are such a coward."

"Not so." Humor tugged at her mouth. "All right, let's do truth."

"Are you lonely?"

"Sometimes," she admitted. "It's nothing new, but this is different."

"How is it different? Describe it to me."

She sat up, drawing her knees against her chest. "It's a good feeling in a strange way. Exciting, sometimes."

"When is it exciting?"

He was right. It sounded silly, and yet . . .

She hugged her knees and sighed. "When you left the other night, and it was so quiet here, for example. I was really alone, but I was kind of . . . vibrating somehow. Like being buzzed."

"Drunk?"

"A little."

"Me, too," he said. "Definitely buzzing."

"But we weren't drinking." She licked her lips. "I used to get that same feeling when I was working with you out at the estate. It just sort of starts in my head, moves to my chest, goes so deep I can't breathe, then . . ."

"Then?" His voice had gone softer, impossibly lower.

"That's enough truth for you," she said with a sniff, and he groaned. "Don't stop now."

"It's your turn to be victimized." Sexual tension edged the game, but also a poignancy, as it had the night they'd played it on the merry-go-round. "Truth or dare, Colm?"

"Hmm." He hesitated. "Dare, just to shake things up."

He wanted to shake things up, did he? She could do that for him. Feeling brave and reckless, she said, "What are you wearing?"

"I like the way this is going already." The smile in his voice made her warm all over. "T-shirt. Pajama bottoms."

"Take off the shirt."

She heard a faint rustling, then he said, "Okay."

"Now lay your palm over your heart."

"Done."

"Is it beating fast?"

"Worthy of cardiac arrest," he said wryly.

Desire leaped within her like a flame, stoking courage, feeding frank admissions. Only honesty could exist in this galvanized space between them. All pretense crumbled at her feet, and this time she didn't scramble to pick up the pieces. "That fast beat—that's what my heart is doing, too, Colm. So fast, it's stealing my breath. Now put your hand on your stomach."

The laughter had left his voice when he said hoarsely, "Done."

"That's where I'm feeling the ever-clichéd butterflies."

He was quiet a long time, too long, until heat flooded her face and she swallowed a twinge of dread. She was playing a dangerous game. Maybe she had gone too far. "Are you there?"

"I'm here."

"What are you thinking about?"

"The way you touched me in the studio," he said.

Sydney breathed again, deep and trembling. She pictured him, somber and focused, as he cradled the phone against his ear. Where was he? Lying in his queen-sized bed with the rumpled sheets? In the dark? Or was a single lamp shining a wan amber glow across one half of his face, his muscled shoulder, his bare chest?

He was the next to speak. "Truth or dare, Syd."

"Dare," she whispered.

"Take off your shirt."

Pulse racing, she shucked off her sweatshirt. "Okay."

"Put your hand over your heart like I did."

She ran her hand over her naked breast and did as he told her. Beneath her palm, her nipple was hard. Her heart felt like it would hammer through bone and muscle and explode from her in fireworks. "And now?"

"Now let me in, Sydney."

Heat slid through her, lighting every nerve. "How?"

"Tell me to come over."

She straightened, her hand gone moist where it gripped the phone. "Colm . . . if I let you in, where do we go from here?"

"I don't know, Syd. We'll figure it out."

Her lips touched the receiver. The fight was over. "Call when you get to the door and I'll buzz you up."

"Give me thirty minutes."

Sydney had never moved faster in her life. She jumped in the shower, shaved her legs, blow-dried her hair, then slathered on a sultry musk-scented lotion and dressed in a pair of snug jeans and a maroon silk sweater that draped off one shoulder. He would strip off her clothing, and she couldn't wait.

What are you doing? demanded the voice of reason as she applied a light touch of makeup with a still-trembling hand. Before she could snap back at that inner voice, the intercom buzzed. She glanced at the mantel clock. He was right on time.

She slid across the bamboo floor in stocking feet and hit the intercom. "Is it you?"

"It's me," he said.

"Come up." She pushed the entry button and then raced back to her bedroom to pull on black, knee-high boots. A quick glance in the mirror and she was satisfied. Casual but not affected, something she could have thrown on without much thought when she got up that morning. She wanted to squirm free of every garment and get naked and feel his flesh against hers. Soon enough. Oh, God. She'd waited much too long for this.

When she answered his knock at the door, the blood was racing through her veins.

"Hi," she said breathlessly.

"Hi." As his light green gaze slipped down to the tips of her boots and back, his face wore a look she would never forget. No man had ever regarded her that way, with approval, appreciation, desire, and softness all at once. Sydney braced herself as she backed up to let him in, expecting him to slide his arms around her and whirl her against the nearest wall, where he would fuse their mouths with a kiss, one hand slamming the door and turning each of the four locks without him even bothering to look.

Colm closed the door and clicked the locks into place all right, but then, instead of kissing her, he placed a narrow box in her hands.

She studied the package with its huge silver bow. "This is the only present I've gotten that I haven't bought myself this Christmas."

"Open it."

Still discombobulated, her entire body vibrating with want and expectation, she perched on the arm of an overstuffed chair. Her fingers moved over the professionally wrapped gift, but she hardly looked at what she was doing. Instead she watched him unzip his jacket and find a seat on her couch, the Christmas tree lights casting rainbow colors on the left side of his face. Every time he took her breath away she thought she might never inhale again, and yet here it came, and with it his scent, as piney as the tree, as warm as the flames in the fireplace.

She finally freed the ribbon, then opened the paper. Inside was a bottle of Shiraz. Instantly Sydney let out a laugh and hugged it to her. "Do you know I haven't had any Shiraz since . . . well, since the last time I had it with you?"

Pleasure played around his mouth as he watched her examine it. "You still like it?"

"I love it."

"How about at—" He glanced at his watch, his leather jacket sleeve creaking with the movement. "One in the morning?"

"Works for me." Unable to sit there another moment without tackling him against the cushions, she stood and headed for the kitchen, where she rifled through a couple of drawers before she found a corkscrew.

And jumped when his warm hands closed over hers.

"Let me." His body moved against her from behind, holding her subtly captive in the circle of his arms as he took the bottle and corkscrew. God, he was hard, perfectly made for her. His erection pressed against the top of her buttocks as he worked with the wine bottle. The cork released with a resolute pop, and then his lips nuzzled her ear. "Glasses?"

She blindly reached for a cabinet door.

His arm slipped around her waist and drew her tighter against him as she grabbed two glass goblets and set them on the granite counter.

"You pour," she said weakly, her head tilting when his tongue flicked her earring and then slid along the sensitive side of her neck.

Instead, he brushed his mouth over her naked shoulder where the maroon top bared it and slid a hand beneath her breasts to hold her motionless. "Sydney."

"Yes."

"Yes?"

The universal question of Man to Woman hung in the air. They both knew why he was there, and still he was giving her a final chance to back out, to change her mind.

Her fingers dug into the granite edge of the counter, her pulse hammering. "God, yes," she whispered.

CHAPTER NINETEEN

He slid aside the bottle, the glasses, everything in the way, and turned her to face him. His mouth nudged hers once, twice, then opened over hers, and Sydney was lost. They'd waited so long to taste each other with nothing and no one between them.

When he lifted his head, she nearly cried out a protest. But the look of dark intent he wore shuddered through her, made her weak and glad for the strength of him and his resolution. He knew exactly what he was doing, what they both wanted, and no conversation or questions were necessary.

He grasped her waist, lifted and settled her on the counter top. His hooded gaze never strayed from her face as the sound of her boot zippers rent the silence. He never spoke as he drew the boots from her feet and tossed them aside so they thudded somewhere across the kitchen. Next came her socks, then his warm touch on her ankles. Cool air slid across her skin as he lifted one of her bare feet against his hard belly and caressed the top of it with both hands. She watched the drop of his dark head as he focused on what he was doing to her, the faint lifting and lowering of his lashes, before she realized that she could touch him, too, some irreverent part of him the way he was caressing her. Guilt existed no longer. No reticence. This wasn't about her independence or her past. Only certainty that she had to have him, and now.

Her fingers reached for his hair and slid through it with experimental ease, measuring its thick, lush texture. His scalp was warm beneath its softness, the tendons in his neck tight as she dipped inside the collar of his jacket and traced them like a musician caresses her instrument. He closed his eyes and buried his face against her breasts as she massaged the tension from him, even as the heat flamed higher.

When he looked up at her, she cupped his face in her hands and let her eyes search his, finding desire and need shot through the spokes of green and gold. She felt more than saw herself reflected there—her own desire and need—in the way his expression softened and his lips parted, and knew she had never in her life allowed the passion for a man to cross her own face as it did now. She'd never felt safe enough. But with Colm . . . oh, with Colm . . .

She was more than safe. She was adulated.

Leaning forward, she took his mouth again, and the soft thrust of his tongue, and smiled at the spastic twitch of his fingers on her ankle, a subconscious response to the same jolt of sexual electricity that flowed through her.

Sydney's pulse danced wildly, fire raging through her nerves, through sacred, female parts of her that she had shared on canvas but never as unabashedly as she would offer herself to Colm. Yes, she was softer than she'd painted herself; she was soft and wet and shivering as he pushed up her sweater and unfastened her jeans.

Then she realized he still wore his jacket. His clothes. His shoes.

She wanted to laugh aloud. There was something so illicit and delicious about having a fully clothed man undress her.

But Colm didn't strip her pants off her legs. He bent his head and found her bare stomach with wandering lips, the glide of a tongue circling her navel, fingers bracing her hips. And when he straightened and drew the hem of her sweater up over her breasts, up, up the arms she'd raised over her head, she fought to breathe evenly and failed. How many times had she viewed his naked skin, delighted in the bare sight of him? Now she offered herself to him, and it was his turn—his right—to look her over, to examine what he would soon claim. What was he thinking as he let his gaze rake her from her tousled hair down to her breasts?

He studied her with such intense concentration, his hands hovering without quite touching, as though he didn't know where to start. She reached out, grasped his fingers and cupped them over her breasts. "Touch me," she whispered.

They were nose to nose, their breath rushing together as his hands moved, caressed her through her strapless bra until her nipples peaked and she squirmed in delight. Then he bent to draw the tips, one, the other, into his warm, wet mouth, and she was surprised to feel her bra sliding away. When had he unfastened it? No awkward groping. No delay. He was practiced; he was perfect. And tonight he was hers.

"You're beautiful," he murmured, the tip of his tongue flicking the sensitive underside of her left breast. He bit her gently, moved to the next breast and suckled it, dragged his tongue over and over it until she squirmed with the hot sensation his caresses ignited between her legs. Then he straightened and brushed his mouth against her lips. "What do you want next?"

Her throat was too tight to answer. God, she loved this play. Her own partial nudity. The anticipation of his nakedness to come.

"Tell me, Sydney. Anything you want."

She finally found her words. "Take off your coat and stay a while."

He stepped back, shrugged out of his jacket and let it drop into a careless pile on the floor.

"Now shoes," she ordered.

No one else in the world could make this awkward part of things so sexy. With a slight quirk of his mouth, he stepped out of his loafers and shucked off his socks. Even his feet were just right. She'd missed seeing these pieces of him, such benign areas and yet so intimate.

"Next?" he asked, bracing his hands on either side of her.

"Next you kiss me, then the sweater comes off."

He followed her instructions; caught her mouth in a lush, hungering kiss, then backed up and drew his sweater up and off, followed by the T-shirt beneath it.

Sydney was enchanted. Colm had never been so desirable, standing before her and slowly, intently stripping with his gaze locked on hers. Her throat went dry as his hands skimmed his own chest in a light caress, then arrowed down to the buttons on his fly, which he flicked open with his thumb.

He was beautiful.

"Do you ever touch yourself?" she asked, brave and trembling at the same time. "You know what I mean."

"I know what you mean. What do you think?" His hand lingered on the erection rising from his fly.

She smiled, her cheeks hot. Someone as sensual and uninhibited as he was . . . "I think maybe."

"Maybe. When I'm thinking of you."

She thought about her own forays into self-satisfaction and how intense they seemed since she'd met him. From now on, the sacred parts of her body didn't belong under anyone's hands but his.

"Be naked," she said quietly.

He pushed down his jeans, taking his boxer briefs with them, and kicked the clothing free.

Restraint crashed and burned at her feet.

"Show me how you touch yourself," she ordered.

He didn't seem to mind. He wrapped his fingers around his shaft and stroked once, twice. So wanton. So ready to please her.

And too soon or not, she loved him.

Colm had been naked before, but never like this, never so naked inside. Goose bumps spread over his skin, partly from the cool air but mostly from the emotions tightening his throat as he stood before Sydney, caressing himself when he only wanted her hands on him. He would please her, do whatever she asked, even if he burst from the wanting.

He thought she might hop off the counter and come touch him at last, but she only tilted her head and watched him, her gaze skimming him head to toe. He knew what she was doing. She was painting him in her mind.

Her lack of self-consciousness washed him with a wild mixture of lust and admiration, her utter concentration on him unyielding as she finally slid, bare-breasted, pants open, off the counter and approached. He abandoned his own flesh to slide his hands around her hips and inside her jeans, but she gently pushed him backward until he stood on the soft kitchen area rug.

"Like this," she instructed. "Don't move."

He closed his eyes and swallowed, his fingers balling into fists to keep from touching her as she circled him, one hand gliding along his naked ass as she went. When she appeared before him again, she pushed down her jeans, stepped out of them, and stood there in a pair of pink lace bikinis and nothing else. He lifted his gaze back to hers and waited, and thought he would die from wanting her.

"Don't you dare move." The repeat order came huskier this time in the thick silence. Her fingers slid over his chest, his abdomen, then down to encircle his hard-on, and he jolted from the firm, deliberate surprise of it. For three years he'd done the pleasing, the handling. Now he stood helpless, tortured, and he loved it.

Before he could recover, she knelt on the rug before him, one hand curled around his cock and the other around his hip. She rubbed her soft cheek against his erection, her warm breath skimming its throbbing length, and Colm squeezed his eyes closed, waiting for that searing, wet heat.

It came slow, slippery sweet. She took him in deep and then pushed him out again, her long lashes lifting to meet his eyes. Everything in him fought to keep from thrusting between her lips. Her tongue slid beneath the head of his cock and down to its base, flicked, explored, then back, and when she closed her lips around him and sucked, he came to life, unable to help himself, and buried his hands in her thick, silky hair. His stomach muscles jumped as she withdrew in a slow pull, then took him deep, stroking a rhythm with one hand and gripping his hip with the other to guide his helpless thrusts.

Don't come, he thought, the pathetic adolescent mantra he hadn't used in years. *Don't come, don't come.*

"Come," she whispered.

Not like this. Not before her pleasure. He would give her everything before taking more, for he had taken so much from her already. Granting ecstasy was what he knew. She would find out what he was eventually, but for tonight he could master his skills and give her all of his knowledge, and beyond that, every part of himself.

Gritting his teeth, he withdrew from her mouth, dropped to his knees before her, and took her face in his hands. He let his gaze search her flushed features, committing them to memory, because he would lose this reality eventually, the picture she made kneeling on her kitchen floor, lips parted and waiting for his kiss.

Seized by need and a stomach-twisting grief, he bent his head and plundered her open mouth, slid his tongue along the inside of her bottom lip, and when her head dropped back in surrender, he caught her waist and lifted her just enough so that she straddled his thighs.

"Sorry about these," he growled, and before she could speak, shredded her pretty lace panties right off her and tossed them over his shoulder. She was trembling, but he was, too, and for the moment there was nothing expert about his reactions despite his intentions to keep things a smooth glide. His mouth fastened on her nipple, sucked and stroked until she cried out. His hand fumbled between them to grasp himself and rub against her wetness, and oh, she was hot and slick against his tip, drawing him forward . . . almost in . . .

Condom. What the hell was wrong with him? "Wait," he said, and lightly bit her breast, holding tight to her with one hand on her backside. With the other, he grasped for his jeans and found his wallet, his fingers shaking while she waited, poised above him and breathing fast.

"Let me," she said when he straightened, and took the packet from him. When she tore it open with her teeth, he shuddered. He'd only seen these uninhibited parts of her when she was painting. He'd known she would be like this, hot and flushed and gorgeous in her passion.

She was no novice. She rolled the condom down his shaft with one quick movement, and before he could draw a breath, she rose up on him, poised herself, and then slid down again, taking him in . . . deep . . . deeper, to the very heart of her.

"Oh . . ." she breathed.

"Yes," he groaned.

They locked gazes, her eyes wide with the shock of pleasure, his sleepy with the weight of desire. With his hands on her hips to steady and guide her, she lifted and lowered and found rhythm, graceful and so, so slow. And when the need became too great, her legs untangled from his waist and she anchored her knees on either side of his thighs to gain leverage.

Colm thrust into her each time she rose up so that there was no surcease of pleasure, only a building momentum that scooted the rug beneath them and eventually sent his back colliding with the nearest cabinet. They laughed into each other's mouths and re-arranged themselves, and he kissed her breasts, her neck, while she stroked his hair and ears and then clung to him as the ride grew wilder.

He looked down between them, to the place where they meshed so perfectly. He'd never known such sweet, hot bliss from being buried inside a woman. It wasn't deep enough. He released her and braced his palms on the floor behind him and pushed his hips hard to meet her, watching the ecstasy on her beautiful features as it flushed her cheeks, her throat, the tops of her breasts.

Sydney clung to his shoulders and cantered upon him a few more short strokes. Then a cry quivered on her lips and she dropped down, grinding, dancing. Colm caught her as she arched backward and bent to her, his mouth on her left breast to taste the untethered thrum of her heart and hold her tight through the quaking.

No warning. There was no warning as his own simmering orgasm shot free. He pushed into her once, twice, lifting her high on him, and shuddered helplessly before she'd even stopped coming. He wanted it to go on forever, the greatest climax he'd ever known.

Her pleasure had become his own.

CHAPTER TWENTY

They made love again, this time in her bed, where he propped a pillow beneath her hips and showed her what he knew about the play of a skilled tongue between her thighs. She was shuddering and limp by the time he rose over her, but with the aid of the remaining condom in his wallet, managed to wrap her limbs around him and take him inside her, and come to climax again, then again. Colm only came at the end, but the orgasm blew his mind, shaking the bed and drawing helpless sounds from his throat. Ah, she undid him. He lost sense of both sides of himself—the whore and the man—and became someone new under her hands.

At dawn they sat naked in the middle of the bed with a haphazard feast of pizza and chicken wings. They half watched a morning talk show, then lay on their sides, arms folded under their heads, and gazed at one another without speaking, too absorbed in each other to sleep. When they finally did doze off, the last thing Colm remembered was Sydney whispering his name as she brushed her lips against his cheek, his temple.

If he could ever love again, it was now, with this woman.

* * *

Hours later, he stirred and opened his eyes. Sydney was sprawled next to him, one knee crooked and an arm flung over his chest. He smiled. She was a bed hog.

His humor faded he glanced at the wall of windows and recognized the angle of the sun, and his stomach sank. Time to get to Avalon. He was a man falling, too soon, too deeply, and still he had to go to work entertaining other women. *Not have to*, he thought. *You could quit.* And then what? The cutting-edge treatment available to Amelia would eventually stall; she would end up in some shabby extended care facility when his savings ran out. It didn't matter if he found a job in the architectural field or any other. Even with his education and experience, nothing could pay like being a whore in Azure's harem.

Sliding out from beneath Sydney's one-armed embrace, he eased from the bed and headed to the shower, then crossed naked to the kitchen, where their clothing still lay in a sloppy heap. He hated to leave her sleeping. All he wanted was to crawl back into bed with her and take her again.

After dressing, he folded her clothes on the counter, rifled through a drawer, and found paper and pen.

I want more of you. I'll call soon. He found a spare key in the same drawer and not wanting to leave her unsafe, quietly locked the door behind him when he left.

He dialed Amelia on his way to Avalon.

"Where'd you go last night?" she asked, nosy woman that she was.

"Out," he said.

She laughed. "All night? You slut."

He changed lanes and stared ahead at the red, blinking lights of insane, after-Christmas traffic.

Slut. Wretch.

"All true," he told her finally. "I probably won't be home tonight, either."

"I won't ask where you're going."

"Thank you."

"Is she the new love of your life? I can do your tarot cards to find out for you."

"I'm hanging up now," he said, and she laughed again.

At Avalon, Colm dressed and breathed himself into character. When his client arrived, he met her at the foot of the staircase and made to kiss her hand, but turned it over at the last second and brushed his mouth against her wrist instead. They all liked that kind of thing, the start of seduction before they even made it up the stairs. Azure, who had greeted the woman when she first stepped through the pleasure club's doors, watched with a satisfied smile from her station at a nearby Chippendale desk. Colm avoided her flinty blue gaze, a knot of disgust tightening his throat.

He thought of this particular client as a blow-up doll with jointed arms and legs. She didn't want to do anything for herself. Her companion for the evening had to strip her, bathe her, arrange her limbs for sex. He recognized her delectations as a lack of confidence, but it hardly made them bearable. Tonight he wasn't in the mood to deal with a helpless little girl.

"Where shall I put my things?" the woman asked in a timid voice, lingering inside the doorway of his quarters. They went through this script every time she scheduled him.

"Allow me." He set her purse on a nearby console, then slid the coat from her thin shoulders and hung it in the closet. She was an attractive forty-five-year-old socialite with fair skin and wavy red hair, but he never saw her beauty except when she laughed. Then he liked her. Then he could screw her. Her humor showed itself so rarely, though, this wasn't a job he ever relished.

And now . . . he would never be the same.

He stood there and looked at her for a minute, knowing there was no way in hell he could have sex with her ever again, then regained his congeniality and crossed the room to the kitchenette. "What would you like to drink?"

"Just a glass of wine tonight would be nice."

Shiraz, he thought, tasting its memory on his tongue. Tasting Sydney.

"Chardonnay," she added. "I like the cheap stuff."

He withdrew a chilled bottle from the wine refrigerator and uncorked it, then poured her a taste like a restaurant server and waited while she sampled it. At her nod of approval, he filled her glass and on second thought, one for himself. Tonight he needed all the help he could get.

He knew she would stand in the middle of the room, looking helpless until the end of time, so he downed his wine, set the glass on a table, and approached to take her elbow. "Sit down and tell me about you. We haven't seen each other in a while."

"I've been traveling with my husband," she said as she seated herself on a nearby wingback chair. "And with the holidays, I had so many parties to prepare for—very important events. I'm still feeling overwhelmed."

He sat in the matching chair opposite her and watched her face as she spoke, reading the little lines carved by anxiety that Botox or Juvéderm couldn't banish. She was one of those social do-gooders that never stopped. Charities, parties, clubs, and five children at home. She didn't like nannies. She liked control, except at Avalon. No wonder she was a rag doll when she got there.

Colm let her go on for a while about parties and her husband and friends who stressed her out until he couldn't take it anymore. Then he stood and drew her to her feet. "I know what you need to take your mind off things."

"What's that?" She allowed him to take her wineglass, which he set aside, and stood stock-still while he came around behind her, removed her suede blazer and laid it over the back of the chair. Then he circled her slowly, his fingers tugging lightly at the blouse tucked into her tailored slacks.

"A bath," he said at last in a low, practiced voice that promised multiple orgasms. The voice of a liar. He was in full-fledged escort mode now, although only half of him stood there. How the hell he was going to do his job after last night with Sydney, he didn't know.

As expected, she stood with arms dangling at her side while he undressed her slowly, drawing each piece of clothing off as though uncovering one of Sydney's paintings. Only what lay beneath was a canvas of a lonely, stressed human being, painfully thin to suit the latest fashions, and with none of the tactile, sensuous flow of Sydney's work.

Get her under the bath bubbles, he thought. *Ply her with wine*. It could all be accomplished without giving a single bit of himself.

When she stood naked and shivering, he took her hand and led her into the opulent, gold-toned bathroom. Gilded mirrors on every wall shot reflections all around them so that there was no hiding, only naked flesh. Normally he loved the mirrors, loved to watch pleasure consume a woman's face. But tonight the reflections showed a skeletal female form and Colm, fully dressed but weary, frustrated. Who was the more pathetic of the two, he couldn't have said.

While the client waited with her arms crossed over her breasts, he wrapped her in a thick terrycloth robe and leaned to start the gold-leaf spigots on the tub, several of which gushed water so generously, the wide tub was filled within a couple of minutes. He added a small bottle of the finest bubble bath, rolled his shirt sleeves to his elbows and checked the water temperature, then reached behind a Greek statue in one corner and activated the jets, which churned the water into an angry cauldron that both daunted and invited the weary.

"Ready?" he asked, and when she nodded, he moved behind her and slid her robe off, stopping to press a perfunctory kiss on her bony shoulder as he did so.

Clinging to his hand, she let him lead her into the bathwater and sank into the tumult with a groan. "Oh, Colm. I don't know which feels better—this bath or you."

Even though she hadn't put her hands on him. The thought of her touch brought a wave of nausea.

He tried to think of the proper provocative response and came up with nothing, so he rose, poured her another glass of wine, and waited while she downed it. Then she opened her legs. She was a pro at this as much as he was. The purpose of the tub jets was to stimulate a woman as well as relax her.

"Stay just like that," he said flatly, and when he adjusted a particular jet so that it hit her just so, she groaned and arched in the roiling water.

Colm suppressed a sigh as he watched her pleasure from miles away.

When she'd had her fill, he grasped her hand and helped her climb out.

"I need a little nap," she said, sliding into the robe he held for her. "Will you come with me? You know how I love for you to hold me while I fall asleep."

He nodded, a smooth liar. "I'll tuck you in."

In the bedroom, he drew back the down comforter and waited for her to climb beneath it. She collapsed against the pillows, stretched, and gave a sigh of delight. "Oh, this is amazing." Reaching out her hand to him, she added, "Come to bed. We still have two hours."

"I'll be right behind you after I drain the tub," he fibbed easily.

She would fall asleep before he got there, and he wouldn't have to strip, cradle her against him, stroke her back, and listen to the even sound of her breathing. Those things, suddenly excruciatingly intimate, belonged only to Sydney.

Christ, his entire existence was unraveling.

When he had finished with the tub, he paused in the bathroom doorway and let his gaze drift over his client's sleeping form. She hardly made a lump in the bed. One thousand dollars for tonight, and all he'd done was give her a bath.

Despite the heavy price for so little, when she woke, she looked rested and beatific. He walked her downstairs and offered her the standard good-bye, with promises spoken through a long gaze.

Then he gritted his teeth and headed to Azure's office.

"How is Mrs. Weiss?" she asked, waggling a pen between her fingers as she sat behind her desk.

"Fine." He paused. This wasn't going to be easy. "I used to worry about asking anything from you, Azure."

A smile curved her mouth. "And now?"

"Now I need something more than this job."

"Darling Colm," she said, twirling that pen between her manicured fingers, "I can be kinder than you think. Sit down."

"I prefer to stand." He braced his legs apart and crossed his arms over his chest. "I want some time off."

"I see." She set aside the pen and sat forward, propping her elbows on the leather blotter. "Why?"

It was none of her business, but he needed this favor. He needed Sydney, and time with Amelia, and time to decide what the hell he was going to do to avoid the implosion of his world.

"I'd like a few days to settle some things in my personal life, unless you want to fire me now."

"You're thinking of quitting me?" She stood, her ankle-length white vest flowing gracefully around her. Displeasure had hardened her expression. "What is it lately with my boys falling in love with these mindless women? You're the third this year."

He fought against showing his surprise. How did she know him so well? She could read the male animal more skillfully than any being he'd ever encountered. He knew better than to argue. It would make him look like a fool.

"If this continues," she said bitterly, "Avalon will be a shell of its former self. Maybe I should hire younger men who have no desire other than to screw fifty women a week. There are a million in this city who would appreciate the job, believe me."

He kept his face carefully blank.

"Fine," she sighed at last. "I won't ask how long you need. I'll tell you. One week, Colm. One week to work out the mess you have obviously made of your life. Sydney Warren is a dangerous choice for you. She'll find out what you've done eventually, and she won't bear it."

He didn't bother to deny it was Sydney. Time with her was counting down, minute by precious minute. The truth from his own lips would come, and then her heart would break, and his, too, and she would hate him forever, but never as much as he despised himself.

It would come. But, God, not yet.

Azure flipped open an appointment book. "Do you have anything on the schedule for tomorrow night?"

"One," he said. "Senator Foley."

"She's a good customer. I'll give her to Garrett and pray to God she finds that acceptable after anticipating you. He is, after all, good with the hard-edged ones."

He waited, knowing there would be more.

"Two things I want you to remember as you slog through the next seven days." She came around the desk, the frown she wore marring the smooth space between her carefully penciled brows. "One, you'll miss New Year's Eve, which is quite a lucrative night for Avalon."

"It doesn't matter," he said.

"I had three women scheduled for you. You would have left here with a nice paycheck, Colm."

"This is more important."

"Sydney is more important than maintaining care of your sister?"

Colm clenched his jaw and didn't speak. It was a low blow and none of her goddamned business.

"Two," she went on, her flawless features drawing tight, "if you want to keep your position here, you should remember that you are mine. If you can't accept this truth, you don't belong here. Don't waste my time."

Hers? His brows went up. He didn't belong to anyone, not even to himself.

"Maybe that's what's wrong with you, Colm," she continued with a sigh, as though she'd heard his rejoinder. "Maybe you've never realized that in this world we all belong to somebody. Our hearts, our bodies, our time. Think about it. I'm only one of many who own you. Sydney Warren is apparently the latest, and the most dangerous. Whether I fire you or you resign, she could cost you your job, and then I may not own you anymore, but you'll wish I did."

They stared at each other, the air crackling between them.

And just like that, her granite expression vanished in favor of a catlike smile. "Enough mothering, hmm? I only do it because I love you. Kiss me, darling. I can't bear a week without you."

He leaned to brush his lips against her cheek, the exotic scent of her filling his senses, cloying, too rich. At the last minute she turned her lips into his and swept her tongue inside his mouth, her fingers curling around the nape of his neck, nails digging in. When he jerked back, she hissed out, "Come back to me, Colm. Don't forget your responsibilities."

She knew too much. About his life. About Amelia, and now Sydney.

It was time to tell Sydney the truth.

CHAPTER TWENTY-ONE

Waking to an empty bed was nothing new to Sydney. She shouldn't have cared that Colm was gone when she awoke. She hated it.

His note was on the kitchen counter, her clothes from last night neatly folded beside it, the rug they'd scooted all over the floor back in place, as though two people hadn't found excruciating pleasure in that exact spot.

I want more of you, he'd written. She carried the note around the loft with her, laying it on the bedside table when she changed the sheets and then atop the dryer as she did laundry. She tried to picture where he was—he hadn't left any indication. Was he modeling for some artist? What secret, mysterious world swallowed him when he left her presence?

It was ten o'clock when the buzzer sounded. Her heels clicked briskly on the wood floor as she hurried to answer it. "Yes?"

"It's Colm."

"Come up."

His knock sounded so quickly, he must have sprinted up the

stairs. When she opened the door, he stood there, smelling of leather and the cold night.

The smile on her face faded with the dark purpose on his. "I need you," he murmured, and leaned to catch her lips with his.

It wasn't enough. She drew back to look into his eyes, found them heavy-lidded and oh-so-green, and said, "I missed you. Make love to me."

He shucked his jacket, grabbed a condom from his wallet, and then drew her against him, spinning her to trap her between his body and the wall as she'd once envisioned. They didn't bother to undress, just unfastened strategic garments, and he dropped to his knees and put his mouth on her, his tongue inside her, soft flickers on her aroused flesh like the slow drift of butterfly wings.

Too much pleasure to bear. When she came, she bucked in his hands. There was little time to recover before he tore into the packet, sheathed himself, then lifted and entered her right there beside the door. They forgot the locks. They forgot the sounds they made, which might float into the hallway for anyone to hear. Everything except his flesh inside her, hers around him and drawing him deep, his hands on her backside, hers on his, so muscled and smooth.

It only took a moment before she climaxed again. His mouth was soft, sinuous against her arched throat when she cried out, and still he kept the rhythm, clutching the backs of her thighs as he buried his face against her breasts and thrust, and thrust, so she slid against the wall, its plaster cool and hard, rucking up her thin sweater.

"Sydney," he groaned, breathing heat through its knit to warm her nipple. "Sydney!"

She buried her fingers in his hair, held his lips to her breast. Held him through paroxysms of pleasure too great to silence.

Slowly she slid down his body and found her footing. He kissed her, easy and sweet, and said with a rueful smile, "That could have been more romantic. Sorry."

"Don't be." She watched with avid eyes as he kicked off his shoes and stripped, leaving his clothes in a pile by the door.

"Take a shower with me," he said, lacing his fingers through hers, "and this time I'll show you romantic."

In the late, languid morning, they lay entwined, her body fitted just right against his. Her nose found the warm curve of his neck, his hand stroked her back. In return she let her fingers play the hard muscles of his abdomen and marveled at his physique.

"Your body is so hard," Sydney said. "All over."

Colm's cheek brushed hers, and their mouths slid together as naturally as if they had always kissed like this, lay like this, reveled in one another's company like this.

When his lips found her earlobe, he traced its curve with his tongue and then lightly sucked it between his lips. Sydney sank her fingers into his shoulders and released a shuddering sigh.

"We need to talk," he murmured.

It sounded serious. She didn't want serious. "Hmm. Okay. Can I go first?"

"Uh-oh," he said under his breath, and she laughed.

"Truth or dare, Colm?"

He was quiet, and when she raised her head to look at him, his features seemed dark with an emotion she couldn't identify.

"What's wrong?" she asked, her brows lowering.

He cupped her cheek in his hand, his thumb sweeping her bottom lip while he searched her eyes, deep, so deep, she thought he would turn her inside out.

And just like that, the darkness lifted. "Dare."

She smiled. "Oh, you're brave."

"Dare me something dirty," he added, sliding a hand up her thigh and between her legs.

Sydney arched into his touch, but quickly grabbed his fingers and drew them to a safer place. "Truth."

"I don't get to choose?"

"No. I want to know more about your life."

His throat moved when he swallowed, and she wondered at the sudden tension in his body beneath her arm, but she plunged onward.

"How did you meet Azure Elan?"

"At a party." He responded too quickly, as if it was a question he was used to answering.

"Do you date her sometimes?" She already knew the answer. If he lied, she would call him on it.

He smiled down at her. "Nowadays that would be a solid 'Hell, no.'"

"But you did before?"

He shrugged. "Once or twice. It didn't last. You saw what she was like."

"Yes." She angled her head to look at him. "You're too honest for a woman like Azure."

Beneath her cheek, his chest vibrated with silent laughter.

"Stop laughing." She lifted her head. "Why did you go out with her?"

"To help my career."

"And not because she's incredibly hot?"

"I thought she was at first," he admitted. "But not now. Not after this. Not after you."

She laid her cheek on his chest again.

For a moment they lay in silence, hands drifting over each other in languid strokes, then he spoke. "There's more, isn't there? I can hear the wheels turning between your ears."

"Tell me about Jill." As soon as the words were out of her mouth, she winced. Maybe Jill was the last person he wanted to discuss.

But he merely smoothed back the mess of her hair and gave her a curious smile. "You remember her name."

"I remember everything."

He thought for a long time. "She was a force," he said finally.

Curiosity mixed with a pang of something like envy jolted through her. "How did you meet?"

"In college. She was studying interior design, I was finishing my masters in architecture. We acted on young idiocy and hormones. We didn't really consider the reality of marriage and the real world past graduate school."

Sydney listened, gently stroking the spot over his heart as he spoke, her gaze reading every nuance of expression that crossed his features, from humor to tension to sadness.

"So we got married, and it was rough. Always. We fought like the kids we were. My sister used to say—" He cut himself off.

"Your sister used to say what?"

"That Jill and I were the best and worst thing that had ever happened to each other. I think she was right. But at the end . . ." His jaw flexed, his hands holding her a little too tight. "We were fighting, even seconds before the accident. It was pouring rain. I hydroplaned on a slick bridge and skidded sideways into a concrete barrier. Her side of the car took the brunt."

"I'm so sorry," Sydney said softly.

She watched his eyes, but they were shuttered.

"It's the past," he said quietly. "Mine. And one of many secrets."

When she pressed a kiss to the sharp line of his jaw and said, "Tell me another secret," he stirred and looked down at her.

"You," he said. "You are my secret."

Sydney smiled. "From whom?"

"From the ugly world. I want to know more about you, too, Syd."

As the sun poured through the vast windows and then rose higher over the city, Colm gently drew Sydney's stories from the dark recesses where she'd tucked them away. They talked about her growing up, her mother, and at last her relationship with Greg Brantley, the man who seduced her so early in her life.

"I still have enormous shame," she murmured, her fingers drawing swirls on the smooth skin of his chest. "I've been through a handful of therapists who tried to help me work through it, but it's the kid in me, I guess, who won't let go of it. The one who was hurt."

"And your mom?" he asked, caressing her hair. "What does she say to you now, after all this time?"

"I haven't talked to her since I left Nebraska. When I got to Washington, I promised myself I'd never live another lie. Yet I stayed with Max, and it was . . ." Her gaze locked on his. "I shouldn't bring him up, Colm."

"Yes, you should, Syd. You loved him once."

"But I think he stopped letting me, months ago, and the distance between us became insurmountable. Maybe it always was, long before his accident, and I just couldn't see it."

She lifted her chin and looked into his eyes. "People might think I was cruel to leave him, but I wouldn't stay with him just because he's a paraplegic. I wouldn't disrespect him by feeling sorry for him. I wanted to marry him once, to have as normal a life with him as we could manage, and for a while, it worked. But then he changed, and I couldn't abide it anymore."

"So it really had nothing to do with me?" he asked, sounding relieved.

She shook her head. "Even though you were there, you weren't the reason I finally left. I just couldn't be the old me anymore for anyone."

"Thank you," he said. "I like the new you."

She rose up on her elbow again to meet his eyes. "You know what? Two months ago we were strangers."

"And now," he said softly, "now . . . my God, Sydney."

That was all. He lifted his head and kissed her.

Blue-sky winter sunshine danced off the white walls and rug as Sydney hummed to herself, pouring two glasses of orange juice. The sound of the shower made her feel warm all over, banishing the usual solitude that plagued the loft.

I have a lover, she thought, and for the first time in four days, it felt real.

Colm finally emerged from the bathroom in last night's jeans and unbuttoned gray shirt, wet hair combed back from his face. "I used the extra toothbrush in your drawer."

"That's fine. It's for you."

"I get my own toothbrush?"

"You get more than that." She met him in the living room and gave his warm, minty mouth a lingering kiss, ending it by nipping his lower lip.

"Just keep that up and watch what happens." He drew her back to kiss her again, longer this time, hungrier. His hands found her breasts through her pajama tank top; hers slid down his hard body to his fly. She had become some kind of sex monster, partly because of the months of chastity, but mostly because this was Colm, beautiful, loving Colm.

He was backing her toward the bed again when the doorbell rang.

"No one called to be buzzed up," she said. "Who could it be?"

"Let me answer it." Colm crossed the floor and said in a none-too-pleasant voice, "Who is it?" His protectiveness made her warm and shivery at the same time. God, she adored him.

She couldn't hear who was on the other side, but Colm flipped the locks and opened the door, swung it wide, and stepped back.

Max.

For a moment, no one said a word. The three of them lingered there in the booming silence until Sydney finally spoke. "I guess they fixed the elevator."

"Hennessy," Max said. "Why am I not surprised to find you here?"

"You could have called first," Sydney said from behind Colm, folding her arms over her chest.

"I tried. Your cell phone's been off for the last two days."

Colm moved to step between her and Max. "What can we do for you?"

"Button your shirt, to start."

"Max," Sydney snapped.

He smiled the smile she used to hate. "I came to tell you I have a buyer for the ménage painting from the show."

Colm glanced over his shoulder at Sydney, his fingers fastening the buttons on his shirt. "I can wait in the other room while you talk about this."

"No need." Max's flinty gaze shifted to Sydney, skimmed her tank top, her braless state, her low-slung pajama bottoms. "I won't discuss business when you're so obviously . . . indisposed. I'll call you later so we can set up a meeting. The buyer wants to meet with you over dinner."

She didn't care about the damned business deal. She just wanted Max to leave.

To her relief, he wheeled backward, his face stony. "I'll be in touch. Will you answer your phone?" It wasn't a real question. He smirked at Colm. "Always a pleasure, Hennessy."

"Wish I could say the same, Max." Colm waited until the man had wheeled himself in the direction of the elevator before he shut the door and flipped the locks. Then he returned to Sydney.

"Pleasant surprise, huh?" He brushed the hair back from her cheek, tucked it behind her ear until her eyelids slid closed and her head listed to the side.

"I would so much rather have dealt with him over the phone this morning," she sighed. "You know why it was off, don't you?"

"We were doing it," he whispered, slipping his arms around her waist.

"Colm."

"He came here because he can't forget you." His lips brushed her forehead. "Go to dinner with the client and sell that painting. Then come home to me, because I can't forget you, either."

"You make me cry, Mr. Hennessy," she said around a lump in her throat.

"I'll make you cry with pleasure. Come to bed."

The first thing Sydney did was staunchly unbutton his shirt in defiance of Max's contemptuous observations and push it off his broad shoulders. She let her hands skim his bare chest as her lips found the side of his throat and nipped him lightly until an urgent sound vibrated from him. He clutched her hips as her fingers slipped down to unfasten his fly, pushed down his jeans and boxer briefs so that he was naked, naked and shivering, even though his smooth skin was hot all over.

The thought of making love this way, with him bare and her still entirely clothed, sent a surge of searing arousal straight through her. "Do you mind if I don't undress?" she whispered, bumping against his erection as her hands slid around to cup his buttocks. "I'd like it like this, with you so very naked."

"Anything you want." His voice was husky, lower than usual. It shivered through her as he backed her onto the bed and crawled over her. Sliding his hands inside her pajama bottoms, he pushed them down around her hips and then slipped his fingers inside the leg of her panties to find her wet, swollen flesh.

As he stroked, stroked, his kiss was light, almost chaste, leaving her mouth open and hungering for more. His words brushed her lips. "What else do you want, Sydney? This?" He probed her with a single finger and slipped it inside her.

She arched her hips to meet him, but it wasn't enough. She shook her head. "I want more."

He kissed her again, her mouth, her chin, her throat, as he inserted another finger. "This?"

"Getting warmer," she breathed.

"Tell me. Let me hear you say it, no holds barred."

She paused. He was asking for something she'd never done: dirty talk. She didn't know if she could manage it. He made her wild, made her want to be everything he craved. But those words had never left her lips.

Her breath quickened.

When Colm shifted up beside her and withdrew his fingers, she groaned. "I want you, Colm. Inside me."

"There's another word for that," he whispered against her ear, "far more to the point." Then he bit her lobe, hoop and all. The small of her back left the bed as though a sizzling line ran between her ear and the wanting place between her legs. "One phrase, Syd. You know what I want. Say it. For me."

She swallowed and turned her head to stare into his eyes. Everything good in the world was written in their green depths: pleasure, the desire to give, the need for more, the need for her to answer his one simple request.

Clearing her throat, she gripped his shoulders and said low and shaky, "Fuck me."

He moved so quickly she barely had time to draw a breath. He grabbed a condom from the bedside drawer, sheathed himself, and, true to his word, didn't remove a single piece of her pajamas, just pushed aside the leg of her panties, found her and pushed into her, slow, deep, to the hilt. Breathing out, Sydney dug her fingers into the hard muscles of his back and met his slow thrust, feeling the slide of him, deep, ever deeper, until she couldn't stand it. She needed him pressed tight and unyielding inside her. Then she lifted her hips and rocked up against him, and somehow, without being guided, Colm knew the pace she needed. He gripped the iron spindles of the headboard above her and adjusted his rhythm to short, tight jabs, and covered her mouth with his when she came, swallowing her cry of pleasure as she shuddered once, twice, three times beneath him.

She hadn't quite recovered when he murmured some intelligible adulation and picked up speed, buried his face in the curve of her neck and pushed in again, again, as wild as though he'd never known control.

Sydney buried her fingers in his damp hair and held him tight, reveling in the delight she brought him as he quaked and muffled his cry against her throat. So many emotions battered her at once. They seemed suddenly foreign to a woman like her, she mused, tears stinging her eyes as she stroked her hands up and down the long line of his spine. And most foreign of all was the sweet, terrifying feeling that for a second time pervaded the silent satisfaction in which they both drifted.

L ove.

The next morning dawned with a gloomy, icy drizzle. It didn't bother Sydney a bit. She and Colm were holed up in their own little world that turned on waves of pleasure and the growing bond between them. Of course, there lurked the ever-present knowledge that at some point the sweet solitude they shared had to end, and the real world would invade with all its noisy, vexatious reality.

But not today, she thought, as she drew on a long, slim sweater dress and belted it around the hips. Today Colm had just slipped out to buy bagels and coffee. They planned to have breakfast and then catch a movie in the afternoon. He had no modeling appointments this week, and Sydney had no commissions due any time soon, and her head was so far in the clouds, she barely heard the phone when it gave a muffled ring from the living room. It rang again, then again as she searched under the sofa and finally found it hiding beneath a cushion.

"Is this a convenient time?" Max asked, his tone dry.

The real world, invading her good time. Sydney sighed. "Perfect timing as always."

"You sound breathless."

"You sound ornery. What do you want, Max?"

"As I was telling you before, the client wants to meet with you and talk out the details of acquiring the ménage."

"Why?" she said, sliding into a pair of boots. "Why are we not doing this the regular way, with me paying your percentage and you dealing with the client?"

"I don't want your money," he snapped.

Her spine straightened. "Well, you'll get it. I appreciate you finding the client."

"Are we doing the dinner or not?"

Sydney's eyebrows went up. "So you'll be joining us, then."

"This man is a stranger to you. Of course I'll be joining you. How does tonight at Claude's sound? Seven o'clock?"

A trickle of foreboding slid through Sydney, but she glanced at her studio where portraits sat scattered and shook it off. The sale of this painting was a milestone. The last of her erotic works to go, except for the one version of the ménage, which she was saving for Colm's birthday in May.

"That will be fine," she told Max. "See you then." But when she disconnected the call, she sank to the sofa and stared at the phone, unable to shake the sense that she'd just committed to something too big to grasp.

CHAPTER TWENTY-TWO

Sydney drove through the streets of Georgetown, looking for a parking space near Claude's Restaurant. She finally snagged a prime spot less than a block away, slid her Mazda sedan into the space, and sighed. A few deep breaths, a quick glance in the rearview mirror to make sure she didn't look as uncomfortable as she felt, and she climbed out.

Dimness reigned inside the rich leather and mahogany-enhanced restaurant. Max waved to her from an intimate, candlelit table, and for a moment, as she crossed the restaurant to meet him, it felt like the old days. The usual lift to her heart upon seeing him was missing, though. Gone for good. In its place sat a leaden sense that somehow she'd been bamboozled into this dinner.

"Hello, Max," she said when she reached the table. "Where's the client?"

He glanced at his watch. "Not here yet. I haven't heard from him, so he should be here any minute." Pulling out the chair at his right elbow, he said, "Take off your coat and stay a while."

Those were the same words she'd said to Colm the first night they made love. Cheeks warming, Sydney slid out of her coat, hung it on a nearby rack, and waited while he wheeled back, drew out her chair and helped her sit. Everything stiff and oh-so-polite. She wondered what Colm was doing. When he'd heard she was meeting Max, he made other plans to check his house and to visit his sister, who Sydney wanted to meet. Instead she was stuck here with her past staring her in the face.

At first they didn't say much. She ordered a glass of Shiraz, to which Max said, "So the new Sydney drinks wine, eh?"

"I've always liked wine." She didn't have to explain herself to him. Truth be told, hard liquor would have done a better job of making all this bearable.

He sat back to look at her. "Tell me more about yourself. How's the portrait business?"

"It might surprise you to hear it's going really well."

"Maybe I was wrong to doubt you. I've heard your name in certain charity circles, and people are anxious to get their hands on a Sydney Warren portrait. It's almost as though the erotic artist has dissolved into thin air."

"That phase would have fallen out of favor at some point, Max. It's a fickle crowd."

"Yes. You did the Marilyn Monroe trick. Step out while you're still shining. And now look at you. You've never been more beautiful or successful. You've got a whole new life."

Sydney frowned and took a sip of wine, her gaze skimming the group of people standing in the entry. "Max, I can't wait all night for this man."

His hand slid along her blouse sleeve. "He'll be here. Talk to me a little, Sydney. Tell me about your life."

She sighed and glanced at him. In the flickering candlelight, he was the same handsome Max she'd met four years ago. He still turned female heads, and the wheelchair seemed no deterrent. If anything, it fascinated people, especially because Max radiated the same charisma and power he had when he could walk.

"Tell me about *your* life, Max. That would be much more interesting."

He shrugged. "I've got three new artists who are keeping me busy. I'm looking for a condo in the city since the commute has become tiresome." He slid his gaze over her. "The house in Virginia is for sale."

A soft nostalgia swirled through her. "Oh, that's too bad."

"You could buy it."

"What would I do with all that room?"

He smiled. "Well, you wouldn't be alone there, would you? Not anymore."

Sydney stopped and looked at him. "It was too much space for you, me, and Hans. It needs a family."

A waiter interrupted to refill their water glasses and inquire about the still missing third party.

"Let's go ahead and order," Max told Sydney. "The client will understand, considering he's almost a half hour late."

She glanced briefly at the menu then ordered a salad. Her stomach felt strangely queasy. "I'll eat with you, but then I have to run."

"Ah," he said, smiling at the waiter as he handed back the menus. "Hot date?"

"Max, don't start."

"I'm just curious how long you've been seeing him, that's all. Would you humor me?"

"No. My life is my business, especially because I know how you feel about Colm."

Max laughed, a harsh, humorless sound. "Any man would feel the same. After all, I hired him to model for you, and look how it turned out?"

"Don't—"

"Did the relationship start right away with him? Working in that isolated studio, just the two of you, him naked, and you—"

"Max!"

He went silent, but his cheeks were flushed, his gray eyes black and piercing in the candlelight. "There are things you don't know about your new boyfriend, Sydney."

"I don't have to sit here and listen to this."

She pushed back her chair and started to rise when he said, "I paid him to do more than model for you."

A chill slid down her spine. She reached for her coat and scowled as she slid into it. "You'll say anything to hurt me. I knew I shouldn't have come to this meeting. Is there even a client?"

"Yes, damn it. Me!"

"I knew it. I knew it! Then the painting isn't for sale." She paused in the midst of wrapping her scarf around her neck and offered him an arid smile. "Anyway, what would you do with an image of Colm hanging in your living room? Throw darts at it?"

"Sydney, listen to me." His hand shot out and caught her wrist firmly enough to make her wince. "Sit down for just a second. There's something you should know before you get hurt."

"You honestly think I would trust anything you tell me, Max? You only have your best interests at heart."

"Listen to me—"

"No. Max, I swear to God, if you don't let go—"

"I hired Hennessy to test your fidelity."

Everything went silent. Sydney sank to the chair and stared at him. "You hired Colm because you thought he might tempt me to cheat on you? My God, Max. I know things hadn't been good between us, but were you really that insecure?"

"You're misunderstanding me, Sydney." His fingers around her wrist went from gripping to caressing. "I hired Colm to seduce you."

She jerked free from him, her pulse commencing an erratic thud. "I don't understand what you mean."

"He's a prostitute. His job was to try to sway you. According to Azure, his pimp, he failed. Yet I don't understand why he was at your condominium in such a state of undress—"

She didn't hear the rest. The room spun. Perspiration broke out on her upper lip. "Colm's not a prostitute, you bastard! He's not . . ."

And just like that, all the disjointed pieces fell into place. Colm's hazy background. The women she'd seen him with. Azure . . . his pimp?

While she sat there in stunned silence, Max withdrew a business card from inside his suit jacket and slid it across the corner of the table to her. "You don't have to believe me. Call Azure Elan and ask her. She'll undoubtedly set you straight."

Sydney blinked and focused on him. "Why, Max? Why would you do something like this to me?"

"Simple," he said. "I knew eventually you'd leave me. And I wasn't wrong, was I? Given the right circumstances—one week with a man like Hennessy—and off your pedestal you go."

Hollow. She'd gone hollow inside. Tears burned her eyes, but she wouldn't cry in front of Max. She stood slowly and reached for her purse. "Thank you, Max."

"For what?"

"For saving me from spending the rest of my life thinking you were capable of love. You never were, even before the accident. I guess your assumptions about me leaving you are coming true, because you really are alone."

She didn't give him time to speak before she slipped through the crowd and out into the December night.

For a long time she didn't know where to go, just paced up and down the street, her brain on pause. Then she stopped.

It was one thing that Colm was a prostitute. It was another thing entirely that he had been hired to deceive her and that he had followed through. For deceived she was, and in love, and shattered.

It couldn't be true. Max was just cruel enough to concoct something so horrendous. Her fingers were trembling, stiff with cold as she stopped beneath a streetlight and dialed the number on Azure Elan's business card.

"Hello," said a sultry feminine voice.

Shivering, Sydney said, "This is Sydney Warren. I got your number from Max Beaudoin. You know who I am."

"Of course," Azure exclaimed. "How could I ever forget so lovely and talented an artist?"

She grimaced, her stomach roiling. "I'm calling to talk to you about Colm Hennessy."

Pause.

Let the games begin. Sydney clenched her teeth to keep them from chattering. "Please don't lie to me. Max said . . . Max told me everything. He told me what Colm is, and what you are."

"Mm-hmm. Oh, and what I am, as well? Shame on Max."

"I'd like to give you the chance to tell me he's lying." Sydney closed her eyes, her heart beating in her throat. "What are you?"

"I am a club proprietor."

"What club?"

"A pleasure club for women, darling."

Sydney braced a hand against the metal lamppost to hold herself up, its chilled steel seeping through her skin and into her bones. "Colm does work for you, then."

"Make up your mind, Sydney. Would you like me to say yes or no? After all, I'm in the business of fulfilling women's fantasies."

Sydney hated her almost as much as she hated Max. "Colm's a prostitute?"

"He's a fine companion. It's not always about sex, darling. You should know that. After all, he claims he failed Max's directive, which was to get you into bed. I'm not sure I believe him, but that's what he says."

Sydney might hate the players in this game, but the one thing that still felt sacred—even though its memory had crashed and crumbled—was the lovemaking she'd shared with Colm. She wouldn't hand it over to someone like Azure, no matter how defiled the memory now felt.

Anger revived her, although the tears kept coming. "I would like to speak with him."

"I'm afraid that's not possible just now," Azure murmured.

"Is he there now? At your . . . pleasure club?"

"He's somewhere around here, but busy."

"He's working?" The tears clogged her throat, thickened her words. "He's with a client?"

"He's doing his job." Silence fell between them, and Sydney couldn't stop the sobs welling in her chest. The phone slipped from her numb fingers and cracked on the sidewalk. For a moment she left it there, then she snatched it up in a fit of rage. "Are you still there?"

"I'm here, waiting for you to tell me if there's anything else I can do for you."

Sydney shook her head. "I don't know. I'm so . . . I'm . . ."

"You're curious about his world, aren't you, Sydney? Any red-blooded woman would be."

Sydney closed her eyes. If she let herself cry the way she wanted to, she would throw up.

"I'm willing to allow you to make an appointment with him," the other woman said gently.

Sydney sucked back a harsh laugh, a fresh wave of ire reviving her. "You think I would come to your—your club and—?"

"Careful, darling. I'm offering you an opportunity to put this all behind you and set your life on its proper path. Most women, even lovely, talented ones like you, don't receive invitations to Avalon. Consider before you insult me."

"You were part of this game."

"And it's nothing personal. Surely you can understand that."

Damn Colm Hennessy. Damn all of them.

And then a soul-sickening idea began to form in her mind. She let it swirl, and though it stripped another piece off her very being, she finally said, "You're right, Azure. I'm . . . curious. I'll make an appointment."

"And you understand you'll have to pay handsomely for his services?"

She closed her eyes. *I already have.* Heart. Body. Soul. She'd given them all.

"Money is no object," she said.

A group of giggling college girls danced by her on the sidewalk and she turned to shelter the call from their raucous good time. When the noise had faded, she added, "But I have one more request."

"What's that?"

"I want one more of your men there to . . . to service me. At the same time."

Azure gave a laugh of delight. Sydney could picture her applauding. "Really, darling? How fabulous and uninhibited of you. Shall I handpick him for you?"

Agony sharpened and twisted her thoughts. "No. It's Garrett. I want Garrett there, and I don't want Colm to know I've made this request."

"Speaking of surprises, are you planning to shock Colm with your appearance?"

"On the contrary. You can warn him I'm coming. In fact, do it as soon as possible. I want him to think about it for a while."

"Your desires are of utmost importance, Sydney."

"I'd like this appointment as soon as possible. Tonight. Now."

"That isn't possible, Sydney. We're booked tonight."

Colm's booked tonight.

A silent sob shook her shoulders.

"But what about two nights from now, darling?" Azure said. "I see Garrett has a cancellation, and I can move clients around for Colm to accommodate you." She paused. "Of course it's New Year's Eve . . ."

"I have no plans," she said, tears turning cold on her lashes as she thought about the romantic dinner she'd planned to cook for Colm at her loft. "Two nights from now will be fine."

"Splendid. My secretary will call you to arrange a time."

Sydney pressed the Off button and stood there, her chest heaving. A homeless woman passed her, matted head turning to stare at her in the purple-white light. Sydney felt naked suddenly, stripped to the bone, the way Colm had always left her feeling when his eyes slid over her. Flayed and bare. Now she knew where that ability had been honed. Azure had taught him everything he knew.

She climbed into her car, blew her nose, and wiped her eyes, resisting the urge to simply weep and weep. She would step into Colm's world, invade his soul space the way he had hers.

By God, she would bring him to his knees before this was over.

CHAPTER TWENTY-THREE

For two days, Colm's calls to Sydney went unanswered. Consternation wound around his insides at the realization that he'd already waited too long to tell her the truth. Of course he would lose her. No human being could stand such betrayal, not even a beautiful, loving spirit like Sydney. No matter the outcome, he had also made a decision about Avalon. His life was unraveling, and the line of love and trust between his heart and Amelia's would do the same. He might lose her as well, but the time was long past to cleanse himself of lies, prostrate himself before the consequences, and bear what came to pass.

At noon on New Year's Eve, he met Azure in the corridor at the back of Avalon's lobby. She was dressed in a white catsuit and diamonds, her ebony hair swinging lose around her face. She reminded him of a very beautiful, very deadly wraith.

"Welcome back at last, Colm. Tell me, are you coming to work for New Year's Eve?"

He studied her pale blue eyes. She had saved him in her own

way. As much as he wanted to hate her, he never would. "I'm out, Azure. I can't do it anymore."

Her fair features didn't change from their slight expression of forbearance. "What will you do?"

"Look for a job in something legitimate."

"I see." She paused. "Colm, my darling, we're friends, wouldn't you say?"

A faint alarm sounded in the back of his mind. "In a manner of speaking, yes."

"Then would you humor me one last time?"

"In what way?"

She folded her arms and leaned a shoulder against the brocade papered wall. "You have a special client who has come a long, long way for her moment with you. Will you meet with her tonight?"

He drew a breath and thought about the lie of omission that would soon end his relationship with Sydney. "No. I'm sorry, Azure."

"But wait. Don't you even want to know who she is?"

"I'm sure she's someone outstanding. But I'm not interested."

"Oh, I beg to differ."

Anger crept through his nerves. "I'm not in the mood to play games, Azure. I'm quitting this job, and it doesn't matter who the—"

"Would Sydney Warren persuade you?"

Colm stilled. Ice filled his being. "What?"

"Sydney has called and requested you specifically."

Oh, God. Not like this. Not like this. He stepped closer, teeth gritted, every muscle tightened. "What did you do, Azure?"

She shrugged. "Nothing she didn't ask me to do. I fit her into the schedule tonight, this night of myriad clients, because as I'm sure you can guess, she's a woman hurting."

"You told her what I am."

"No, darling. Max Beaudoin obliged you."

Of course. Somewhere deep down, Colm had known it would play out this way.

His hands clenched into fists and he whirled, looking for something to hit in substitute for Beaudoin. There was nothing except the white, brocade-covered wall, as white as the flowing dresses Azure favored.

His fist went right through it, sent plaster and dust drifting to the carpet. He hardly felt the scrapes on his knuckles.

Azure straightened and her features softened. "Don't worry about that, darling. We'll just take it out of Sydney's payment."

He closed his eyes and leaned his forehead against the marred wall, his breath rushing in and out, heart racing.

Behind him, Azure approached in silence and he jerked when she spoke softly next to his ear. "Will you meet her, Colm? I think this can't end any other way for you."

Colm wanted to die and take Beaudoin with him.

"Colm?"

It was time. Everything was unraveling, and he would stand and take the blows he deserved.

He turned his head to look at Azure. "I'll meet her," he said.

CHAPTER TWENTY-FOUR

Sydney hesitated outside the inconspicuous red-lacquered door and smoothed the front of her leather duster. She was dressed in black from head to toe, black pencil skirt and form-fitting, off-the-shoulder sweater, black thigh-high stockings, stiletto heels. Her blond hair was slicked back, her makeup applied heavier than usual. She would see Colm's whoredom and raise it a level of her own, because she had already sold her soul to love him.

She grasped the brass knocker and tapped lightly, her pulse thundering everywhere. Right away the door swung open, and a handsome, dark-haired man led the way inside the dimly lit lobby. "You're Ms. Warren?"

Lifting a hand to her throat, she nodded.

"I'm Tim," he said.

She forced a tight smile. "It's a pleasure."

"The pleasure is all mine. Let me get Azure for you. She's been awaiting your arrival."

She tried not to feel abandoned when he slipped through the vast, elegant room and disappeared down a dark corridor. Her feet felt rooted to the Persian rug as she stared at her surroundings: the Queen Anne furnishings, the brocade walls and upholstery, the massive crystal chandelier. Cherubs adorned the ceiling in swirls of pale blue skies and cotton clouds.

Across the lobby, soft voices touched her ears and she glanced sharply to the right to spot a man and woman sitting close together on an ivory, velvet-looking settee. Their lips were so close, they seemed to kiss with their low words. The woman turned her head and looked directly at Sydney, and the man followed suit, and they both smiled.

Sudden reticence crawled through Sydney. *I can't do this.* She whirled toward the door and wrapped her fingers around the brass knob, yanked at it. A draft of ghostly cold air swept in, and quickly she stepped onto the threshold—

"Sydney, darling."

Oh, God. She turned back to face Azure, who stood before her like a vision in a tight-fitting white gown with a fishtail flare at the bottom.

"Welcome to Avalon." Reaching out to grasp Sydney's hand in her cool, manicured fingers, she subtly shut the door at Sydney's back. "We're so pleased you're joining us for New Year's Eve. There will be a party later, if you care to attend after you meet with—"

"I won't be attending the party," Sydney said sharply.

Azure's crimson lips tipped up. "I see. All right then, come sign in. Just a brief contract to dot the *I*s and cross the *T*s of your arrangement."

Numb, Sydney allowed herself to be led to a Chippendale reception desk, where she accepted the pen Azure handed her. She glanced briefly over the contract and scrawled her name at the bottom, and it felt as though she had signed away her very heart all over again.

Smiling at her in an oddly triumphant fashion, Azure picked up a phone and pressed a button. "Your client has arrived," she said, and gently hung up. "Colm will be down to greet you momentarily. Would you like something to drink?"

Sydney tasted the memory of Shiraz, tasted the memory of Colm's skin . . . and shook her head.

Her gaze was drawn to the top of the staircase, where Colm had appeared from the shadows. He descended slowly, running one hand along the banister.

She swallowed hard.

"I'll leave you now," Azure said when he reached the foot of the stairs. "Enjoy your visit, Sydney."

When they were finally alone, Sydney shifted her gaze from Colm's probing one. "Let's get this over with."

He held out his hand. "Will you come upstairs?"

A millennium passed before she raised her chin and met his eyes.

And finally put her fingers in his.

Colm's apartment was elegantly decorated, all beiges and ivories, damask and suede. The king-sized bed sat high, its striped duvet adding an additional five inches of fluff.

"Want a glass of wine?" he asked, his hands clasped behind his back.

"Just water." Her parched throat grew dryer when she noticed for the first time how he was dressed, in tailored beige pants and a white button-down shirt. She'd never seen him attired so blandly, but his beauty was excruciating. The warm light from the bedside table lamps gilded the highlights in his hair and set off his pale green eyes so that they glowed preternaturally. His shirt was opened at the throat, showing just a triangle of skin, a glimpse of the tender place her lips knew so well. It occurred to her she'd seen him naked as often as she'd seen him dressed, and the thought brought a bitter laugh rising in her chest, one she swallowed. Tonight would be the last time she ever laid eyes on his bare skin . . . on him, all of him.

Colm crossed the room and retrieved a bottle of water from a small stainless steel refrigerator, poured its contents into a crystal tumbler, then returned to hand it to her.

Being careful not to touch his fingers, Sydney took it from him and sipped, her eyes avoiding his. She couldn't stand the unhappiness etched in his features. Anger began a slow curl through her senses and she turned away from him to set her drink on a low table, a fresh surge of restlessness seizing her. Tonight's plan seemed so smart at the time she concocted it, but now all she wanted was to get away, to leave the deception and agony behind, leave him behind and never look back.

No. She had to see this through. Garrett would be here soon, and she would take control and show Colm what it felt like to be gouged to the core.

Then she felt him close behind her, close enough that she imagined the heat of his body seeping through the leather of her coat. His hands rested briefly on her shoulders and she tensed, but he only slipped the coat from her arms and folded it over a nearby wingback chair.

She turned back to watch him, willing him to keep his distance.

When he said, "May I touch you?" she shook her head and tears burned her eyes.

"Do you want to talk?" he asked.

"No. I want . . ." She crossed to the table near the door where she'd left her purse, making a wide berth around him as she went. Inside the bag, she'd packed a small drawing pad and pencils. "I'm going to draw you."

Surprise lifted his eyebrows. "That's an unusual request."

"Really?" She gave a short laugh. "I find that hard to believe in a profession like yours. Doesn't anything go? Chains and whipped cream? Come on, Colm."

He dropped his head and rubbed the bridge of his nose. "I would have come to you for this, Sydney. It didn't have to be here, where Azure—"

"Money is no issue, as you must remember, and I wanted to pay for your services, as well I should. Can we get on with this?"

Colm pressed his lips together, nodded. "Where do you want me?"

"On the bed will be fine."

"Sitting?"

"Yes. Propped against the pillows."

He did as she ordered, kicked off his shoes and climbed onto the bed, where he arranged the wide pillows behind his back.

She grabbed a small gilded chair from a desk to her left and turned it to seat herself near the bed. She propped the drawing pad on her lap and began to sketch, her bottom lip caught between her teeth as her gaze flicked between Colm and the paper. All the while her heart thudded in her chest and her fingers quaked ever so slightly, enough to mar the lines so that they spread across the page in a useless scrawl.

"Are we ever going to talk again?" he asked. "Really talk?"

She stared down at the pad. "No. Never again." When she looked up, he was staring at her. She held his gaze, chin lifted, refusing to look away until her hand began to move over the pad again, laying down a haphazard sketch that reflected the chaos within her.

A tap came at the door, and immediately Sydney's pulse picked up a panicked speed.

Frowning, Colm climbed off the bed. "No one should disturb us. I apologize."

She sat in silence, watching. She couldn't see Garrett when Colm opened the door a crack, only heard the low murmur of the two men's voices before Colm swung the door open and stepped back to let Garrett in.

Colm's expression was darker than she'd ever seen it.

Good, she thought, and rose to her feet.

What the hell was going on? Colm stood aside and Garrett cast him a passing glance as he closed the door quietly behind him and crossed to greet Sydney.

She wants both of us, Garrett had told him, and Colm's mind shifted from confusion to denial as Sydney rose, smoothed the front of her pencil skirt, and offered a tight smile.

"Sydney." Garrett took her hand and brushed his lips over her knuckles. "It's a pleasure."

Anger scrabbled through Colm. "Get your hands off her," he said, barely keeping his cool. For the first time, he hated his friend. He wanted him gone.

"Don't talk to him like that," Sydney snapped. "This is what I paid for."

Colm gritted his teeth, his fingers curling into fists.

"Let's get down to business, gentlemen." She looked from one face to the other, her tone deadpan. "I started the drawing, but it's not what I want."

Colm couldn't speak. He was too busy watching the way her eyes skimmed Garrett from head to toe and back. Hungry. *As though she could eat him whole*, Beaudoin had said once, and for the first time, Colm understood his panic when Sydney observed other men.

"What do you want, Sydney?" Garrett avoided Colm as he kicked into smooth mode.

"I want you to unbutton Colm's shirt," she said.

Colm's mouth fell open.

Garrett moved before him, muttered beneath his breath, "Sorry, buddy," and skipped his fingers down Colm's shirt so fast, Colm barely had time to draw a shuddering breath.

Garrett tugged Colm's shirttails from his pants, then turned to look at Sydney. "What now?"

It took everything human in Colm to keep from knocking the other man across the room.

Sydney seated herself again, crossing one long, sleek leg over the other. Colm spied the top of her black thigh-high stocking and his rage deepened. Why the hell was she dressed like that? God, had his sins completely killed off the Sydney he'd loved?

"Now Colm unbuttons your shirt," she told Garrett. "Then he unfastens your belt."

"No," Colm said staunchly, but Sydney merely smiled.

"Don't worry. I'm only going to draw you. Remember the ménage? It wasn't so bad, was it?"

"No," Garrett said, glancing at Colm. "It wasn't bad at all, right, Colm?"

Colm just shook his head and looked down. *It's a job, just a job.* But he stood icy with shock, his hands shaking as he reached for the buttons on his friend's shirt and undid them as quickly as he could.

"Now his belt," Sydney reminded, swinging her leg, her pad poised on her lap.

For the first time Colm did as he was told without hesitation, the clink of the belt the only sound in the thick silence. When he finished, he glanced up to find Garrett watching him. Colm had never seen his friend blush before. God, this was awkward.

"Now remove the rest of your clothing and get on the bed," Sydney ordered.

The men finished undressing in silence. Garrett was the first one done and climbed onto the bed. When Colm joined him, shivering more from nerves than the cool air, they looked at Sydney, waiting to see what kind of hell she'd put them through now.

"Sit facing each other," she said. "Garrett, angle a little to hang your leg off this side of the bed, and put your hand on Colm's right thigh." She paused to watch before she added, "Higher."

Garrett's fingertips all but brushed Colm's pubic hair.

And then Colm understood. Sydney was trying to humiliate him the way she had been hurt. He had torn her to shreds, and only the deepest shame on his part would satisfy her. She would have her way. He could read the determination in the set of her chin.

He opened his mouth to stop the fiasco, but Garrett flashed him a hard look and shook his head almost imperceptibly.

Sydney flipped to a fresh page and began sketching again, those blue eyes moving back and forth from the pad to her models. If Colm didn't know her, he would have thought she was an automaton. But the fire in her eyes burned with rage, and he knew she would never forgive him for what he had done, no matter his reasons.

She worked for a while, the men sitting in utter stillness until she shifted and looked up.

"I don't like this. I want something more."

When Colm didn't speak, Garrett said huskily, "What do you want, Sydney?"

"Put your mouth on Colm's."

Colm froze. Garrett sucked in a breath. Then he leaned forward and spoke against Colm's ear. "It doesn't mean anything, James. You know it. It's all an act. Everything here is a figment of our imaginations."

Colm shook his head, but Garrett simply drew back and waited.

And Sydney waited, too, with her blank mask staring at them, gently swinging that long leg, her pencil poised above the sketch pad.

Colm closed his eyes, felt the mattress give a little as his friend leaned forward again. Garrett's breath touched Colm's lips. "Okay?" he whispered.

"Just get it the hell over with." Colm's whisper came out tortured.

Garrett carefully touched Colm's lips with his own.

"Open mouths, please," Sydney said lightly, and Garrett, mindless, uninhibited Garrett, obeyed.

Sparks of outrage flew behind Colm's eyelids. The heat of humiliation too great to bear suffused his body and he jerked away, twisted and scrambled backward until his back hit the headboard with a resounding crash.

"Jesus—Garrett." Breathing hard, he shot a glare at Sydney, who had set aside her sketch pad and was watching it all with that cool blonde impassivity. "Go downstairs and get your money back, Sydney. I won't do this for you." He glanced at Garrett. "I'm sorry."

"No, it's okay," Garrett said quickly. "Colm, it's okay." He climbed off the bed and grabbed up his clothing. "No harm done."

But he was wrong. When he'd dressed and left the room, closing the door quietly behind him, Colm jerked the sheet from the bed, wrapped it around his waist, and glared at Sydney. "Humiliation gets you off?"

"Just yours." Still no emotion, only the slightest twitch of a frown between her eyebrows.

And suddenly he was so tired. He didn't want to fight her. He wanted the game to be over. "Are we going to fuck? If not, get out." He'd never addressed any woman like that. He'd never wanted or despised a woman more.

"That's not a very nice way to speak to your clients, Colm."

"My name isn't Colm."

And then there it was at last—the shine of tears in her eyes. "Who are you, you lying bastard?"

"It doesn't matter."

"I want what I came for, damn you!"

"Then get on the bed and I'll show you what I can do. Let's make this a freebie. I'll pull out all the stops. Will that make you happy? Then you can go downstairs, lie, tell them you want your money back, that nothing happened."

"I'm not the one who's so skilled at lying. You owe me the truth, Colm. Whoever you are."

He stalked her and stopped just short of knocking her over, his hand dropping the sheet at last so he stood before her, raw and naked. "The truth? Here it is, short and sweet. I've been a prostitute at Avalon for three years. It started after my wife died in the accident. My sister—my twin—was in the car with us. She's a quadriplegic now. Paralyzed from the chest down because of her injuries."

Sydney seemed to stumble, confusion, pain, and shock crossing her features all at once, and then her expression darkened even more. "And this whorehouse is the answer to your guilt?"

"Maybe. But I needed the money for her care. Enough to accept when Max promised me double the pay if I could get you into bed."

"Bastards!" She threw her pad and pencil at him. "He's so twisted, but you're worse. You slept with me, made me believe you cared for me, but you wouldn't have told me the truth, would you? You would have kept it from me forever."

"No. I would have told you. And I would have betrayed your trust, and lost you."

"Screw you, you manipulative liar."

He stared at her. "Keep talking, Sydney. Get it all out. I'm no better than Max, or Greg, or any of the men from your past. Maybe I'm worse."

"You're right. I really hate you. I want you to see it in my face before I walk out of here." She was trembling, sobbing now. Tears burned his eyes, too, but he hardly felt them. He could only feel her rage, not his own. He was empty inside. Dulled to the pain.

"I see it," he said. "I see that and more."

"There's nothing more. This is all there is. Hate. Disgust."

"I don't believe you. You cared for me, and it's not over, Sydney. It's still happening."

She gave a harsh, choked laugh. "Oh, you are a real bastard. Were you like this in your former life? You—"

He caught her wrist in a vise grip so painful it brought a cry to her lips. "Look at us. This is exactly what Max wanted in the end. He wins." He released her and wiped his face on his naked arm. Christ, he was destroyed. He'd destroyed himself, his wife, anything of value he could have offered Amelia in her young life. And he could have stopped it. The accident, Jill's death, Amelia's suffering, the games he'd played with Sydney's heart, everything. This broken moment—none of it ever needed to happen. He'd bought into Max's game, and Max had won.

The world between them came to a standstill except for their harsh, strident breath. Down the hall, the grandfather clock chimed ten, ticking off the silent seconds to the New Year while everything they'd built between them turned to ash and blew away.

"It was a job you needed, then?" Sydney whispered, hanging her head so that her blond hair hid her tortured features. "Even when . . . even afterward? At Christmas? And this past week? Was Max paying you then, too?"

"No." His heart turned over. "Syd—"

"Don't call me that!"

"I fell for you."

"I don't believe you."

"It's true."

"So why are we here? In this place? I could have been another woman tonight. You would have slept with some other woman tonight—"

"No." He shook his head. "What few clients I've had since you and I made love I've been able to put off. I took this past week off, then I quit Avalon tonight, except for you. One last client. I owed you."

"You're a liar. How can I believe you?" she cried. "And even if it were true, there's no going back from this. When I think back to all those moments between us, those intimate moments—I feel so sick. I feel dead inside."

He thought about reaching for her hands, dropping to his knees in front of her, burying his head in her lap. He wanted her fingers in his hair. He wanted her tenderness, but she was right, he deserved nothing. Watching her retrieve her coat and grab up her purse, his pain bled him dry, leaving a skeletal heart.

"Before you leave, hear me out," he said, his voice shaking. "No more lies. Will you listen?"

Her coat hugged to her chest, she reluctantly rested her back against the door.

"My real name is James Hanford. Three years ago I put my sister in a wheelchair. She . . ."

A sob seized his chest and he shook it off. "Amelia had no money when the accident happened. No insurance. The government's help is a drop in the bucket, so I fucked my way through half this city to keep her in my home, to hire nurses, to make ends meet, to keep my soul with her instead of here. But I lost it anyway."

He lifted his head and looked at her. "I lost you. You should know, Sydney, I would have loved you."

She shifted and looked away. "I could never love a man like you."

"—James," he finished for her.

"James. You are a sad, sad man, James. I won't be dragged into your hell."

"Then you should go," he said. "Get out of here, Sydney. This is no place for you. Go home."

Her coat rustled when she slid into it. The door squeaked slightly when she opened it. Her voice cracked when she said, "Good-bye."

But he didn't look up until it closed behind her with a resounding click, leaving him alone with agonizing silence his only companion.

CHAPTER TWENTY-FIVE

Two hours into the New Year, James came downstairs. The lobby was deserted of clients. They were all upstairs getting their money's worth. Confetti and streamers littered the room, leftovers from the party. The house attendants cleaning up the mess raised their heads to look at him as he walked through the vast room for the last time. He found Azure working in her office, a single, dim lamp illuminating the file in front of her.

"It's hiring time again," she said without looking up. "What do you think, Colm? A college boy this time? Someone young and hungry?"

He sank to the chair in front of her desk and looked at her. "Anyone. Just no one like me."

"No," she said slowly. "No one like you, darling."

"I've cleared out of my room."

"Here's your share of the payment from Sydney Warren." She slid him an envelope. "I won't bother to ask you how it went. She was weeping when she came downstairs, but she paid. Fifteen hundred dollars for her time with you and Garrett. Expensive to come away so devastated." She glanced up at him and her eyes narrowed on his face. "And you, Colm? Are you devastated, too?"

He wouldn't answer. Everything inside him was knotted and sick. Instead, he opened the envelope, flipped through the bills, and handed it back to her. "Give it all to Garrett."

"Are you insane?"

"No. I'm beat." He stood and shoved his hands into his jeans pockets. "I have to thank you, Azure. It's been an interesting ride."

"Hasn't it, though?" She rose to her feet and came around the desk, and this time he didn't pull back when she kissed him. His lips twitched beneath hers, the urge to cry welling up in his chest, and then it was over. All of it.

"Oh, and Colm?" she added, stopping him at the threshold of her office.

He looked back at her. "Happy New Year."

James smiled a little. "Happy New Year. Good-bye, Azure."

He headed out of the club through the rear exit, his belongings packed into a large duffel, which he slung over his back. The night was moonless, blacker than black. He breathed deep, coatless, letting the cold wind shiver through him.

It was time to go home. Home to Amelia, to a new existence he couldn't begin to predict. All he knew was that Sydney was gone from his life, and the emptiness was greater than he knew how to bear.

The two men sat in silence, one with a beer in his hand, the other with a scotch and soda.

The dimly lit bar was sparsely populated on a Monday night, soft rock playing overhead and the low murmur of a newscaster on the LCD screen above the bar.

"Thanks for meeting me," James said.

Garrett nodded and took a drink of his scotch. "I figured we should talk at some point, but I also figured you should be the one to do the talking."

"Yeah." James cleared his throat. "I owe you an apology for what happened the other night at Avalon."

"You don't owe me anything, James."

"Yes, I do." He finally looked at Garrett, gripping his beer with both hands. "I would have beaten the hell out of you if I'd had half the chance, you know that, right?"

"Yeah, I know." Garrett gave him a sad smile. "I should have walked out, but . . . the money, you know. The job. I can't lose it."

James nodded. He understood. He'd been just as desperate that night—anything to keep from losing Sydney.

"I'm sorry you got pulled into things, though," he said. "I could have stopped it sooner, but I didn't. I wasn't thinking straight. I would have done anything she wanted for a minute there, but in the end . . ."

"I understand."

"Don't think bad of her, Garrett."

"I don't. She was one pissed-off lady, and I can't blame her."

James gave a nod and took a long pull from his beer bottle. For a moment they were silent. Then Garrett said, "Have you talked to her since . . . ?"

"No." He would never speak to her again. The realization sliced a hole through his insides and tightened his throat. "She won't ever talk to me again."

"I wouldn't call her if I were you," Garrett said, and James gave an arid laugh.

"Don't think I haven't considered it about once every five minutes."

"You've got it bad for her, huh?"

"Something like that. Something mindless just like that."

"What's your plan, then?"

"No plan." James took a swig of beer and swallowed. "Just put one foot in front of the other until I'm done slamming doors and burning bridges."

"Look, James." Garrett leaned on an elbow and ducked his head to catch James's gaze. "For the last three years you did what you thought was right. When you came to Avalon, you were desperate and broke with a wheelchair-bound sister you couldn't afford to care for."

"Some kind of blessing Avalon was, huh?" James finished his beer and gave the bottle a restless nudge.

"It was, in the beginning. Don't knock it. You earned that money for Amelia, and along the way figured out some things about yourself—starting with, you're not meant to be a male whore."

"True." James half laughed. "Then what the hell am I?"

"An architect. Look, buddy, you've faced the impossible before. Here you are again, same scenario. Find a way to earn a living with what you know best and take care of your sister. Maybe this time, you'll find something that won't strip your dignity away."

They fell quiet again until Garrett said, "I'm going to miss you. At Avalon, I mean." As soon as the words were out, he drained his glass and motioned to the bartender for another drink.

James's chest ached. "Yeah. But we'll stay in touch."

"Good." Garrett grinned. "So after that night with Sydney . . . we're okay here?"

"We're okay."

"Let's hug."

"Touch me and you're dead," James said, and this time they both laughed.

*   *   *

Coming clean was a new experience for James. He'd lost Sydney, cast off Avalon, and now it was time to face Amelia. He owed her the truth more than he owed anyone. How he was going to take care of her when the savings ran out, he didn't know. He only knew the right thing to do—tap into honesty and take the bitter medicine.

On a crisp January day, he wheeled her out into the afternoon sun, its rays seeping through his jacket, and parked her where she could look out over the lawn. He tucked and re-tucked the blanket around her, paced, and came back to face her.

"What is wrong with you?" she asked finally. "You're acting like you've got ants in your pants."

For a long time he didn't say anything, then he grabbed a nearby patio chair, set it backward before her, and straddled it. "There's something I'm going to tell you, and I'd rather you hear it from me than from someone else. Not that you would, but . . . it needs to come from me."

"Should I be worried?" she asked, with a smile that didn't reach her eyes.

"No." He rubbed his hands on his denim-covered thighs. "I should. You're not going to like me anymore after this."

"Stop scaring me."

"Okay. Look . . ." He licked his lips. "I—"

"Take off your sunglasses so I can see your eyes."

Jesus. They were his last bit of armor. He removed them, methodically folded and slipped them inside his jacket. Then he leveled his gaze on hers with all the courage he could muster. "You know how I work a lot at night? And I'm gone for weekends a lot, and sometimes for days?"

Her frown stole the sunshine from the afternoon, replaced it with roiling clouds of doom. "You've been lying about it?"

He nodded, withdrew his glasses from his pocket, fiddled with them. Tucked them away again. And then he braced his hands on his knees and said, "Yes. Lies. All of it."

"So what have you really been doing?" A vague, hopeful smile, the silence before the storm, crossed her cold-flushed features. "Exotic dancing?"

"Worse." He drew a breath, tried to swallow and couldn't. "I've been working in a women's pleasure club."

For a moment her expression was a total blank. Then she burst out laughing. "You are so full of it. Even though this joke's sort of cruel. You've gotten really twisted in your old age—"

"I'm telling you the truth, Amie." He reached beneath the blanket for her limp hand. "It's an underground club in D.C. called Avalon. I have—had—an apartment there where I entertained clients."

All humor fled her features. "You're serious."

He exhaled and closed his eyes.

She didn't speak for so long, he thought he'd imagined the whole conversation. Just another nightmare and then he would wake up. But this was no dream. The tears in her eyes spoke for her until she managed, "Don't tell me you're doing this because the pay is great."

His fingers closed tighter around her hand. "Amie—"

"The pay is great to keep me out of a nursing home?"

"The pay is good for a lot of reasons."

"Are you punishing yourself?"

"I don't know. Amie. . . ."

"Don't touch me." No doubt she would have ripped her hand from his if she had the choice.

"I deserve your contempt," he said, regret burning his insides.

"At first I gave myself no choice in this job. But then it became part of who I was. And now . . . I don't know who I am."

"I can tell you. You're no brother of mine," she snapped. "I hate you for making me the source of your pain. And don't deny such a job isn't painful. You think you've helped me, but it was selfish, James. Selfish."

She was right. He lowered his head and rubbed the aching space between his brows.

"Well," she said, "now that you've cleansed your soul to me, I should tell you that you can cast off your damned hair shirt. Roger wants me to move in with him." At his stunned silence, she went on, her face darker than he'd ever seen it. "You think you're all I have in this world, James, but you're wrong. You can't stand like the concrete wall you are between me and a real life. Roger and I still love each other. The wheelchair hasn't stopped that."

He couldn't think of anything to say except, "He left you after the accident. He left you alone and hurt, Amie."

"And now he's changed, and I have, too. No—I take that back. I'm the same person I was before the accident, except my limbs don't work. But everything in me is the same. I deserve as normal a life as possible, damn you."

"But how can he possibly take care of—?"

"How can he possibly give me the care you've provided? I would never have accepted your brand of help if I'd known what you were doing to yourself. You knew that all along, James. So you lied to me. You made me part of your unhappiness, and I don't know if I can forgive you." She was crying now, hard. James's throat was tight, too. He closed his eyes again and swallowed his pain.

"Roger knows what I need, and we're deciding together how to go about it. So you're likely off the hook. You can stop being a . . . a gigolo, or whatever you call it."

He gave a defeated nod and got to his feet. "For what it's worth, I've given it up."

"That doesn't do much to help," she said wearily. "You and your darkness. It's always been the worst part of you."

He wiped his eyes and gazed down at her. She was formidable in that wheelchair. She made Max Beaudoin seem like an invalid inside and out. Amelia was the strongest person he knew. "I'm sorry, Amelia. So sorry. I didn't mean to hurt you."

"I love you," she wept. "But you have to stop. Stop hurting the people around you and stop hurting yourself. Who will you have in the end? No one. Not even me, who you thought would be by your side forever."

He laid a hand on her head in silence, and her lashes fluttered closed, her face wet with tears. Then he left her alone in turmoil for all he'd told her. And realized . . . all along, he'd needed her far more than she'd ever needed him.

Who knew the passage of time would move so slowly, or that joy would bleed, drop by drop, out of everything Sydney reveled in? Paintings, the ones she did for the sheer joy of the art, sat untouched in her studio. Even the charity shows had lost their satisfaction. She dutifully attended one or two and ended up with a commission for the president of a corporation and one of two unruly children who preferred scampering around her studio to sitting still. She ended up snapping a few cursory photos of them to finish the picture, and when she was done, she took a break from public events in general.

For a couple of weeks, sitting on her sofa in her pajamas and staring out the window in bleak despair became her choice of self-indulgence, but then she rediscovered her anger and went back to work, breaking out of the seclusion and recognizing it for its ability to heal.

She wouldn't allow herself to wonder where he was, what he was doing. Had he really left Avalon? For the first time Sydney thought hard about the situation with his sister, how he'd struggled to take care of her, and a twinge of compassion pierced her. But no . . . her propensity for empathy had always led nowhere. She was empty inside where he was concerned, and she would get over him if it was the last thing she ever did.

Two months to the night the world had dropped through the floor, a knock came at the door. She had finished the children's portrait and was washing her brushes in the bathroom sink when she heard it. Memories of Colm—James—admonishing her to be safe flashed through her mind, and whoever this was had found his way into her building without being buzzed up. She gingerly tiptoed across the apartment to the door, leaned against it and demanded, "Who is it?"

"It's Hans," came a faint, accented voice from the hallway.

Hans? She unbolted the locks and swung the door open. Indeed it was Hans, dressed in jeans and a Washington Redskins sweatshirt. For once his sandy hair wasn't neatly combed back from his patrician face, but fell over his forehead. He looked . . . normal and relaxed.

"Hans," she exclaimed. "What are you doing here?"

"I have something for you," he said, polite as always. "May I come in? I'll only take a moment of your time."

Sydney stepped back and gestured him into the living room, her gaze dropping to the rectangular canvas wrapped in brown paper he held under one arm.

"Max is turning your studio into a garage for his motorcycle collection," he said, his tone dry. "He's not selling the estate after all."

"He . . . what?" She stared at him, her lips parted. "What is he doing with motorcycles?"

"Gazing at them lovingly, I suspect." Hans set the canvas against a nearby wall. "It's sad, really. He's a sad man. He spends a lot of time alone these days, but seems to prefer his own company to anyone else's."

Sydney wouldn't allow herself to feel sorry for him, damn it, any more than she did for Colm.

Hans didn't wait for her acid response before he added, "I was clearing out the few items remaining, and found this painting in the studio closet. It occurred to me you may have accidently left it behind."

She approached it with some reticence, already guessing what it was, and carefully stripped the brown paper away. "It was no accident," she said softly.

Colm gazed back at her, pale green eyes alive, skin luminescent, face half in shadow, displaying both sides of him: the Colm she had known, and the dark truth she didn't all those months ago when her brush stroked the paint on the canvas.

"Take it back," she told Hans when she found her voice. "I don't want it."

"I'm sorry, but no," he said in a staunch voice she'd never heard from him before. "Pardon me for saying so, but I think if you keep it for a few days, you'll change your mind. It's some of your finest work."

Sydney turned away from it, wrapping her arms around herself. "We'll see." Then, because she knew the two men had developed a friendship, she asked, "How is he? Colm, I mean."

"His name is James Hanford."

She waved a hand as if the truth didn't matter, as if that name didn't race through her and quicken her heart.

"Filled with regret," Hans went on. "Destroyed by it, frankly. But then, I'm sure you knew that."

"I truly don't believe it."

"Sydney," he said gently, "The time for lies is over, I believe."

She heard his double meaning, dropped her head, and closed her eyes. "Does he tell you this, Hans? That he's unhappy?"

"The few times I've seen him, no. But I can read it in him. He doesn't look good." Hans stared her up and down. "And if you won't take offense, I would say the same about you."

His comment stung. "And the fact that I don't look good means I should throw aside my . . . my betrayal and run back to him? I don't think so. He's a prostitute, Hans. Did you know that when he was out at the estate?"

"I did not," Hans replied. "Only after you left did Max mention it. He actually admitted to what he'd done. The only reason I remain on with him is that he doesn't really have anyone else. Clients he represents, certainly, but no one to call family."

"What Max did was evil."

"Yes, Sydney. And James was a pawn, as were you. The difference is that he's right to regret his actions, and you're not. You did nothing wrong in your relationship with him."

Who was this brutally straightforward man standing before her? She loved him as much as she hated him. He was indeed a friend.

She cleared her throat, her words caught in confusion and sadness. "Thank you for the painting, Hans."

"It was my pleasure, Sydney." He glanced at the rendering of Colm's face and added, "If you don't mind my saying so—and despite everything—I found him to be one of the finer men I've known. His error was enormous, and he's paid a heavy price by losing you."

She merely looked at him, so he went on. "I don't know how to reach him any longer. After the last time I saw him, he moved on from his, ah, former place of employment, but to where, I don't know."

"It doesn't matter," she said. "I won't be seeing him."

Hans merely smiled and stepped out into the hallway. "We all make mistakes, Sydney. All our lives. It's only forgiveness that gives us the impetus to continue on."

"Thank you, Hans . . . for . . ." Tears burned her eyes and choked her words. "Thank you."

He nodded, and she gently shut the door after him.

CHAPTER TWENTY-SIX

For a full week, she kept the portrait turned to the wall. She painted, created new works, participated in a show, and returned home to find the picture waiting patiently for her. At some godforsaken hour, after a restless night, she climbed out of bed and crossed the living room to finally look it over. Holding it gingerly, she turned it around and lifted it to her easel.

The painting remained undone, but the outline of the pose was there, the utter seductiveness of him, the way he had looked the last time he'd been in her studio out at the estate—the first time she'd put her hands on him and brought him pleasure.

She snatched it up, ready to toss it aside in a fit of frustration . . . but then she stopped. He looked at her from the depths of the canvas, the way he used to watch her when she painted him. Deeper, even. Deeper. Nostalgia speared straight through her and she sank to the floor holding it before her, cursing the man in the portrait and reliving every moment between them, because she hadn't forgotten a single second.

"Truth or dare, Sydney?" she murmured, wiping her eyes on the sleeve of her nightshirt. Truth. *You want to find him, to start over, to forgive, to give both of you, as Hans said, the impetus to continue in this life.*

She would find him, but how? Hans didn't know. Sydney had long since deleted his cell number from her phone, and she knew he wasn't listed. Not long ago, on a dark, lonely night when she couldn't sleep, she'd spent a few pathetic moments perusing the phone book for his name. Just for curiosity's sake, she'd told herself at the time, but had come up empty.

There was only one way to track him down.

Hopping to her feet, she crossed to the kitchen and rifled through a drawer to pull out her address book. Tucked inside the book, in all its engraved glory, was Azure Elan's card, the one Max had given her on that awful night so long ago.

Azure would know where to find Colm.

It was one o'clock in the morning.

Sydney didn't care if she woke the woman from a coma.

To her amazement, Azure picked up on the second ring, her voice not sleep-fogged, but crystalline, smooth.

"Ah, Sydney," she cooed. "What a joy to hear from you after so long."

Torn between a surge of old anger and new relief, Sydney said, "I'm sure you wonder what I'm doing calling at this late hour."

"You don't wake a child of the night." Azure gave a pointed pause. "Tell me, darling, are you calling for Colm?"

"I don't know how else to find him."

"Much to my regret, Colm has left Avalon. Had you heard?"

"I'd heard."

"I see."

"Do you know where he is, Azure?"

"Hmm." Sydney could imagine Azure tapping one crimson fingernail against her lips. "I believe he's hung out his shingle as an architect. Does that help?"

"Yes." Sydney released the breath she'd been holding. "But do you . . . have his phone number?"

"Let me see what I can do." Azure laid down the phone with a soft thud and didn't return for a long time. The low murmur of voices reached Sydney's ears through the phone. Time ticked by, second after painful second. Just when she was ready to give up, Azure returned. "Forgive me, darling. We're busy at this time of night."

"Of course. I'm sorry for my timing."

"Don't apologize. But you do know, Sydney, it's against policy to give out a companion's contact number, no matter that he's no longer employed with us."

Sydney gritted her teeth. "How much do you want?"

Azure laughed, a light sound that trickled down Sydney's spine. "Oh, Sydney, there's no charge. I just want you to be aware that what we're doing is a no-no. And I'm assuming you deleted his cell phone number from your records in a fit of rage, so you've had it before."

"That's right." *Please, God, get on with it.*

Azure gave her the number at last.

"Thank you," Sydney said, loathe to talk to the woman any longer. "I do have one more question."

"What's that, dearest?"

"The night you confirmed that Colm worked for you, you said he was there with a client and couldn't come to the phone."

"I hardly recall."

"Was it a lie?"

Please tell me it was a lie.

"Maybe a tiny one," Azure said. "At that time, I was trying to protect him. Will you forgive me?"

Never. Sydney didn't reply.

But Azure wasn't finished. "Forgiveness is a lovely thing, isn't it? And Colm is so deserving, darling. Good luck to you both."

Sydney hung up and stared at the phone. What in God's name had she just done to herself?

By Saturday afternoon, she'd nearly worn a groove in the living room floor from pacing. She crossed the expanse of her loft a few more times, then stopped, and in a fit of courage, tapped out the cell phone number she'd played and replayed in her head for the last month like the lyrics to a song. Her heart threatened to leap through bone, muscle, and skin as she listened to the ring. *One. Two. Three.*

On the fourth ring, to her disappointment, his voice mail picked up.

"You've reached James Hanford. Leave your name and a brief message. I'll get back to you as soon as possible."

She nearly missed the beep as that wonderful voice washed over her. Clearing her throat, she said, "James"—it was so strange to call him that—"this is Sydney." Her gaze darted to the unfinished portrait. "I have something that belongs to you. Give me a call if you can. I'm home tonight."

Sydney had just stepped out of the shower when the phone rang. She grabbed a towel and dashed, dripping and shivering, to snatch it from the living room table. "Hello?" she said breathlessly.

"Hello, Sydney."

Colm. No, *James.*

She couldn't speak, so she waited, her eyes closed, trembling as water slid down her back and legs to pool on the floor.

"I got your message," he said, his voice huskier than she remembered it. "You said you have something that belongs to me?"

"That's right." She bit her lip to keep from telling him what it was.

"My toothbrush?" he asked solemnly, and she almost laughed. Almost.

"I'd rather see whatever it is in person," he added. "I'll pick it up."

"No," she said.

He hesitated. "No?"

"I mean, I'd like to bring it to you." *See where you live. Meet James Hanford without the lies and pain between us.*

"I live in Silver Spring," he said.

"I remember."

"It's a hefty drive for you."

"That's my problem," she said archly. She heard him blow out a breath and quickly tempered her tone. "I mean . . . I'd rather just bring it out to you, if that's okay."

"It's fine. My address is 4212 Kepler—"

"Hold on, I need to find something to write on."

She skidded naked and wet across the floor in search of a pen and pad, found them, and jotted down the information when he gave it again.

"Got it?" he asked.

"I've got it." She drew a breath and released it, the heat of memories thawing her despite the draft. "James?"

"Yeah?"

"Nothing," she said. "Just wanted to try it on for size."

His smile softened his voice. "What do you think?"

"It feels strange."

"The truth feels strange between us."

"Yes."

"Not all of it was a lie."

Here came the trembling again. A mixture of remorse and lingering doubt threaded through her, but she would battle it with the courage Hans had instilled in her. It was time to set her life right again. "When should I come?"

"How about tomorrow morning? Ten o'clock?"

She straightened, her gaze straying to the kitchen where they'd made love the first time. "That will be fine."

"It'll be good to see you again, Syd," he said.

"See you tomorrow, James." She pushed the End button and drifted back to the bathroom to dry off and brush the tangles from her hair, to study the woman in the reflection with the flushed cheeks and uncertain smile. She didn't know her, but she wanted to.

It was this same strange woman who drew on sweats and curled up on the sofa with cell phone in hand to make another call, this one to information. And when she had the number she needed, she dialed without hesitation, her pulse hammering.

The voice that answered sounded only vaguely familiar.

"May I speak with Hannah Watson?" she asked hesitantly.

"This is Hannah. Who is this?"

Sydney closed her eyes. "Hello, Mom," she said.

The redbrick house on Kepler Street was a bungalow, its landscaping winter-dry but immaculate. Sydney pulled into the driveway behind James's SUV, then changed her mind and backed out to park on the street, arranging for an escape if need be. She turned off the engine and sat in the silence for a moment, breathing deep and trying to calm her nerves. Flipping down the visor, she checked her appearance in the mirror and found she looked fresh and relaxed, almost soft. For a woman whose heart was in her throat, it came as a surprise.

Her knees felt weak, her stomach a little light and floaty as she crossed the recently swept sidewalk and climbed the stairs to the small front landing. She gave the door a polite knock, which sounded preternaturally loud, and waited, clutching the wrapped portrait, hardly hearing the sweet song of winter birds in the front yard's maple tree.

She waited.

And waited.

Knocking again lightly, she stood there and bit her lip, doubt filling her. This was a bad idea, a sign from God to get out of there while the going was good. But before she could turn and flee, the door swung open, and there he was. James Hanford, regarding her with that old, faint smile and those pale, beautiful eyes.

Colm Hennessy was gone. Here stood someone she didn't know. She wondered if he was thinking the same thing about her as his gaze searched her face and he said, "Sydney Warren."

She cleared her throat. There was no more room for untruths. "It's actually Sydney Watson. I renamed myself when I moved to Washington as a teenager."

He stared at her for a moment before his smile widened. "I see. Well, then, Sydney Watson, would you like to come in?"

She stepped past him and into the living room, where a crackling fire lent a comforting warmth. The room held a beige chenille sofa and two overstuffed chairs in patterns of tan and brown. A bit monochromatic but handsome, not so different from his apartment at Avalon.

Sydney didn't want to think of that awful night. The man standing before her wasn't the same person any longer. She found him watching her with mild amusement curving his mouth when she finished her examination of the living room.

"What do you think?" he asked.

"It's lovely. I mean, you know, masculine."

"My sister left and took all her girly-ness with her, thank God."

The sister in the wheelchair, the one he'd given himself away to protect? "Where did she go?"

"She's moved in with the man she's going to marry."

Sydney's eyebrows went up. "How wonderful for her. Does she still have the same care you provided her?"

"Her fiancé is a millionaire. How's that for kismet?"

She laughed a little. "The universe works in mysterious ways."

"And she's crazy-happy." He looked down. "I'm finally happy for her. For a while there, I didn't trust the guy she's marrying. They were involved before the accident and after she was injured, he left her. And then this winter, he came back. After everything with you, I realized . . . who am I to judge him?"

Sydney stood there with the portrait hugged to her chest, not trusting herself to speak. She didn't want to talk. She wanted to drink him in, this stranger. He looked like Colm, and yet he didn't. His face was leaner, as though he'd come through a terrible storm, but his eyes were the same: unique, deep searching.

"Come this way," he said, when he seemed to figure out she wasn't going to respond to his statement.

She followed him past a short corridor and into a surprisingly spacious kitchen.

"And this is where I nuke my frozen dinners," he said with a sweeping gesture. "Would you like a drink? Tea? Coffee? Shiraz?"

She found herself laughing, something she'd begun to think would never happen again, and certainly not with James. "Bad things happen when I drink Shiraz."

He glanced at her as he withdrew a glass from a cabinet. "Good things, too." Before she could react, he held up the glass in question.

"Just water." Her stomach was too knotted to handle anything else. She watched him move to the refrigerator, taking in the deep brown Henley shirt stretched over his broad shoulders, the smooth fit of his jeans faded in all the right places. He was barefoot. Something about those naked feet sent a spiral of desire twisting through her.

God, she needed to talk, to move, to do something and distract herself from the delectable sight of him. Leaning against the counter, she laid the portrait atop it and said, "I have your painting."

He turned to hand her the glass of water. "My painting?"

"Your portrait."

She couldn't read his face as he studied the wrapped frame for a moment, then slid it closer and carefully removed the brown paper.

For a long time he looked at it, his lashes moving as his gaze searched it, and she waited, her breath caught in her throat. When he finally looked up at her, his eyes were unnaturally bright. "This is someone from forever ago."

"I know," she said softly. "I thought maybe you'd forgotten him by now."

"No. There'll be no sweeping him under the rug." He pushed a hand through his hair, ruffling it. "I've forgiven myself for the mistakes I made, but I'll never forget them."

"I've done the same," Sydney told him. "The past is behind me, but just a spark of it stays with me. A kind of warning, I guess."

"I blame myself for that," he said softly.

"Don't. It will always be that way, even if I hadn't met you." She braced her elbows on the counter and drew a breath. "I did something really scary after I talked to you the other day. I called my mother. After fourteen years, I talked to her."

He touched the sleeve of her coat with a single finger, rubbed the edge, a comforting gesture. "How did it go?"

"It wasn't exactly the joyous homecoming of a lifetime." She stopped. "That's not exactly true. It was a start. She's mellowed a lot, and admitted she made mistakes with me. She has regrets, too. This world seems so full of them."

"Are you going back to see her?"

Sydney shook her head. "She might come here this summer, but I can't go back there. Like I said, the past is behind me. So is Nebraska."

"I'm proud of you for calling her. That took a lot of courage." The tenderness in his voice surprised and moved her. What he thought still mattered to her. Everything about him mattered.

"So did your leaving Avalon," she said.

Two lines appeared between his brows. "It had ended long before I quit, Sydney. I couldn't stand another minute after you left. Who told you?"

"Azure. She said you're working as an architect."

"Hmm." Arid humor tugged at his mouth. "I don't know how she heard that, unless it was from Garrett. She has her thumb on everyone's pulse, I guess."

"Is it true, then?"

"Azure is always right."

Sydney laughed a little before she said, "I came away from my conversation with her thinking she cares about you."

"She loves all her boys."

Neither of them spoke for a long time, James examining the portrait again while Sydney stood across from him, taking in the wave of hair that fell over his forehead, the straight nose, the sensitive mouth. Ten minutes in his presence and she was falling again, but this time she didn't berate herself. She simply let the feelings wash over her, the freed soul of her speaking its truth at last.

After a while he looked up and grinned. "I was naked a lot when I worked with you."

"Weren't you used to it?"

His eyebrows went up and she hurried, "Modeling, I mean. Naked. Ugh."

She felt like a complete idiot until he looked away, a flush warming his cheeks. She'd never seen him blush before, and she liked his vulnerability. The last of the polish about him, the part she'd never been able to quite touch, fell away. Colm was truly gone.

"This portrait's not finished," he said finally.

Folding her arms on the countertop, she let her gaze drift over his face. "Does that bother you?"

"Well—shouldn't you finish it?"

Sydney hesitated. "What do you propose?"

He gave a one-shouldered shrug. "We could finish it together."

"You mean . . . at my place?"

His smile held the slight quirk of humor she'd so missed. "We could do it here, but somehow I don't think you brought your paints."

"My studio would be best." God . . . what was she doing? She'd come here to resolve the last of her past. In truth, though, she'd known somewhere deep down that he would draw her close again, and oh, she'd craved it.

She glanced at her watch. "I'll be at my place this afternoon. Can you meet me?"

"Sure." He watched her straighten from her leaning position on the counter and finally came around to meet her. "How about four?"

They walked together to the front door, Sydney loathing to leave him even for a few hours. What would she do this time if their relationship blew up in her face? Could she—would she—ever trust him again?

She was borrowing trouble. Nothing about this arrangement meant a reconciliation, and the thought both distressed and relieved her.

They stood too close on the small landing, the breeze nipping at her cheeks.

"I'll see you at your place at four," he murmured.

Sydney nodded, zipped her coat, and headed down the steps, ever aware of his steady regard behind her. When she pulled her car away from the curb, he was still standing with the door open, watching her go.

CHAPTER TWENTY-SEVEN

Anice lady in a fedora let James into Sydney's building, saving him from being buzzed up. *Not safe*, he thought, but caught the door she held for him.

He let her go into the elevator without him and stood outside it for a long while after it closed, the portrait held tight under his arm. He hadn't been able to read Sydney when she was at his house, but he liked having her there. She fit in, he'd thought as he leaned against the counter across from her, both of them looking at the half-finished portrait she'd painted. She fit into his life. There was room only for her.

But that morning she'd been inscrutable, the way she was the first time he met her, and God, he wanted her. It washed him in waves now as he studied the elevator, wondering if this was the worst idea ever.

The building's entry doors swung open behind him, ushering in a cold draft and snapping him to life. A woman with a little boy offered a polite smile and stepped around him to let her child press the elevator's Up button. Before James could ruminate further, he stepped onto the elevator after them and pushed three. Nervousness had him by the throat, but he swallowed the feelings and glanced down at the boy, who was staring at him in that uninhibited, eerily perceptive way of children.

"Hi," James said. The child didn't reply.

"I see you have a canvas," the woman's cheerful voice came too loud in the enclosed space. Her perfume was strong, too. It reminded James of fruit cocktail and Avalon.

"Are you involved with the artist who lives on the third floor?" she asked.

Involved? Hell, yes. Every aching cell of his heart.

"I meant to say are you working with her?" the woman rushed on. "She let me come in once and see her studio. She's so talented."

"Yes, she is." He smiled. "And yes, I'm working with her."

The elevator arrived at Sydney's floor. James touched the boy's head and stepped off. The doors slid closed behind him and he followed the short corridor to the door on the right.

For the week they'd been lovers, Sydney had insisted he keep the key. He'd never given it back, taking it out frequently to torture himself with the memories. They'd lived a lifetime in that one week.

Now he knocked lightly and waited, vaguely aware of the sound of someone's music coming from another apartment. Coldplay. He grinned to himself but sobered when Sydney swung open the door.

"You're right on time," she said, her expression pleasant but distant. "I like that about you. Come in."

There was a time he'd stepped through the door, whirled her against the wall, and made love to her, no holds barred. But times had changed. He had no idea what to expect.

He moved inside and glanced around. The Christmas tree they'd decorated was long gone. The living room looked naked without it.

"Come to my studio." She crossed the floor, slowing as they passed the kitchen. "Are you thirsty?"

"I'm fine."

She took the portrait from him, unwrapped it, and set it on an easel. A few feet away was a small platform draped in black cloth.

"It's kind of cold in here," she said as he sat on the edge to remove his shoes and socks. "Need a heater?"

"I'm fine." He was short on words. *I'm fine* was all he'd said since walking into her apartment. They were both acting so awkward, he could barely stand it.

"Want me to get naked?" he asked bluntly to break the ice.

Her eyes widened a little, the only shift in her expression. "Just your shirt. Same as the old days."

While he tugged his shirt from the waistband of his jeans and drew it up and over his head, he glanced at her. Her blue eyes were averted. She sat in utter stillness, the palette of paint clutched in her hands, looking everywhere but at him. The same remote woman he'd met that October night at the gallery opening.

"Jeans, too?" he asked, his hand hovering over his fly.

"Unbutton them, but not . . ." She flushed and looked at him. "You know. Just like before. Lean back on your elbows, jeans undone, one leg hanging off the side of the platform."

He did as instructed, then waited.

Her throat moved when she swallowed and picked up her brush. For the first time James noticed she had Diana Krall on the stereo, a soft croon that soothed the senses.

Sydney worked in silence, and he began to relax, muscle by muscle. The air in the studio was too cool, but he welcomed it on his heated skin.

After a while she said, "James?"

"Yeah?"

"Want to play a game?"

He smiled at her, but her features held no humor in return. His heart took a leap. "Truth," he said, guessing her thoughts.

She continued to paint, a faint frown knitting her brows. "Did you know the truth would be so destructive?"

"Yes." Their eyes collided. "I didn't want to hurt you. I didn't want to lose you."

"You tore me up."

He looked down. "I know."

"I hurt you, too. I hated myself that night."

"Not as much as you hated me."

"More, James. Much more." Tears sparkled on her lashes, but she gave a small laugh and dashed her hand against her eyes. "I'm sorry for what I did to you."

"I'm sorry for how much I hurt you." He sat up, then thought better and stood, hitching his jeans up around his hips. "Are we still playing, Sydney?"

She shook her head. "No more games."

He took a step toward her. "Forgive me," he whispered.

"I do," she said, and slid off the barstool to meet him halfway at last.

S ydney held perfectly still, trembling as he leaned forward and brushed his lips oh so softly against her cheek. He drew back a couple of inches to meet her eyes, his own a turbulent, darker green.

"I still want you," she whispered, laying a hand over his naked, thudding heart.

"I want you, too." His fingers caressed her hair, his thumbs sliding along her jaw to tilt her face upward. "Should we forgive each other, then?"

She nodded, her breath coming faster as he leaned toward her again and this time kissed her lips once—and waited for her rejection. When it didn't come, he kissed her again, and made a low sound of satisfaction when her mouth opened beneath his.

"I missed you," he whispered between hungry kisses. "God, I missed you so much."

"I missed you."

"Can I hold you?"

"Please," she said, her cheek coming to rest against his hard shoulder, and his arms slid around her to enfold her in sinuous warmth.

This time when he kissed her, she tasted him, and he tasted like Colm Hennessy, but hotter, softer. His tongue was gentle in her mouth, drawing her out, and suddenly desire seized her like nothing she'd ever known. She dug her fingers into his shoulders, feeling the resilient muscle beneath her fingertips. "Make love to me."

He lifted her until her legs wrapped around his waist and walked her, their mouths fused together, to the bed, where he laid her on the mattress and followed her down.

Her palms slid over his bare chest, down his stomach, and he raised himself above her to give her room to caress him, his head lowered to watch her fingers move on his skin.

"I thought of this so many times," he whispered. "Your hands on me."

"I thought of it, too. Too much, I think."

She pushed down his jeans and he lifted his hips to accommodate her, laughing breathlessly when she said, "Commando, I see."

"To finish the portrait, but also for you. I didn't know if . . . but I hoped."

"I didn't know either. But now I've never been more sure."

Her heart took a leap when she realized he was trembling as

hard as she was. He sat up and drew her up with him to tug her silk blouse free from her pants. His fingers skipped down the covered buttons, freeing them one by one, and when she shrugged out of it, he covered her breasts with his palms.

"You're so beautiful."

For him. Only for him.

He let his fingers trace the curves of her breasts, his thumbs brushing her nipples through her lace demi-cup bra until they stood erect. At the same time she drifted a hand down and touched the hot, hard part of him she craved.

When he groaned and his head listed to the side, she smiled in triumph. "You're beautiful, too." She stroked him, base to tip, squeezing slightly, until he sucked in a breath and bit his lip.

Then, to his utter frustration, she slid from under him and stood beside the bed, her fingers lingering on the button of her pants.

James watched her, his gaze heavy-lidded, as she undid the fastening and pushed down her slacks, slow, taking her panties with them, and then undid her bra and let it slide, teasing, languid, from her arms.

Heart pounding, he held out a hand to her and she took it, letting him lead her back to him. He would have drawn her beneath him again, but she shook her head and rose over him, strong and hungry, and settled herself above him.

Together they reached down to poise the tip of him against her . . . and frustration froze him. He closed his eyes and groaned, "Wait. Condom. And I don't have any."

Leaning as far to the right as she could without unseating herself, she reached into the bedside drawer and withdrew a packet. "You're not the only one who comes prepared."

His frown darkened. "I have no right to say this to you, everything considered, but . . ."

"But?" She smiled, knowing what would come next.

"I'll kill anyone who touched you while you were away from me."

Sydney laughed and brushed her mouth over his. "I bought them for you months ago. I was tired of you digging in your wallet."

Breathing strident, he reached between them, tore open the packet, and rolled the condom down his erection while she watched.

"Oh, James," she said, her voice hushed. "You're so hard."

"For you. Hurry."

She straddled him again, and with his hands bracing her waist, she slid down and he pushed up, and they met in the middle of ecstasy too long anticipated.

She moved on him, undulating slow and languorous. He slid his fingers through hers and held her arms out to the sides, his gaze hot with desire as it raked her breasts, her stomach, down to where their flesh met so perfectly.

With a desperate laugh, James seized her waist and stilled her. "Stop . . . I'm going to come if we don't stop for a second."

She paused on the edge of climax, breathing fast, and smiled down at him. She loved his pleasure, his sweet agony. She would do anything he asked, even wait, knowing the delay would propel them into release.

After a moment he lifted his hips and they moved again, faster now, harder, until they danced like a well-oiled machine, and desire became a wild sort of pleasure-pain. This time he didn't stop her when she tumbled over the precipice, crying his name. When she fell forward he caught her, clutching her close as he rolled her beneath him and thrust into her over and over. The pleasure built in her again and another orgasm rolled through her, and this time James let go of his control. She clung to his back and held him tight through the shudders that seized his body, her kiss swallowing the desperate sounds he made.

The sinking sun cast a red-gold light through the wide factory windows, painting their bodies with an ethereal glow when Sydney finally stirred and rose up on an elbow to look at him.

He was watching her, his green eyes drowsy. "Hi," he said.

"Hi." She leaned in to brush his mouth with hers and found herself drawn into another full-fledged, ravenous kiss. And oh, the hunger. She'd never be able to get enough of him.

"Cold?" He reached down and drew the covers over both of them before settling her against him, her cheek to his chest where she could listen to the easy rhythm of his heart.

"I can't believe you're here," she said sleepily.

"Me either. I didn't let myself think about it until I got your phone call. And even then I couldn't tell what you wanted."

"I wanted this. I wanted you."

"Ah, Sydney," he whispered, stroking her hair. "I'm falling all over again."

She swallowed and pressed a kiss to his warm skin, too filled with joy to form words. She was falling herself, this time for a man named James whose secrets were hers, too, to keep.

"Will you trust me again, Syd?" he asked. "Believe in me?"

"I think so." She scooted up to look into his eyes. "It might take me awhile."

"We have time." He gave her an easy smile, though she felt the tension tightening his muscles. "Let's start over, you and I."

This was the moment to let him go, to escape the chance for more sadness, more hurt. But in all her thirty years she'd learned that happiness was a fleeting state, just like grief, and the only promise was peace, if she would allow it to suffuse her. And it did. The fear simply dissolved, replaced by the beginning threads of love and hope as she shifted over him and kissed him again, softly, with tongue and delight.

He blew out a breath of relief. "We'll take it slow, okay? One day at a time."

She smiled at him. "We have to. I don't know James Hanford."

"I don't know Sydney Watson."

"It's a pleasure to finally meet you," she said.

ABOUT THE AUTHOR

Jamie Disterhaupt has written romance since she was a teenager, and was first published in 2003 under the pseudonym **Shelby Reed**. Her contemporary stories are emotionally driven and contain unique premises that revolve around love and redemption. Jamie also writes paranormal romance and currently has several stories published with Ellora's Cave Publishing, Inc. She lives in Florida with her husband and writes full-time.